DMITRY NOVIKOV

A FLAME OUT AT SEA

A FLAME OUT AT SEA
by Dmitry Novikov

Translated from the Russian by Christopher Culver

Published with support of the Russian Booker Foundation
Sponsored by GLOBEXBANK

Publishers Maxim Hodak & Max Mendor

© 2019, Dmitry Novikov

© 2019, Glagoslav Publications

www.glagoslav.com

ISBN: 978-1-912894-22-2

DMITRY NOVIKOV

A FLAME OUT AT SEA

Translated from the Russian by Christopher Culver

Published with support of the Russian Booker Foundation
Sponsored by GLOBEXBANK

CONTENTS

A RAINBOW ON THE WATER

Among the generation of Russian "New Realists", who burst onto the literary scene at the turn of the millennium and were met with a loud welcome from critics and readers, Dmitri Novikov stands apart from the rest.

The New Realists became known as a wartime generation who wrote about the uprising in the Caucasus, about local conflicts, about how the young men who served were broken and came back from the war straight into Russia's brutal 1990s. However, Novikov affirmed a peaceful, everyday existence, with the silence of the northern forests in autumn and fishing on the tranquil lakes of Karelia.

The New Realists were a generation of activity: demonstrations, skirmishes and explosive outbursts. Novikov however dealt in contemplation, in the static and still, and in adoration. Indeed, the collection of stories that brought him fame was entitled *A Fly in Amber* (2003).

The "New Realists" arrived as a generation of unbridled self-biographers. They created a myth about themselves, either confessing or repenting, like Roman Senchin, or building up a tough self-depiction, like Zakhar Prilepin. However, Novikov retreated into the shadows; the image of the author himself was obscured and his characters were allowed to speak instead.

Perhaps this is why, while Prilepin has his expressive "boots full of hot vodka" in that eponymous story, Novikov has his "fly in amber", an emblem of a frozen, enchanted life; while Senchin has his hopeless *Flooded Zone*, Novikov has his "flame out at sea": a flame that arises like the spirit of God over the cold waves of the White Sea, and Novikov refers to the open expanse by its Karelian name, *golomya*.

There is nothing in the world more beautiful
than the shore of the White Sea…
There is nothing more fearsome than the shore of the White Sea…
There is no greater border in the world than the shore of the White Sea…

Dmitri Novikov's new novel is essentially about faith and love. As it should happen, faith must first be lost, and love (of God towards mankind, of human beings towards nature, of kith and kin for each other… I could go on) is put into question.

This doubt is expressed in the form of the novel, which is devoid of linear narration and which fragments into flashbacks, whether to pre-war Kem, to the village of Keret before the October Revolution, or to the 16th century inhabited by hermits and renunciants, or to the fat first years of the new millennium when the descendants of the Karelian fishermen, hunters, camp guards and prisoners come to fish on the lakes in its natural reserves. The protagonist of *A Flame Out at Sea* turns out to be a descendant himself. Grisha is a doctor in a children's ward, a folktale hero with an ample red beard (however, in this portrait one might guess at the appearance of the author himself…). Nonetheless, the book is not so much about Grisha, as about a person's journey towards himself – through history, through time, and through terrible and painful memories. The path to oneself, a path that lies over water, is the principle that runs through the novel and gives it unity: restless Grisha, his stern and moody grandfather Fyodor, the good Konstantin, and the quiet and saintly old man of the place Savvin –all belong to the White Sea, as they all gaze out at the mysterious *golomya*.

Is the White Sea, the open expanse, the *golomya* really the novel's main character? That seems to be the case, especially considering that ultimately the grandfather and grandson, Fyodor and Grisha, must come to the sea and wrestle with it.

In this novel the figure of Fyodor is linked to a certain secret that weighs over everything. Even his wife of many years, Grisha's grandmother, has not disclosed it, "nor why he had received a pension that was as small as a sparrow's tail; nor why some people came to the house without even waiting for the funeral and took all of grandpa's medals, one after another according to a list." Gradually things become clear. Grisha's grandfather, the war hero ("The Karelian front. Private in a penal battalion. Sixteen combat reconnaissance operations. Two medals. Senior lieutenant. Then captain. Commander of the penal battalion. Concussion. Wounded.") was one of those Soviet functionaries who sent men to prison, who castigated landowners and had men shot; this trace of the grandfather's crime immediately sets Novikov's novel apart from other family requiems that are dedicated to people who are ruined or who suffer without doing anything bad themselves. Deep down in the world of *A Flame out at Sea* is a crime: a barge began to sink as it was bearing arrestees – strong Pomors, men who knew the sea – off to the labor camps; they tried to save themselves by leaping into the water and swimming to the shore, but it was none other than Fyodor who shot at them from the barge, shouting "about treason, about running away, about how the country would not forgive us..."

> Bullets spread over the water like a fan. The water turned red [...] One by one these men, who had been bold sailors on icy waters, now sank into the depths. One by one our northern people disappeared, Russia's men of steel. Like fish that flash white in the depths, they disappeared into the sea. Like a flock of salmon that has left its native shores forever, tortured by an incomprehensible, evil force [...] A bright, sinking, heavenly rainbow lay itself over the sea, it was parting now along with life and hope, following after the tribe of fish, which not so long ago had been people, they had left because of human evil.

Was this the same grandfather who brought up his timid grandson and showed the boy the secrets of the sea and the forest? The same one who, wounded and contused, served the whole war and had medals to show for it? The same one who always wanted to catch a bear?

Novikov's *A Flame out at Sea* is a paradoxical novel. Nature, history, psychology, human relationships – everything within it is ambiguous and uncertain, everything is shown to the reader as an unbearable radiance or a pitch-black abyss, as an icy plunge into a stormy sea or as a rainbow rising above the calmed waters. It is no coincidence that an image that runs through the novel compares a man with a fish, and it is concerned throughout with fishing; a series of striking and fascinating metaphorical scenes, in which love proves to be closely linked with death, tenderness with brutality, and the deaths of the precious fish of the north with the powerful life-affirming energy by which these fish burst through the surface of the water.

All of these episodes of fishing are depicted by Novikov with unconcealed delight, something he naturally transmits to the reader too, by forcing the reader to follow with baited breath, not only the symbolic and metaphorical "fish", but also the specific details of a fishing expedition. Here, we have a man bound to an enormous slippery burbot with a triple hook. Here, under a rain shower, he pulls forth from the water a gray Atlantic salmon. Here, he enjoys a veritable feast of pike. Here, a flock of salmon is heading upriver to spawn and no nets, no traps made by man, can stop it. Here, a bullhead catfish puckers its mouth as if to say, "Look-there, watch-out," and thus warns Grisha in his boyhood against a looming abomination from the world of older people...

The scene of violence against a child, just like the scene where the protagonist is rescued after drinking to excess, follows the spirit of the New Realism, as if contrasting with the expressionistic style of the White Sea chapters. Yet, what is interesting is that for any other author this scene would have served as a culmination that ponderously points to the total collapse of our world and an inescapable catastrophe for the main character. However, for Novikov this scene is just one of many, alongside the shooting of arrestees on the barge or a bear killing a full-grown moose during rutting season. Yes, Fyodor's crime ricochets back and strikes Grisha, but Grisha then lifts himself up and becomes a doctor in a children's ward. We kill, we are killed. The fish that are killed give the fishermen a sensation of the sharp, pungent taste of life. Above the icy waters a rainbow flickers. On the shores of the White Sea, among hermitages lost in the forests, a demon appears to Grisha and his brother. The open sea threatens death, but only by coming into contact with the elements can one regain the desire to live. The fishing metaphor is simultaneously transparent and intense, straightforward and sophisticated, and already something one expects from Novikov, but nonetheless unpredictable in each scene:

> Even when I caught and killed salmon, I loved them. I loved to lay their silvery bodies down on the stones at the riverbank and slowly, and carefully, gut them. Inside they were just as fine as they were on the outside. Their flesh was bright orange, with mother-of-pearl innards, always an empty stomach (when the salmon is spawning, it doesn't eat) – sometimes it seemed like all this was just some fine waxwork figure that clung to the highest spirit of beauty that the salmon bore within itself. I loved their smell – they smelled of themselves, alive, their leaps, their raging flights into the sky. They smelled like cheating on the sea...

A Flame Out at Sea smells of blood and saltwater, of our world today and of history. The *golomya* is in fact a place where one can perish, but also where one can be saved. That is our history, the history of Russia in the 20th century (and not only). Where else than in the White Sea – along the coast with its ancient monasteries and Soviet camps – can one remember this and take it to heart?

Elena Pogorelaya
Literary critic

A FLAME OUT AT SEA

He who plows the sea discovers happiness and the world belongs to him. He reaps without sowing, for the sea is a field of plenty.

A nameless Pomor cross on Grumant

I was very pleased to get a rare book, a gift from my friend Grisha, a man who had the appearance of an old style Russian hero: he was tall, with auburn curls and an ample beard. Grisha worked as an ER doctor at a children's hospital. He also wrote some powerful, catchy songs that even brought tears to the eyes of the most grizzled men of the North. He had brought me this book as a token of his thanks after I had recommended some routes along the White Sea shores to him. He wanted to go there to "find healing for his soul", as he put it.

The heavy, dark-blue volume was pleasing to the hand and the eye. Its title, embossed in gold, was also a delight: *Dictionary of the Spoken Pomor Dialect*. I am very fond of dictionaries in general. One can learn many new things from them, unlike some novels. Yet again, I was intrigued by the story of this dictionary's author, Ivan Durov. He was a native of the old Pomor village, Sumsky Posad, and a self-taught man. He was fascinated by the Pomor dialect and began collecting local proverbs, sayings and ritual speeches. He worked on this for five years, compiling a dictionary and ultimately sending it to the Academy of Sciences. Several years later he was shot at the Sandarmokh site in Karelia, the victim of repressions against local historians. His manuscript languished in the archives for eighty years and has only recently been found and published. This was a precious gift.

Grisha would talk at length, and enthusiastically, about what he had discovered in the places I had recommended to him. "You are a good guy," he thanked me, imitating Pomors accent, after he had been given a chance to hear them. He would paint in words the White Sea, the northern rivers and the fields of juniper. Then I recalled the words of my Karelian grandmother: "Juniper is the tree of death".

1975, PRYAZHA

The worst thing was seeing him from behind when he had nothing covering over his back. On his arm, his shoulder and his shoulder blade: three holes. They had closed up, healed, but these were not scars, they were holes. Grisha was afraid to ask, and his grandfather never talked about it. Even though it had clearly been a machine gun, he had been shot in the back and it was unbelievable that anyone could survive that. Yet his grandfather had survived. Only now his steps were slow and he coughed terribly at night. So loud and hoarse in fact, it sounded like a raging lion dying somewhere in the depths of Africa. The coughing would often wake Grisha and his back would feel cold and shriveled. Grisha would just lie there for what seemed like an eternity without daring to even move, holding his breath. Then his grandfather would fall silent again. Grisha too would fall back asleep, his nose wrapped in his grandmother's old blanket.

It smelled strange and tart. The entire house was imbued with the smells of some former, forgotten life. These smells would rush into your nostrils as soon as you came in from outside and they would make you involuntarily reflect, and recall, what each thing meant. For instance, this smell was so warm and dry, with a slight tinge of dust and limestone, like an old Russian oven. Not the bottom part of it –there smells of delicious food always emerged, whether it was pancakes, fish soup or fried potatoes – but rather the top, which in fact was referred to as the "oven top". "Don't climb up on the oven top!" his grandmother would say, not yelling at them but just so none of the numerous small children would fall from there. Grisha was the eldest of all these small fry and therefore responsible for them all. The "oven top" was covered with old, yellowed newspapers with some animal skins laid on top. One skin, Grisha knew for sure, was from a wild boar, it had long, coarse hairs and a yellow inner side that had a pungent smell. This skin could be used to frighten the younger children when they could not control themselves and spent hours fooling around. Other skins came from harmless domestic sheep; these skins were soft and somehow defenseless. All of these things – the warm stove, its whitewash surface, the old newspapers, the wild boar and the obedient sheep – would mix together, to give off that smell of a village home that would remain in one's nose for ever. Years later it could make one recall childhood; the age would rise back up with a note of melancholy and in its fullness.

The oven was grandmother. With its smell, its warmth and with the taste of the food that continually lay within its warm womb in huge black cast-iron pots. It was eerily mysterious how these dishes would appear out of the raging, purple-flickered hell, grabbed by handles that jutted out like horns. With strong tea, sweetened so much it was viscous, every hour from a dark, smoke-blackened teapot. Later, this would be replaced by a shiny new electric kettle, meaning tea was taken more frequently. Black bread, sprinkled with oil and coarse salt, or a white loaf with sugar – this food was also grandmother.

Grandfather was the cupboard. It was small, dark and located on the left after you came into the house, opposite the kitchen. It wasn't even a cupboard but a large closet. A curtain made from rags was hung over the door. That was where the shotguns were. Grisha would go there alone, not letting any of the younger children in. He would sit for a long while in the dark and run his hands over the cold metal of the shotgun barrels and the smooth wood of their butts. The shotguns also had a smell. They smelled of danger and alarm. Also, they called to him with some manly affability, some ultimate responsibility. Grisha immediately felt older when he carefully cocked one and then slowly pulled the trigger. The hammer would give a dry click; if any adults were in the house, especially his grandfather or uncle, they would immediately start yelling at him to not fool around.

Hunting clothes were also hung in the closet. Their smell was similar to the boar skin, just as wild, but with a metallic, artificial twinge. Immediately one could sense how they were all interrelated: the clothes, the shotguns and the boar skin. It immediately became clear why everything was the way it was: the danger, alertness, excitement, a shot, a brief shriek, scurrying legs and a long knife in one's hands. The dry leaves under the animal's body. The hot blood and the autumn soil drinking it up greedily. The closet was Grandpa. A soldier's greatcoat also hung inside it.

There were also many things from the army inside the home. Photographs, in an album, where Grandpa was a dashing lieutenant in a tunic adorned with medals. Grisha already knew that the Red Star and the Combat Red Banner were real medals, deservingly won, something to be proud of. They lay in red boxes in an upper drawer and Grisha would often secretly take them out and run his fingers over their lacquered surfaces. He especially liked how they were attached to clothing not with a pin, like some common badge, but with a sturdy fastener which could only be taken off with a large piece of clothing and one's heart coming off with it. His grandfather never talked about the war and would not let him play with the medals. His grandfather never yelled at him, he just knew how to give Grisha a look that would send chills down the back of his neck and made him want to obey. In another drawer, kept under lock and key, were the bullets.

Sometimes he was allowed to watch when his grandfather and uncles got ready to go hunting. They would take out the fascinating cartridge cases, the shining, precious caps, the shot in various sizes and the funny wadding. All this was set out on the floor, on top of a neatly laid sheet of newspaper. They would sit down alongside one another and begin something that was clear but still somehow secret: they rammed the caps into the cartridge cases and poured in the powder, then inserted a thin cardboard strip and then the thick wadding, and then filled the space with shot. One more strip would be added, then they crimped the cartridge shut. Sometimes, instead of shot, a bullet was placed into the cartridge, mostly one that was round and funny, but occasionally one that looked dangerous, with a sharp tip. The steps proceeded so quickly and deftly that Grisha could not even manage to appreciate the work. They would do this in turns, each seeing to his own; the entire process was blurred into a clear, simple harmony, delighting in guns. Grisha would reach out his hands to help them, but they would only allow him to play with the shot or, rarely, he would get to pick up a bullet that had fallen into a crack in the floor. There were also ramrods with brushes. The adults would clear the barrels of their gun, smear them with a dark oil, look up into them against the light and, satisfied, set the gun aside. Here, a strict custom was observed, a ritual and at its head was grandfather. Occasionally, one of Grisha's uncles would fall out of the rhythm, he would get distracted and move his fingers clumsily. If this happened, grandfather was not afraid to cuff one of these grown men on the back of their necks. If this was done in jest they would laugh, but if grandfather was serious they would say nothing in response, only lower their heads and try harder.

Grisha's father never touched these guns and ammunition. He said that he felt sorry for the animals. He was the eldest son and had moved to the city early on. He would sit and watch the deft fingers of his brothers and his father, but he never picked any of these exciting, tempting objects up. Grandfather would look at him with a mysterious smirk, as if he knew something that others could not know, regardless of their age or peacetime experience. Peacetime experience is experience of life. Grandfather knew something different.

Grisha's father also remembered something that his younger brothers and sisters did not.

The maiden name of Grisha's grandmother was Vlasova.[1] It was an ordinary name, half the village had it. Then a certain era swept everything into place meaning some were honored, some Ulyanovs, while others were considered to be the enemy. How can one grasp that a new era has the potential to bring sin and decay? The laws of humankind are age-old, any speedy attempt to bring about happiness can turn into the opposite, and that a human life would suffice to see all the stages of this process, from the enthusiasm of the young to the dull despair of the old. Between young and old lies the spite of adults, so confident but shameless. This is referred to the demonic "dialectic", but how could one understand it without experience and without God? Yet everyone had to understand it. Even Grisha's grandfather.

Thinking is hard – Grisha realized this when he grew older. While young, when you are full of strong emotions and spite, it is easier, and a spiteful gaze will boldly look for enemies. There are so many of them around; those used to holding a gun in their hands know that.

There was a shout and the crying of children. Grandfather was not grandfather back then but a young hero. A wounded man, a hard man. When Grisha's grandmother protested against something back then, she too was not grandmother yet but a mother, and a young but plain woman who had already given birth to five children. She would protest, and maybe she would say something in Karelian. Grisha's grandfather would forbid her from speaking Karelian, "The Soviet authorities demand we be international". When she spoke out against something too daringly or in a language he could not understand, or when she carped about something sacred to him, he would fly into a blind rage. The veins on his neck would throb from fury. Everything would come rushing back to him: the cries of others earlier, the bread of an orphan, storms at sea and the waves dashing against the rocks. Trust in his elders and in commanders. Betrayal and three holes in his back. Everything came back to him again and goaded him on. Just like the waves crashing on the rocks.

---

1   The same surname as that of Andrey Vlasov, the Russian general who defected to Nazi Germany and was later hanged for treason.

He grabbed his gun and shouted at that damned woman, "You get out of here, you enemy of the people!" The kids were wailing, the kids he called mongrels, degenerates and the enemy. Shoots from a foreign root. Not Russian, almost all Finn.

"You get out of here! I'll shoot, you damned Vlasovites!" he screamed so loudly, as to deafen himself. The children fell silent, they were deeply frightened. Only the eldest sniffled slightly, barely breathing. Their mother stood on the ground of the plowed field. Barefoot. She held the two babies in her arms, the middle children pressed themselves against her legs. Her firstborn was standing slightly to her side. Everyone stood looking at him without saying anything. The gun danced in his hands. Anger danced in his head. It had filled him up completely and pushed everything else out. Then it started to rain. Thick drops fell on the earth, on their white heads, on their dirty feet. Where a drop fell on their feet, he could clearly see how the filth of the soil disappeared and a vivid pink circle of healthy skin suddenly glowed in its place. The children's skin, the woman's. His families.

Cold streams of water were flowing down his face, his shoulders and under his collar. He shuddered and threw the gun down into the dirt. The hatred in his head suddenly shrunk to the size of a grain of sand and his head began to ring like a bell. He turned around and ran, staggering, towards the house. The eldest child rushed after him. "Don't cry, pa!"

The house stood on a low slope, above the river. It wasn't really a river, more of a stream, heavily overgrown with willows and sedge. The stream gaily gurgled among the stones and between the roots of trees, sometimes being completely hidden by these. By hopping from one large stone to another you could cross the stream completely. Only fear stood in the way. The bank near the house was hidden behind the thin trunks of trees, as if Grisha were surrounded by real jungle on all sides. The cries of birds fell silent. Only a willow would rustle mysteriously with its slender leaves, and this rustling too sounded somehow confining and dangerous. Fear, along with an irresistible force that made him want to make his way ever further across, made the stream's spell as spicy and clean as the smell of frozen earth. Indeed, that is what the stream smelt like with its wet earth, tree roots and bushes, its babbling radiant water and the wet moss of stones. Grisha could spend hours observing its life. He would track the fleeting minnows through the swift currents, look for caddisflies in their little homes made from sticks and watch the wonderful frogs that darted about. Once the stream gifted him a real wild animal. The boy had made a few leaps over some stones that his feet knew (further on there were some unfamiliar and dangerous stones that threatened a fall into the water), and he saw the animal. It was small, dark brown, with a pointy muzzle and round ears. It was quite close, just two meters away. Grisha froze. The animal sniffed, dissatisfied, its nostrils flaring. The white points of its teeth stood out. On a stone nearby lay a bird, torn apart. Or rather, it was no longer a bird at all, just a fan of feathers and a few drops of blood scattered over the rough gray surface of this wild countertop. For a second the animal stood there, estimating its strength, but then it turned and disappeared, fleetingly without a sound in the tall grass. Only the long tail of a snake slithered after it. How strange this all was, frightful but attractive, an experience which was both haunting and powerful. It was as if Grisha had been the animal, as if he himself had crept through the grass and devoured its prey. After a minute had passed Grisha began to breathe again, and a few more minutes later he turned around and hopped on trembling legs back to the familiar bank. He rushed past his grandfather's bathhouse. He picked up speed and dashed over the delightfully springy boards laid over a muddy patch towards the house. As he flew in, he cried to his father, "An animal! An animal! I saw it! It was brown! It ate a bird!"

"It was probably a mink," his father answered indifferently. "It must have escaped from the fur farm."

The bathhouse stood right on the bank of the stream, just a step away from the water. A bit further, between two stones, there was a deep channel with water up to an adult's chest, and after steaming oneself in the bathhouse one could leap into it and laugh merrily. Saturdays were generally bath days, a sort of celebration. The bath would be warmed in the morning. Grisha was allowed to watch after the fire and, proud at having this adult responsibility, he would haul wood, feed it into the crackling stove and close its heavy cast-iron door. He would then watch carefully to make sure that, God forbid, not one little piece of charcoal would fall from the red-hot maws of the stove. It was hard to look after the stove due to the heat, as it would become nearly unbearable and he would often jump outside onto the bank of the stream and take a few deep breaths of the air that was doubly fresh after the bathhouse heat: like a stupid fish caught on a hook and intent on breathing to the end. Sometimes his grandmother would come to see how he was doing. She would stroke his head with her eternal "My my, how they're torturing the boy!" and place a lump of sugar in his hand. It was nice when the sugar was rock-hard, barely absorbing any of his saliva. It was much worse when it was professionally refined sugar, for it would instantly dissolve in his mouth, leaving behind a taste of dissatisfaction and fleetingness.

His relatives began to come in for lunch, his aunts and uncles with their families. It got noisy in the home, especially in the yard outside. The children, so happy to meet, started running around. Grisha, proud of his job, looked upon these little ones indulgently. Only when Serega arrived did he allow himself to relax, because the other began to immediately help him. Serega was the same age as Grisha, but Grisha's father explained that he was Grisha's first cousin once removed, so of his uncles' generation. This came as an unpleasant surprise to Grisha, but his "uncle" was unperturbed. The two became friends.

Serega was odd. He was somehow too nice a boy. He would forgive anything. Once he was running and leaping across the clearing between the bathhouse and the house, and a ram that was grazing nearby attacked him. Twice the ram butted him with its sharp head, then pinned him against the fence. Serega tried to push the ram's head away with his weak hands, but the ram only pushed him harder towards the wooden fence, pinning him under his ribs. Serega was already breathing heavily, but when Grisha grabbed a big stick, he shouted, "Don't! You'll hurt him!"

Serega stood in this dangerous vise until the ram grew tired of its victim's weakness and went away. Yet, even after this there was no question of Serega doing anything in revenge, not even throwing a rock.

He also loved birds. He could spend hours watching a big bird soar in the sky, the high blue sky, and seeing how it turned into a tiny little thing in the distance. He could spend all day with pigeons, carrying them on his breast and whispering to them. Men like him easily take to alcohol. They don't have the strength to resist its swift, powerful current. Some twenty years later, after a month-long binge of tearful drinking, he hung himself on a clothesline. On his grave there were always some bread crumbs, the cross-like prints of birds' feet, or downy feathers tangled in the high, wild grass.

They would start going to the bathhouse a couple of hours before dinner. The women went first. Their procession was always led by Grisha's grandmother and it was funny to watch how she solemnly led the column of compliant young people behind her, moving duck-like from foot to foot as she. "My, my, they've made it so hot you can't even go in," came her merry voice from the bathhouse. Grisha and Serega exchanged glances, for her words were to their credit.

The women's turn did not take long, the first session in the steam was hard. When an hour had passed they were already came back inside the house, marching in the same line. Their heads wrapped in wet towels, their flushed faces, their smooth and languid movement were imbued with some rare, uncanny sense of leisure and ease. Some sort of wisdom and detachment. Some sort of firm submission. It did not last for long. As soon as they entered the house, they began to make a fuss, rushing about and preparing dinner. Grisha's grandmother headed this, but not with an aggressive stance, she was soft and in good humor. Here and there one heard her plaintive "My, my!" That simultaneously pitied the slow-moving, inept girls and drove them on.

The men would go into bathhouse when it was already like a furnace. Red-hot heat from the glowing coals lurked within the brick-lined depths, exhaling a gentle and dangerous breath. They closed the little door on the stove. It had become impossible to breathe. Impossible to even exist. Grisha's head grew muddled and he felt an urge to jump outside. His legs buckled and it seemed like he had reached a point where he could only lie down. But then his father or grandfather would gently nudge him to climb up onto the benches. The wood of the benches was so hot it put a bitter feeling into Grisha's mouth. It was impossible to sit, it felt like his backside would catch fire and burst into flames. Grisha put his hands under him, his palms could better handle the heat. He would hardly come to his senses, to perk up and look around, before his grandfather would open the little door to the stove and, after nodding to the other men in warning, cast half of a dipper of hot water into its black maw. There was an explosion inside and a violent but colorless cloud of steam would burst from it and sweep away all of the life in its path. Grisha's ears, nostrils and fingernails were gripped in tongs of blinding pain. He squealed and leaped down from the bench, trying to escape among the bodies of the adults. However, his grandfather was prepared for this. He swiftly grabbed Grisha by his wrist, deftly put him on his stomach and began to whip him with a bath broom that had been made ready, steamed beforehand. Grisha screamed and kicked. His back was burning, he could not breathe and his head was swarming with multicolored balls. "You just hold on, squirt. Hold on, you little greenhorn," his grandfather would say in a serious voice, but somewhere deep down mirth could be heard. Grisha felt that he had reached the end, that his little life was over, but his grandfather would throw on more steam and work through Grisha's stomach, chest and shoulders. Then he would let Grisha go. Grisha's father would pick him up and set him on the floor. His grandfather would take a bucket of cold water and drench the child from head to toe. The sudden sharp cold through the glowing heat, the flowing life over red-hot death forced Grisha to squat down, as if a hand had been placed on him in blessing. After this, he stood up straight on trembling legs and grunted in an adult fashion, surprising himself and making the grownups laugh. His grandfather wrapped him in a sheet and carried him out to the dressing area. "How was it, you little greenhorn? Good?" he asked, and then dived back into that hell. Grisha sat drinking water from a large aluminum mug, listening to the cries and whipping sounds coming from the bath. His head was empty and in a marvelous state, as if it were the shell of an egg made clean. His body was singing, his soul trembled within it.

It was in the bath that he first saw his grandfather's back.

I know, Fyodor, I still remember a whole generation later: you really wanted to catch a bear. Tapio, the forest spirit, the god of marshes and pine forests, you remembered it all.

You were enchanted by the stories of the old; how men would catch bears with a spear. Your grandfather, an old hunter, spoke with firsthand knowledge. How to choose a good birch tree, one with a trunk that split in two. The angle should be the size of a bear's neck. It shouldn't be rotten wood but strong and healthy, because your life is going to depend on it. A spacer could be inserted between the forked trunk, or conversely the forked trunk could be pulled closer with a rope and it would take on the desired shape within a couple of years. You have to do everything right; life can change into death in a flash if something goes wrong. The bear will not give you a chance if you slip up. How to find the beast, how to goad it so that it would move towards you? A bear is not an evil creature; it would rather walk away than fight, as long as its young or its prey is not threatened. For this reason, it is better to catch it through a bait, where it won't want to give up what belongs to it. How do you make it get up on its back legs, so that it will fall upon you from above in its rage? How do you successfully set the spear up so that it will clamp down on the bear's neck, and stick the other end into the earth? All without making any mistakes. Even then, when the bear is about to tear it away from you, you'll get a chance to leap up at it, the Finnish knife must strike its heart. The *veyche*, as the Karelians called this knife, had to be metal and so tempered that it would slice through the bear's ribs like butter.

Your grandfather forged and sharpened knives himself. When the blade was ready, red-hot out of the fire, he would take a birch-bark container, fill half of it with water and the other half with linseed oil. Then he would submerge the knife into the container so that the cutting edge would be in the water and the top of the blade in the oil. It would then be tempered so that it would be flexible but not brittle, and then the blade could cut through wood or bone without being dulled. He would then fine-tune it with a file, tsssh, tsssh, and would then drive a nail into the log wall and cut straight through the nail with the new knife. Afterwards, there would not be the slightest nick on the blade.

Remember how he once caught a bear and brought it back home to carve up? You were amazed at the animal's claws. They were like thick, black needles, long and sharp. Your grandfather was in a joking mood, he put the bear's paw on the crown of his head and the claws reached down all the way to his chin.

"You see, Fyodor," he said, "a bear has such power in it." He spoke with respect and awe. "If a bear gets angry, you can't run away from it, you can't hide. You couldn't get away even on horseback. Sometimes you can climb up a tree to save yourself. When a bear is big, it doesn't want to climb trees, it's too difficult. But it could knock down any tree. It'll tear up the roots and bring the tree down. For that you'd have to really upset it, get it out of its den in winter or wound it. Also, in early spring, a bear can be angry when it is very hungry. Or when a she-bear has to protect her cubs. But a bear is usually peaceful, it walks around and grazes. It gathers berries or different roots. It'll sense if a person is around and try to slip away unnoticed. You won't hear a branch crack under its paws. You'll just sometimes feel it staring at you in the forest. If you get a chill down the back of your spine, that means the bear is looking down on you from somewhere in the mountains. That's why when you walk in the woods, you should make loud noises, sing something, so that the bear can just slip away. Sometimes, if you suddenly come upon a bear without it hearing you, it can get scared and attack you out of fear. That's how God made bears subject to people. They are afraid of us."

Your grandfather said all of this when he was taking the black, heavy skin off the bear. Again, you were amazed to see how much a skinned bear resembles a naked human being. The legs, arms and shoulders. Only the shaggy head with its huge bared fangs emitted an inhuman power.

"No wonder the Finns have sixteen names for the bear, so that they don't have to say its real name, it's too frightful. You might even attract a bear, call it to you, if you say its name aloud. That's why Tapio, the spirit of the forest, is the most suitable name. You don't need to be afraid of it. It's a great joy if you catch sight of any animal in the forest – it means that nature has revealed some secret to you. You don't have to be scared of animals in the forest. Be scared of people."

Your grandfather turned gloomy and fell silent, lost in thought.

You got lucky immediately after. You were walking along a forest path gathering mushrooms. It was early autumn and the birds were still in full force and fluttering among the branches. You could hear tweeting from some places and cooing from others. The leaves were still green, only here and there, on the birch trees, yellow strands glittered like cheap gold. You walked along the path in the forest you knew so well and again you were amazed and delighted by new things: here an aspen had grown and become magnificent in its bright-red garb; a stone that was home to a snake was deserted this time, the creature having crawled off somewhere. The path was an old one. Some strong, old men had uprooted huge boulders and stacked them in heaps on either side of the path. It was probably them who had dug the wide ditch running alongside the path; in marshy places the little road had remained dry. Who knows in what era this all happened, whether it was back when the Karelians still made the sign of the cross with their left hand, or later when they had grown weary of the raids by the northern invaders, so the children of ten Karelian tribes joined together and burned down the old Viking capital. However, today, the forest was a cheerful place. The hardwood trees rustled gently in the warm wind and the age-old pines quietly whistled far above, with their age-old song.

Then suddenly came a terrible roar. It shook the air like thunder at the beginning of a storm. You knew that September was the moose's rutting season, when two powerful beasts would confront each other to fight for love. When they roar like that it is better not to come across a moose.

You started looking around for a strong, convenient tree, but something had instantly changed around you. The roar fell silent, replaced by a powerful cracking sound and the slight birch trees around you began to sway. You had not even managed to jump aside when a moose leaped out into the small marsh only three meters away. Now it was not just walking forcefully, it was running. It tore across the forest cleaning and jumped over the ditch full of water and mud, but it did not make it all the way across and now, with a splash that sparkled in the sunlight, its hind legs got bogged down in the filth. It leaned with its forelegs on the dry earth and struggled to break free. An instant later, a massive thing wrapped in a black hide made a huge leap out of the forest and with a roar, it fell onto the moose's back. One sweeping blow with its paw, a hunk of flesh and skin, still throbbing with blood, rolled right under your feet.

How you ran! The wind was whistling in your ears and your legs bore you galloping over the boulders, over the trunks of fallen trees towards home, towards people. But no one was running after you. The master of the forest had taken its prey.

I did not know you very well. You left when I was six years old. We had gone fishing together a few times as kids. I had heard a few stories about hunting. At night you're coughing, heavy, almost a howl, when you were trying to clear out your lungs that had been shot through and had got too much smoke in them. Your gloomy face and harsh words when you were invited to meetings of veterans and war heroes. "The real heroes are the ones lying in the earth," you would say.

The brief lines of the papers attested to two medals.

Your father's name was Trifon. Your grandfather remained nameless to me. Who were they, where did your mother and grandmother disappear to? Were there any brothers or sisters? I know nothing of this.

Why did you catch pikes on the lakes with Pomor tackle, and set a long line? Is this not the reason why I am so attracted to the White Sea, is this not the reason I love it?

If you originally came from there, how did you end up in the Vologda region when the war broke out; were you in the gulag? Because you were enlisted as a private in a penal battalion. Then suddenly, your father and grandfather disappeared in the Ukhta uprising, when the Karelians, who had earlier been so inclined to the Russians, rose up because they could not bear the bad treatment and heavy taxes, when the Russians were taking away the last meager fruits of the northern lands. Did your mother save you by pushing you into the carriage of a passing train, not caring where it was going to, just so that you would not end up on the black barges which people remember in the Pomor villages to this day?

I know nothing. I have no answers. I can only guess, only seek out the meager traces among those brief lines on those military honors. The Karelian front. Private in a penal battalion. Sixteen combat reconnaissance operations. Two medals. Senior lieutenant. Then captain. Commander of the penal battalion. Concussion. Wounded.

You really wanted to catch a bear, but for some reason this was not granted to you. You even started thinking that if a bear without its hide resembles a human being, then could a man, putting on a hide, not come to resemble a beast? A hide over the soul. Maybe you didn't have enough of the beast inside of you then? Maybe the bear was not an enemy to you at all? After all, you bagged moose, wolves and boars by the dozen.

You remember that time hunting. You had been tracking it for a long time and finally caught up to it. It was quietly grazing over marshy ground, munching on cranberries. You stood downwind of it, a bullet was in the chamber, the safety off. Your hunting dog was silently tearing at the leash, sensing that the prey was near.

Then the dog broke away, the leash could not hold. It bounded over towards the bear. The bear was too preoccupied with its food and had seen nothing. Suddenly a wolf mother leaped out from among the thick firs, grabbed the dog by the back of its neck and dragged it into the forest. You had no choice but to shoot the wolf. You killed it and saved the dog. The bear just slipped away. The wounded dog was incapable of walking, so you carried it in your arms for miles. It was hard, but you still held onto the dog and managed to carry it home. Was that how they carried you, with those holes from the exit wounds in your back? Behind you they dragged a prey squealing from terror. The night was white.

Three hours before that you had been sharpening your Finnish knife, your *veyche*. Sharpening it like your grandfather taught you: "Tsssh, tsssh, tssh." In such a way that it would smoothly go through ribs like butter.

You were probably thinking about many things at that moment. Looking back on your life. Things you never told anyone.

Again and again, I read through your papers. "Personally laid several hundred antitank mines, twice as many anti-personnel mines, even more explosives… Personally led combat reconnaissance operations. In one of them, he was first into the enemy's trenches. With two grenades he blew up a dugout with five enemy soldiers and their officer. While repelling the enemy's counterattack from a machine gun he killed over twenty Nazis. He showed great skill in reeducating the soldiers of the penal battalion."

For a long time I just could not understand how you were capable of this. How, after months of soldiers retreating, after many thousands of men had been taken prisoner, after all the grievances you had against the authorities and the nation, you were able to reverse everything.

I would think about it and couldn't understand, that is until I met an interesting man. He was the same age as me, a colonel, a decorated Hero of Russia. With a gold star on his chest. When we had already drunk a little bit, a half-liter of bitter and vodka, I decided to ask him about that.

"You see," my colonel friend told me, "Russians never wage war for someone or something, but against an injustice. Never for 'the motherland', Stalin, or whatever, but rather against the Germans when they understood that the Germans were enemies to take down. After all, the Germans were no fools, they tried to play on Russians' historical feelings: they re-opened churches. Our guys watched and thought about this for a while. But when they realized how things were, they decided it was time to break skulls. Everything else just wasn't important anymore."

The Germans had marched in merrily and brazenly, like that moose in the autumn rutting season. With a roar and a fanfare. And then they were stopped.

You finished sharpening your knife. You glanced at the clock and muttered, "Let's go".

After the platoon had put on their camouflage hides, they began crawling. Not a single branch snapped under their quiet movement. The platoon spread out but merged into a single powerful forest entity. One which already felt that its prey was near. "Forward!" you shouted in the final meters. The platoon roared as it made its short leap.

KONTAKION IN THE THIRD TONE

Thou didst devote all thy will to God and didst follow him with all thy soul, and didst reject the vanity of the world. Through prayers, tears and suffering, thou didst spurn the flesh and fight the unseen foe righteously, didst defeat him and camest rejoicing to the gates of heaven; now, thou standest with the angels before the Holy Trinity, and after thou didst fall asleep in the Lord, the All-Seeing Eye has seen thy efforts, and has granted thee the gift of working miracles. We venerate thee, we approach and bow in front of thy venerable relics. From thy righteous grave thou healest us invisibly, and thou prayest forever, preserving thy native land and people unharmed from enemies visible and invisible. So, we all cry aloud to thee, righteous father Varlaam: pray for us ceaselessly before Christ our God.

2003, LOVOZERO

"*Syoy, syoy!*"[2] Baba Lena heaps steaming venison onto our plates. She is a Karelian. Old man Andrei is a Komi. An Izhem Komi. He is clearly proud of his origins.

It is warm in the little forest cottage. That is the most important thing – half an hour before, Volodya and I were shivering like animals, completely soaked in the spray of the savage waves on Lake Love (as we nicknamed Lovozero, which really did sound like Love-ozero).

Andrei is a short, wrinkled, easily drunk old man with striking blue eyes. True alcoholic's eyes are dull, constantly tearing up. But in his, there was not the slightest glimmer of such.

"Don't you think I haven't seen anything just 'cause I live in the forest now? I have seen a *lot*." He is constantly on the move: sitting at the table, jumping up to throw more firewood on, stirring the steaming pot on the stove. "I used to live in the village. Before that, I did reindeer breeding, worked as a foreman in a brigade. I had twenty people under me, and all the girls…" He squints charmingly. "I was senior Communist Youth," after a pause and a sip of hot tea, nearly half of the mug filled with sugar, he continues: "I collected fees."

"What kind of fees were they, how much?" I ask, suddenly interested because I had recalled a red booklet with blurry purple stamp marks inside, "Paid. Communist Youth."

"How much? Some amount. One line, one fee." Old man Andrei laughed heartily, he clearly enjoyed his time in the Communist Youth.

"And where did you live before that?" I ask. "Where are you from originally?" I find it interesting, I have been in the tundra only twice in my life. But I already feel how the beauty of this place impresses me. It is an unreal, harsh beauty: the light-blue, fast-flowing river, bordered by a slender strip of vivid-green northern forest in summertime, and beyond it an endless expanse of gray swamp. In the distance the Lovozero tundra, blue mountains with white snowfall melting from their tops, looms over this peaceful landscape.

---

2   'Eat!' in Komi.

"We're from Komi country, Izhem folk. They sent us here to the Kola Peninsula to take care of reindeer. There were eight of us. Only two are left. That's Communism for you."

A gloomy look comes over old man Andrei's face and he suddenly falls silent. I have to pour him another glass of grain alcohol diluted with water.

"What's it like in this part? Interesting?" I know a little of them myself, but I wanted to hear it from a local. Local people are good for an inquisitive sort, they know many secrets and will tell you if they feel like it.

Old man Andrei gave me a significant look. "No place more interesting. Lake Seydozero will be off your route to the side, so you won't see many seidas.[3] But Kuyva[4] will keep an eye on you." He lets out an odd chuckle. "You'll pass the rocks. They're called the Ancestors. There are some drawings there. Some old temple. A very special place is Chalmny Vare. If you get to it, of course."

He fell silent again, chewing a hunk of meat, lost in thought. "Nah, life has been fine. Just hard." The old man gripped his glass in his broad palm and downed its contents. Then he slowly crawled onto the bed, so enormous that it extended along the entire wall and seemed to take up half the house. It could easily fit fifteen people. The blankets were clean animal skins. There was no dank smell of human misery in them. The bed was strong, made from rough-hewn boards, and it lay close to the ground. It seemed to be very cozy and warm – outside the cottage's walls the wind continued to rage, rain streamed down the windowpane. We could hear the roar of Lake Love.

Volodya had been led away somewhere by Baba Lena. Volodya was one of those ethnic Ukrainians whose family had moved to Kazakhstan and he had spent his whole life in the steppes. This was the first time he had ever been in the forest, in the tundra. He was therefore somewhat clueless, like a new bucket on the edge of a well – it stands there on the edge, the zinc sparkling in the sun, unaware of the imminent plunge down. Good thing there is a chain on it.

I hadn't managed to get much sleep. The same jitters, an unbelievable fear for a forty-year-old, which had come over me long before our trip out here and had not let me relax, for even an instant. Sometimes I managed to momentarily quash this fear with a deep draft of liquor, but

---

3   A Saami sacred site, consisting of a large stone placed on several smaller ones.

4   A supreme deity of the Saami people. An image of him can be seen on one of the rocks above Lake Seydozero.

that had just let me fall onto the reindeer skins into a sleep, the awakening from which was even more frightening.

I did not know why, this time, it should be like this. I would try to guess, but I could never entirely pin it down.

Old man Andrei was snoring on the bed. I again took out the map and the route description from my backpack. I unfolded the map and started to examine the bends of the rivers I had already memorized. One of them bore a strange name, Afanasia. We had to reach a second, a huge, desolate and majestic one. Ponoy means 'River of the Dog' in Saami. Not the sunniest of names.

I do not know what strange whim brings me to the North. It is irresistible. Often, you are again preparing for a trip there, stuffing things into your backpack and you wonder, with a mixture of fear and hope, if it is some demon driving you or if it is some divine calling. You are thus tortured by doubt until you get to the end, where everything is revealed. Then you find out whether you should give thanks or flee in terror.

I read the description of our route once more. Holes have had already started to form along the folds of the paper. Yes, uninhabited for hundreds of miles. Yes, category four. Yes, eleven people had perished when rafting years before. But the blue and green map of the northern lands beckoned irresistibly and affectionately. It held promise and mystery, like a beautiful, frightened woman who has already given in, already surrendered. One needed to take a good, sober look at her to discern; behind her gentle yielding, the flash of a gaze as sharp as steel under the eyelashes fluttering in fear.

"Mom, I know what to do to make a boy chase after you," said the four-year-old charming daughter of an acquaintance of mine. "You have to go up to him, smile, and then run away…"

Enough. The map goes back into the backpack. My boots are on my feet. I am standing at the door and then outside. I have a tick-repellent layer over me, a knife on my belt, a firmness in my gait, determination in my breast and enthusiasm in my mind. After I take a shot of liquor and eat a bite of venison, I leave the house.

The cottage stood black against the white night in the northern wilderness. The house was black because the plywood walls were covered with roofing felt on the outside, such is the Kola Peninsula style. On top was a camouflage netting, most likely for decoration. The low roof made of slate darkened by time was flat — snow heaping on top of it in the winter would provide extra warmth. The small windows also sheltered the life within from the severe cold. There was a shaky fence, woven together from slender birches, which was not meant for warding off neither man nor beast. By holding the snow back, it would take on the blows of the wind coming off the lake. There was also a garden, two meters of dug-up earth from which a pair of onion shoots stuck out and strawberry leaves timidly pierced through the soil – the berries would have to wait until September.

The cottage was not supported on stilts. Or maybe it was, but it squatted low above the ground like a bird ruffled up.

Two friendly dogs, huskies, paced around the yard. I immediately won their friendship for the price of a deer bone. Further along the mean dog was chained up. It was a mixture of a St. Bernard and Caucasian Shepherd; it had once been hurt by a human being. It would therefore rush upon one silently, without warning. Only the sudden ringing of its thick chain could save one from mortal danger. However, the cat, Vasily, had not sensed this danger and now its back had no fur on it – the dog's fearsome teeth had torn off the skin on the top and along both sides. Now the cat was black and pink, a miraculous survivor, but still as affectionate and hopeful for some fish. The friendly dogs would sometimes grab the cat by its head or its scarred flesh. The cat would playfully fight them off without even extending its claws. When walking around it would give the chain a wide berth.

"Come on, Volodya, let me show you the dog," came Baba Lena's voice from the fence. "So that you don't accidentally get bitten."

Volodnya followed after her obediently. He was a former swimming champion, well over six feet tall, and generally a somewhat pensive sort – the aquatic environment is more slow-moving and viscous than out in the air. He had long hair and a black beard, and for sheer swankiness, when going into the forest he would wear a track suit, a remembrance of his past achievements, with KAZAKHSTAN on the back in gold lettering. The track suit's main colors were yellow and blue, perhaps symbolizing this swimmer's ancestry. "Well then, the pirates have landed in town", is how he had been greeted by the first person he met in the Kola Peninsula the day before. Indeed, a large earring would have suited Volodya.

When we were still at home preparing for the trip, I had talked a lot about the North. About my worries and the dangers. About how it was really unclear how to even reach Ponoy, there were too many bends on the way to it. It was just as unclear how to leave – the river flows into the White Sea at its very neck, where it borders on the Barents Sea, solely inhabited by the coast guard, and the only way to get out was the steamship *Klavdiya Elanskaya* with its mysterious schedule and its helicopters that carried Americans on elite fishing trips. "It's a way out that is actually a way in," Volodya said thoughtfully.

I started to joke. "Volodya, we can't really rely on the coast guard, and even less on the *Klavdiya*. The only realistic way out is a stern helicopter pilot. You're a handsome, impressive guy, your job is to charm the pilot. We don't have enough money for a greedy Icarus. So, think of something."

"It's a way out that is actually a way in," Volodya chortled, now in a happy mood. Why can't two grown men have some locker-room talk? But I laughed more when in the shop, the clerk had handed Volodya a light-blue sleeping bag, the inside of which was lined with pictures of kittens. Volodya was frowning now. He turned another one down because of its funereal black color.

We laughed together when, in another shop for real men, there were no tick-repellent layers available in Volodya's large size. "Take this, it also helps against ticks…" in the girl's hands was a netting meant to be worn right against the skin, which could also highlight an athletic manly chest.

"The stern helicopter pilots would shout out with joy from seeing a handsome guy like you. And they'd take you anywhere you wanted to go. I'll just ride along in the corner." That is an especially good quality of Volodya, he never gets offended. On expeditions that is very important.

This all came back to me for some reason while I was watching little Baba Lena authoritatively lead Volodya towards the chained dog.

"It's a bloodstone," she said, pressing a greenish stone with red spots into his hand. "We call it 'Saami blood' here. It's a present for you."

"Let me introduce you, Berik, this is a friend, friend," Baba Lena started to firmly pet the mutt, pushing his head down towards the earth. The dog began to growl quietly. "Don't you be afraid, Volodya. Reach down and pet the dog." There was a certain quirk in her voice, which had suddenly become much younger-sounding.

Volodya obediently bent down. Like a swallow that has successfully swooped and is now setting off for somewhere with its prey, Baba Lena surged up towards Volodya and landed a heavy, powerful kiss on Volodya's big lips.

From the suddenness and horror of this my friend froze for an instant, then fell backwards onto his back, rolled over quickly like a hare, and tried to dash away on all fours.

"Hey, stop!" Baba Lena tried to grab him by his yellow-and-blue track suit, but he tore away and rolled around the corner of the cottage. Sticks cracked under him.

Baba Lena glanced around, straightened her gray hair, and returned to the house. Some ten minutes later, still amazed by what I had seen, I went inside too. After another ten minutes had passed, Volodoya, out of breath, tiptoed in cautiously. Old man Andrei was not sleeping, he was sitting on the bench. Baba Lena was setting the table again.

"She's *my* woman," said old man Andrei in a grim voice to the frightened Volodya, who only blinked his big, intelligent eyes.

I spent the rest of the night in half-delirium. Again the wind roared outside the window. Again rain fell. But my *chuyka*, my inner sense did not let me down and I lay on the edge of the bed, close to the wall. A friend of mine with Cossack roots told me that a *chuyka* is a stick with a black ribbon on it, and when Cossacks avenged one of their own, they would stick in on his grave to say it was done. But I know another meaning: a *chuyka* is a feeling and it important to heed it.

Volodya lay right next to me, and after him, old man Andrei. He had drank again and then raved all night. Then he suddenly said in a begging, thin voice, "Don't touch me, don't touch me. I'm a normal guy." He then subsided for ten minutes. I immediately sank into a deep sleep, only to be awoken from it, as if with a bucket of cold water, by a rough and heavy command, "Just lie there quietly. Wait." My hair stood on end. Behind me Volodya tossed about restlessly. Old man Andrei again fell silent, only to whisper after another interval had passed, "Volodya, Volodya, get up, pour this old man another drink."

I could not hear anything coming from Baba Lena, but I knew, I sensed that she was not sleeping, that she was nearby and gazing intently through the darkness with her cold, sharp eyes. And then suddenly she began singing quietly:

Priest Varlaam prepared his lady,
For burial as if for a wedding.
Her hair lush on her brow
He braided with care:
"Sleep, priest's wife,
Sleep, beauty beyond words!"

This was repeated again and again. I could not tell any longer if this was a dream or real life. At the bottom of the dark pit, into which I was falling, lay some terror, but after I shuddered and woke up, I realized that real life was even more frightful. Whether I dreamed it or remembered it, I again saw you drinking my blood. We had parted, or rather, you had left. But I needed to show you that I didn't care, that I wasn't afraid of anything. Even this, which seemed equal to death. I was fearless back then. I boldly drowned my sorrow in vodka. I invited a friend of mine, a hard-drinking doctor, on a bender. We were drinking in the car. I went into a pharmacy and bought a drip bag. "Pump some blood out of me, bro. Bloodletting ought to help." When we had got about half a liter, I took some more vodka and went to your place. I had such a desire to scare you in some profound way. I mixed the vodka with the blood and barked, "Drink it!" All I expected was some crying, fright, indignation and disgust. But not laughter. You laughed and drank it. One shot, then another, then a third. You laughed and gazed intently at me with a cold, sharp look.

Morning finally came. As soon as the light of the white night gave way to a sunbeam suddenly coming through the heavy clouds of Lovozero, Volodya and I leaped to our feet at the same time. We quietly slipped out of the cottage and washed in the lively gray water. We sneaked back in to grab our things, but now the kettle was already boiling on the stove. Old man Andrei was sitting at the table and smiling. Baba Lena was cutting the pink, translucent flesh of a big, fat whitefish into slices.

"Sit down and eat breakfast," old man Andrei said, clearly in a good mood. "Volodya, pour this old man a drink."

"*Syoy, syoy,*" Baba Lena was putting heavenly-tasting foods onto plates.

"Here's what I think," said old man Andrei. "I haven't gone too far upstream. Give me the map. Yes, the Mariyok River, then another twenty miles or so. The Volok, the Koyniyok…" Then he concluded merrily, "It'll be a bit hard for you, but at least one of you will make it back. I don't know about the Ukrainian, but the Russian definitely will!"

"Where? How do we get back?" I poured the old man some more liquor, but he only smiled in reply.

"Old man, are you perhaps the river keeper?" Volodya asked cautiously.

The old man's smile disappeared from his face and he suddenly said in a serious and harsh tone, "Don't you ever say that again!" After a minute of silence he told us, "Well, god speed. It's a long way."

We quickly brought out our canoe, threw our things into it and loaded it ourselves. The cat, Vasya, meowed a farewell. The dogs barked. The

St. Bernard's chain jangled. I pushed with the paddle off the river bottom. Volodya, who was sitting at the canoe's nose with the other paddle, swayed.

"Balance with your rear!" I shouted to him; this was the trick with canoes.

"A tailwind is blowing on your asses," old man Andrei said, his arm around Baba Lena's shoulders.

After a few paddle strokes we were far away. With some difficulty I turned around in the narrow canoe and saw two figures, now very small, watching us go. The dogs were running around near them, and the cat, black and pink, curled around their feet.

1971, CRIMEA

The grape bunch was bright, glowing from within, as if it consisted of several dozen little electric lamps painted in a light emerald color. It hung over the rough planed boards of the table that was flanked by two benches. The benches, like the table itself, rested on thick blocks of old, mealy-gray wood with a thin edge of damp black at the ground. If Grisha managed to seize the opportunity and clamber up first with his knees onto the bench and, after a cautious look around, onto the table-top, he would then only need to stand up on the tips of his toes and pick one of the grapes. But there were always grown-ups sitting at the table from morning until evening, either playing cards or dominoes, and at night Grisha had to sleep. Therefore, for several days now Grisha, like a stubborn little shark, hovered in alternating narrow or wide circles, but he never forgot about the grapes. At home he had sometimes tasted them, but always did during the big celebration at the end of the summer, that is, on his birthday. He could remember two such celebrations, and judging from how old people said he was, there must have been a third, the very first, but whether there had been grapes then, he could not remember. When there were grapes, Grisha stuffed himself with them, though he always had the feeling that a few more could have fit in his stomach. He ate them with the seeds and skins and could not fathom the strange habits of the older ladies, who pursed their lips into a chicken's rear and sucked out grape after grape, and then spat the grapes' hard hearts, somewhat shamefully, onto their palms. Grapes were sometimes sweet like tea, which made his remember when his mother had her back turned and he could pour as much sugar in as he wanted. Sometimes grapes were sourer. But they were always sweet, and after Grisha had finished them, he would still nibble on the soft stems remaining on the branch that had been ripped out of the transparent flesh of the grapes.

Unlucky yet again. The neighbors were sitting at the table, the same regulars, along with one man that Grisha did not know. "Who might you be?" the man asked him. "I'm little Grisha" – mama had always told him that he had to be polite, even when he did not feel like it.

He thought that perhaps he should no longer say "little" but simply "Grisha", as that would be somehow better, more grownup. He turned to run away, and fortunately, just then, his mother invited him to walk down to the sea.

First of all, the sea was nearby. Secondly, swimming was not just fun, it was also something good for him, two things which rarely coincided. Thirdly, he had to walk through the marketplace, where mama always stopped to buy something yummy. Grisha only knew of peaches here, in the south, and they made him very happy. They were so sweet and juicy, which would get him to thinking how many more pleasant things in life there were to discover. After all, they had just got here, and already he had discovered the sea, peaches and the real grape bunch hanging on a vine, waiting for him.

When they reached the beach, he saw something else that was nice and he immediately remembered: Marina. The two of them had become acquainted the day before, here on the beach. Mama said that this was a girl and Grisha asked what her name was. They went swimming, then Grisha noticed that she was somehow different from him. For some reason, Grisha generally found it nice to look at Marina and he immediately wanted to be friends. They had played for a long time the day before and now he ran towards her like an old friend. However, Marina seemed angry today. As if she did not even recognize him. He would try to speak to her, and she would pout and not want to play. She did not want to swim today either, she just sat all dressed up with a big panama hat. Their mothers spread out a blanket nearby and chatted about something, but Grisha was thinking about how he could cheer Marina up, because he wanted things to be nice like yesterday and for her to smile and not pout. He finally thought of something! His father had caught two insects several days before and pinned them. One was called a solifuge and the other a scorpion. His father said that they are dangerous if they are alive, but Grisha was not afraid of them now that they were dead. They were amazing.

He liked the solifuge less, it was a pale yellow thing with funny teeth at the front. The scorpion was his favorite: dark brown, something that looked fine as if it had been lacquered, and from the front it resembled a crab, with the same pincers. On its tail there was a spike with venom that it used to kill its enemies. His mama had told him all this. Here it was lying in its box, so magnificent and dangerous, like a little attacking tank or some kind of machine gun – the claws jutting forward, the tail bent overhead and aimed, the creature all covered in armor. He really liked the little scorpion.

Grisha decided to cheer Marina up this way, he would show her his wonderful insects and give her one. When it came to which one to give her, he naturally thought about the solifuge, because he already loved the scorpion with all his heart. He was already thinking of how he would go home and brag to all his friends. He would not miss the solifuge that much. But Marina was clever, she saw right away how things were. She also liked the scorpion, of course. First she screamed to show how frightening it was for her, but then she lay down next to Grisha and started to look, and Grisha told her everything. Then he reluctantly gave her the scorpion, because he really liked Marina, even more than he liked the scorpion.

Then came happiness. The little woes that Grisha felt vanished at once. Marina became cheerful and nice. Their mothers were absorbed in their conversation about grownup things and the two children started doing whatever they wanted. First they ran around and bathed in a small saltwater puddle cut off from the sea by a strip of wet sand. Then they decided to go swimming without the adults, because the puddle was too small and the water in it was warm like mama's hand. They splashed around and laughed, and Grisha taught Marina how to build castles out of sand, when you take the sand together with water and let a little stream run over your palm, and the towers of the castles rise higher and higher. Once a larger wave came and the sand castle slowly sank under its influx – then things became a bit sad. Marina suddenly tried to run away from him screaming, but he ran faster and always caught up with her. They fell onto the sand, but instead of getting up they wallowed in it and ended up looking like people made of sand. Then they ran back to the water and the sand immediately fell from their bodies, which again became identifiable. The sun was not too hot, they did not burn, and no one made them put their panama hats on. Marina's mother told her to change out of all her clothes, and for some reason Grisha again found things interesting and happy. He himself had been running around naked now for some time, and when no one saw, he showed her how he had to pee. The wind was also nice, not too hot and very light, and when Grisha looked carefully out at the sea, he saw that somewhere in the distance it merged with the sky and you could not distinguish which was which. He was amazed at this and he told Marina too, but she did not understand what he was talking about. They continued playing for a long time, but then their mothers shouted that it was enough already, that they had turned completely blue. They were not blue at all, they were the same color they always were, but they had to get out of the water. Then they lay down on the same blanket and started looking at the scorpion again, and Marina's mother put her black eyeglasses on her, which made her somewhat mysterious and even more beautiful. All of this was so nice for Grisha that he did not even care about drinking anything, and he had completely forgotten about the peaches. He only remembered when his mama took the peaches out and he shared them fair and square with Marina. They bit into one after another and the juice ran down their faces. Their noses were tickled by the fresh, sweet smell, and if one of them sneezed, they laughed together, although their mothers said that they were not to set another foot in the water. The sun was shining so warm on his back, he wanted to do something bold and funny at the same time to make her look at him, so that things would always be like that. It seemed that things would always be like that.

Then a man ran past them towards the beach and stepped on the box. The box was immediately crushed; Grisha himself felt scared and crushed inside. He could not think about anything. He grabbed the box and opened it, all that was left of the scorpion were some small choco-late-colored fragments. Grisha could not even cry, because Marina was crying, wailing with all her might. After all, it was her scorpion now, he had given to her. It's all your fault, she cried; Grisha fell silent, for he had not expected any of this. It wasn't fair that she was yelling at him, because even if things were sad for her and the scorpion, it was the man who had stepped on it. No, it's your fault, she wailed and her face became ugly somehow, wrinkled. I'm going to tell mama everything, and she was already running off to tattle on him. Grisha tried to catch up and explain everything, but this time he could not, she did not want to lis-ten. She only shouted that she didn't want to be his friend anymore and that she didn't care about him. At this moment they were packing up to go. Everything was over. Now he felt a twitch in his nose, not from the water, not from the peaches, but from his wanting to be her friend, and how nice it had been, but now he could not say anything to her, because she was walking away with her mother and they did not even look back.

Now Grisha's mother started to get ready to go. "Come on," she said, "let's look for your father, he's not coming for a long time." They first walked down the beach along the sea, and then a bit further away from it, closer to the marketplace. They found him there. He was lying with some men and two women on a carpet, talking and drinking beer. Or wine, Grisha still did not know the difference, both tasted bad. The women were nothing special, they were pretty but mama was better. They were just talking, but mama has such a severe face that Grisha felt that he might cry, and she said something to dad that made him shrivel up completely. She gripped Grisha's hand tightly and they walked back towards the house so quickly that he almost had to run. Now mama was yelling at him, that he was raising dust with his steps or that he was whining. But Grisha was not whining at all, he was only thinking about how awful and unfair everything had been – first there was Marina, and now he was being yelled at because of his dad. It was not his fault at all and he had been a good boy, he had listened all day, he had eaten what they told him to for breakfast. He knew about the sun, that it was a red-hot ball, and about scorpions and many insects and what they were each called. But now they were yelling at him, such a smart and nice boy. He remembered the scorpion and again tears came to his eyes, but he did not cry, he held the tears back. Everything had turned out so bad, so unfair, like never before in his life, probably. Everyone had told him to just behave and be a good boy, but in reality things did not turn out that way. Grisha could not understand this, though he tried.

When they got back to the house, mama was again yelling at him for wanting to pick up a cool stone from the road. She stopped in the yard and said "Stand here", in such an angry voice that it was scary to even look at her face. It somehow reminded him of Marina's voice. His mother went into the house alone. Then his father arrived. He patted Grisha on the head and walked into the house, but he walked with a guilty hunch like a stray dog. Grisha felt sorry for him: imagine, he had only been talking with some guys and drinking beer. If Grisha had his way, he would be allowed to do that every day, there would be nothing wrong with that. Only now his parents inside had started to fight and Grisha grew bored. At first when they fought he got very worried, but then he got used to it, he saw that it was not a serious argument. First they would fight and then they would kiss.

He started walking around the yard. He looked at the chickens which were kept across the fence. He turned a big stone over and watched the ants, how they dragged their eggs into burrows. He found a good stick, one straight as a sword. Only then did he suddenly notice that there was no one sitting at the table in the yard. It was the first time he had seen such a thing: no one at the table and the yard empty. But high above, just like before, the bunch of grapes hung, sparkling in its fullness. It was bright and seemed lit from within, as if it was telling him "eat me". Grisha looked around. The yard was still empty. Then he resolved to do it. He found a box lying outside the house and dragged it up to the bench. The bench was high, but he managed to climb up, he only lightly scraped his knee on the rough edge. He climbed up and thought about how not everything in his life was so bad. Maybe there was something worth behaving well for. He only had to wait, it seemed, and then the well-deserved joy would come. The whole bad day had become a good one.

Then he climbed from the bench onto the table. It was a little scary, but he did not fall. It would be scarier if someone came now and yelled at him, but those grapes were meant for him. He had known this for a long time, from the very first time he had seen them. It was such a wonderful bunch of grapes and it grew and called out to him. Grisha stood up on the table. The bunch was now right there, right in front of his face. It seemed nice and delicious from up close, much more so than from far away. Through the transparent skins, through the smoky flesh, Grisha could glimpse the little seeds, so tart, that lay within. The grapes were stuck to each other so harmoniously, as if they were afraid to part, as if they knew that the most frightful thing in the world would be to part. The whole bunch had such a wonderful oblong shape, so full and neat, that it made Grisha squint. A wonderful feeling of happiness came upon him, wrapped him from head to toe, like a salty sea wave. Such happiness made it seem as if there had never been an argument and misunderstanding with Marina, as if his parents had never fought and the weather would always be so fine, the sun so gentle, the wind so cool and the sea so warm. A happiness that you know will never end and that will last forever. Such a happiness that he now understood: be a good boy and you'll get your recompense.

Grisha opened his eyes. He stretched out his arms and took the bunch in his hands. It was cool and tight like a nice, brightly-colored ball. Grisha tugged. The bunch did not come off, he had to twist it, then he felt the precious weight in his hands. With a slight cracking sound he pulled one grape off and gratefully popped it into his mouth. He smiled happily and bit down. His mouth filled with a burning, pungent acid. Grisha's face wrinkled from the burning, from the pain, from the hurt, and he burst into tears.

MID-16TH CENTURY, VILLAGES OF KERET AND KOLA

Oh, it is funny now, my brothers, even though such a little amount of time has passed. I laugh with tears and the sharp wind blows them from my cheeks into the sea as if they were a paltry, drizzling rain. I laugh at myself, at my cares, my experiences and hopes, though a man is not a creature to hope. He has no such right to think that he will be compensated for righteous deeds. Only by going through many trials will he understand that he should be saved by faith and all else he should reject, for the world is too cruel, there is little love in it and God is righteous among men, so curb your pride.

I was, my brothers, Varlaam, a priest of Kola. Though the wise, seeing my strength and happiness, said, "You, Varlaam, are like unto a *shalamat*,[5] you live too at ease, you are toying with death, you fear nothing, you know nothing of fear." I did not heed them. For all things, I thought, lay in a man's strength and the grace of God. How well I lived in my native northern land. God gave me everything: he gave me faith, he did not deprive me of hope and he endowed my body with strength. Most of all I thanked our Father for my Varvara. She was such a wonder, such a beauty, that at times I could not believe my fortune and I would lay sleepless through the white nights asking, "Is this for me, is this not a mistake? For what deeds was it given me?" But in my pride I would feel at ease and tell myself, "It is mine." We lived together happily, in the summer the river Kola ran and in the winter it froze over, but it gave us sustenance, beauty and contentment – it nourished us with salmon, it ran its course among the hills and was a pleasure to the eyes; it brought all manner of guests, mainly good people, to satisfy my interest in life, in its varied forms. In wintertime, even though it was cold in our parts, everything was still joyous: you stoke the bathhouse and then plunge into a hole cut into the ice, praising the Lord, you put skis on and hunt creatures great and small. I served my ministry wholeheartedly, I taught

---

5 *Shalamat*: a deer meant for sacrifice.

the people to lift their hearts in praise towards their Creator in happy times and in woeful times alike. I believed with thanksgiving, my brother, but clearly that was not enough.

The river Kola twists and turns, it whirls like a wheel, just as our lives – one cannot riddle anything out, one cannot foretell. You walk along its banks, through the bright forest of pines, as if you are strolling through woods edenic, but suddenly you see that step by step you are falling into an evil mire. The sparse forest now rises like a wall about you, the black alders and aspens are dastardly, with their thin branches they flail at your eyes until tears come to them, they flail again. Now swarms of biting flies assail your ears, your nostrils, uncountable numbers get into your mouth and such a frenzied buzz arises that after an instant it is no longer a buzz but a roar. You wander among the mosses, you fall into the foul water up to your knees, but you must push through the dense foliage with your shoulders, your throat dry from thirst. Such dense foliage arises around you that your head spins; you understand nothing, you no longer know which direction is which or even your own name. Then you stop for a moment to catch your breath and raise your eyes to heaven: "Lord, save me". Then lo! Your heart is calmed, your despair departs, you easily come forth from the accursed foliage and your fear is behind you. Only you have no conception of what lies ahead, when and where you will again be borne into evil places and the evil one will confuse your soul. Then you will give in to doubt.

Thus, in my happiness, my brothers, I did not notice in time that something was wayward. In our parts it has always been so: your gaze cannot be distracted, you must be attentive to the world. If you forget yourself, even a little, let your guard down, you will immediately pay for it, you will howl like a wolf, but it will be too late. When I noticed the bad things, everything had long since come to pass already. Everyone around me knew of this and they were silent, wagging their evil tongues behind my back. But I was like a senseless child. Because I loved my Varvara greatly. After all, as the learned teach us, even if you love, you cannot trust, because people are enemies to each other and there is no true love between them. Yet we are prideful – "Love exists!" we cry, and we sell our souls for the sake of those whom we love. I began to notice that Varvara was not like herself sometimes. Her habits had changed like the water in the river: if the sun shines the water is bright, but as soon as a storm cloud comes, the water becomes blacker than black. She began to hide her eyes from me, not from fear but from some deep-seated thoughts. I would question her, but she remained silent. If she gave an answer, she still seemed far away from me. I suppressed my evil thoughts and trusted her like I trusted myself, my mother and God.

I felt ill at ease on that day. My soul was not in its right place, though I celebrated the liturgy diligently and I tried to quell my disquiet with work. Nevertheless, the seagulls cried with such lamentation that it struck me deeply. I felt my whole being in the grip of foreboding. Varara had left that morning to go to the nearby village, for we had run out of salt and soon the salmon would come. She was gone for a long time and now the sun was preparing for sleep. I could not bear it any longer, I gathered my things in an instant and went off in search of her, but I cursed myself – I should not have allowed that weak soul to walk alone through savage nature and among evil men. I flew to the village so fast that the oars bent in my hands. I threw myself into searching for her and I asked people. Yet no one would speak, they only looked away with a strange grin. Finally, my patience was at an end, I grabbed at the shirt of a bearded parishioner, and he then pointed at a Norwegian ship that stood nearby.

I again got into my boat and headed for the ship. I rowed up to it and there I witnessed a hubbub, merrymaking with neither care nor decency. A drunken crowd reeled on the deck and scurried about their cabins. There were seven men there and among them was my Varvara. At first I did not even recognize her. Her hair was let loose, her eyes shone with a demonic flame and her cheeks were red, not from shame but from these lowly entertainments. The outsiders were grabbing her and carrying her around, but she remained mirthful. She would go round and round with one man, and then cling to another man as to another darling. Now they noticed me and everyone came to stand together, and she was there in their midst. I attempted to admonish her, but only briefly – she laughed like a witch, she would not give herself over to me and she was whirling there like a top. The foreign men jabbered something in their own language and came towards me. I forgot about God in that moment, I forgot my faith and hope. Only black wrath remained within me and I surged forward like a heavy wave. It flooded through me, blinded my eyes and made my hands heavy as lead. I grabbed a cask of wine, weighing some fifty pounds, that stood on a bench and I hurled it at this gang of men. They scattered across the deck like spray and hugged the walls. I could no longer hold myself back – a small anchor came into my hands and I lashed out with it to the left and to the right. Whoever tried to stand against me, I hit him with all my rage. Neither did I spare those who whimpered. I killed her first.

When I came to my senses, somewhat, I did not think long about what to do. In an instant everything was gone: my life, my love; the devil had taken everything from me and he took me along with him. I rolled my Varvara in a piece of sailcloth that was lying nearby, as if it had been expressly prepared. I placed her at the prow of my boat and pushed away from the terrible ship. I made my way, first along the twists and turns of the river Kola, then into the bay and the northern seas. There was no longer a place for me on this earth, let the deep devour me, for my dead love lay before me as an eternal reproach, the outline of her body shone through the sailcloth and behind me was a foreign vessel that I had filled to its broadsides with blood. I knew nothing before about the path of wickedness, but I knew it now. Forgive, lord, this sinner.

Oh, I found it funny, my brothers. I laughed with tears and the sharp wind blew them from my cheeks into the sea, like the slightest drizzling rain. I found my sudden journey funny and my fortune, until just recently; the sea waves splashing into my boat, the gray sky above my head and the terrible cargo at the prow of the boat. This humor lasted several days, but the Lord gave me no relief in madness, he did not take away my wits, but instead forced me to follow his road to the end, in cold knowledge and despair. When I realized this, my laughter died away and from then on I began to live in a grim silence and stubbornness. I, a feeble creature, resolved that I understood God's plan, I began to direct my boat to the North, ever further from land and men. There was no forgiveness either from them or from myself and I was to be punished in an exemplary manner: swallowed up by the icy abyss without anything left of me, not even in the memories of others. I cannot remember how long I spent like this, waiting insensate. I constantly prayed to God for a quick death, for each new day began with the sight of the terrible bundle at the prow and each night was filled with memories of what had happened. I sometimes cried out with a beastly cry from the anguish and the pain in my soul, but the waves gave no heed to my cries. I saw terrible storms, my brothers, where the depths of the sea exploded madly upwards towards the sky. I rejoiced each time I suspected the end of my suffering, yet it was as if some unknown force lifted my boat up over the abyss and bore it further along. I shouted blasphemies and cursed God as cruel. I writhed in spasms and then fell asleep exhausted, but when I woke up, the sea was calm around me and I still lived. I went hungry for many days and drank no water, but then the northern seas began to feed me, though I did not ask them to. A storm had ripped a sea kale away and then driven it to my boat, or I was brought to shallows where I dug up lobworms, it was enough to know how to throw a fishing line into the water – cod were abundant, about me. I fashioned a fishing line by winding up the sailcloth that covered my cargo and a hook from a nail. This crude tackle worked, I caught such a richness of fish I had never seen before. I pressed fresh juice from the fish, drank it, then rain too began to deliver me water. The Lord did not will for me a quick death, for it is not possible to repent for one's sins without suffering.

I traveled long on the sea without peace – everything within me was rent apart and crying out, while on the outside my hands were ceaselessly laboring at the tasks of seafaring. As soon as my boat reached the neck of the White Sea, I recognized it from the tales of my forebears. The place was well known for shipworms, which eat the wood of vessels and have drowned countless ships. This is where you led me, Lord, this is the death you have prepared for me. And again in my pride I was blind and I congratulated myself for my farsightedness. Yet my boat passed through these straits, and I saw not a single worm on it. My boat remained unspoiled, as if it had just come from the boat builder's hands. The wind was slight, gentle – and a warm and sharp gust suddenly blew the canvas from the prow, so I averted my eyes in horror. When I dared to open my eyes again, there was nothing there. The wind had borne away my wife's mortal dust away with it. I realized then that another road awaited me, not towards death but life, so that I might seek salvation and labor endlessly, tirelessly, remembering everything, in good health and caring for others. In tears, I gave praise to God.

Now a small bay was revealed to me, where among the abundant rocks and forests, a lively, bright river fell into the sea. My wanderings had come to an end. The name of this river was Keret.

My solitude was no burden to me. I settled in these fertile places and the song of any forest bird was sweeter to me than the voice of man. Our kind can only be tolerated because of our children and the various animals, which are also our kin, which means that they are in some degree our justification. Otherwise, we are a foul race, and we need – goodness, we need – the mercy of God, for without it there is no meaning to existence. But we live, busy ourselves, labor, and it is not in vain, there is divine providence in it, only it is inaccessible to our meager wits, otherwise our pride would lead us astray. Thus, I lived with the memory of the terrible events, with pain in my heart and tender hope. I thought nothing of my sustenance – everything was already there, prepared all around me. I firmly remember one thing from my life and the experiences granted me – things are happier and easier when you have compassion for others. Therefore, I prayed hour after hour – Lord, accept my prayer for children and animals!

1978, PRYAZHA

It was nice to remain behind as the eldest for the first time. The grownups were having a wedding. Not all of them. Uncle Igor was marrying the young and beautiful Valya. Everyone else was the guests. That morning they had spent a long time getting ready and running about nervously. The children were also agitated and ran around at the adults' feet. It was only Grisha's younger brother, three-year-old Konstantin, who calmly sat at the table drinking tea. From his earliest days he had been serious and judicious, he always thought for a long time before doing something or repeating after someone else. For that reason he did a lot of things right, something that his parents loved him for. The others, loud and of varying ages, did not grasp that this celebration was not in their honor and that they would be staying home under Grisha's supervision. He had been immediately told of this and everyone, whether mama or grandma, came to him with instructions. Don't poke around in the stove, don't let the little ones out into the street, give them their food on time, have everyone lay down for their nap. "I know, I know," Grisha said, already tired of answering them. They might not realize it, but he was already big and responsible.

Finally, everyone was ready. Grandpa was the last to leave, he looked at Grisha carefully but did not say anything. They walked down the road, a festive, orderly crowd. The village was not far from their hamlet, so they went on foot. Only Uncle Igor had sped off earlier on a motorcycle, looking all happy and scared.

Grisha got down to managing this household. He quickly quieted the noisy children, putting a toy in one's hand and cuffing another on the nape. He was helped a bit by Svetlana, his cousin. Though she was a couple of years younger than him, that didn't matter, she was smart. They took care of the small things, then fed everyone and had them lay down to sleep. The two of them then played chess. They got bored. They went down to the stream, but there was nothing interesting there. Then Grisha remembered that he knew where Grandpa kept the ammunition for hunting. In the second drawer of the chest, the one locked with a key. Svetlana suddenly said that she knew where Grandpa hid the key: on a nail high behind a curtain. For some reason Grisha did not even think – maybe he couldn't. He got up and ran into the house and found the key. Svetlana was right behind him. With his heart anxiously and joyfully beating in his chest, he opened the drawer. A treasure like Aladdin's cave lay within. He turned the casings, wads and shot around in his hands, then put them back – they didn't interest him much. He spent more time looking at the bullets, he took several for himself and gave little Svetlana one for her assistance. Then he opened a small box – it held caps shining with gold. Next to them was a full tin of black powder. This was something else completely, something for grownups. Now Grisha's joy made him completely forget any shame at going through other people's stuff, and any fear that he was taking forbidden things. He rolled a newspaper up into a cup and filled it with a handful of caps and a generous helping of powder. Then, he and Svetlana ran outside and exploded the caps. He knew how to do this, some guys had done it in the yard once. This was a lot of fun. You put the cap on a stone and then you smash it with a small rock. There's a crackle, a boom and pure bliss. This is no child's cap gun. It's a whole different kind of fun.

He spent half an hour having fun like this and blowing off steam. But there were a lot of caps and there was no suitable company around; Svetlana didn't count, she was still small, plus she was a girl. Grisha felt bored. He went into the house with Svetlana following after him. He opened the stove. There were red coals inside, they were ablaze with heat. He took the rest of the caps and hurled them into the stove. He hardly managed to close the little door before there was such a boom. He was even scared a bit, but then he saw that it was nothing: after the boom it was quiet again. A strange whim came over him. Complete recklessness; his head had completely stopped thinking. He wanted even more explosions and fun. So, he took a handful of powder from his bag and threw it into the stove. Now it went off for real. The stove shook. A cloud of smoke from the powder came roaring out and hung over the kitchen. Svetlana let out a loud scream. Even Grisha was slightly taken aback. That's enough, he thought, I've had enough fun. No need for more shocks. He sat for a while, caught his breath and then thought of something. He took a matchbox, removed one of the sides and poured powder into it. It would be great, the powder would catch and then through the open side flame would roar out, so the matchbox would fly like a rocket. He was smart, he had thought of everything, right, no wonder that he did well in school and read smart books. He did everything with careful precision and then he set the box on the edge of the table and stood slightly away from it. Little Svetlana also kept her distance. Grisha lit a match and carefully put it into the box. He waited, but nothing happened. The match burned out, but the powder didn't catch. What in the world? He was very surprised at this absurdity, so he bent down to see how this could happen. He looked into the box from the side. Then it hit him right in the face.

He had never felt such pain in his life. Even when he had gone down the slide and bit his lower lip. Grisha fell to the floor next to the door. His face was burning. He couldn't open his eyes, it hurt too much. The babies woke up. They started crying. Smoke hung all around, the place reeked like a battlefield. It was a good thing that little Svetlana jumped up and ran to fetch the grownups. Grandpa was the first to arrive, he came hobbling in. He was lame, not fast on his feet, and he was wheezing, but he was the first back. Grisha had already started crying from the horror. Grandpa picked him up and carried him outside. Soon an ambulance came. While Grandpa was hobbling up to it, Grisha heard, through his own wailing, his Grandpa saying, as he rocked him, "Oh, you little fish. You little fish…"

He soon became known as one-eyed Grisha. That is what his local friends nicknamed him almost immediately after he left the house, for the first time, with a bandage over half his face. Fortunately, he kept his eye. His other eye had emerged completely unscathed, apparently it was capable of squinting much faster than the first. The skin on his face had been seriously burned, but after a stage of blisters and raw red flesh, it too started growing and became clear and rosy-colored again. Everyone felt that Grisha had been extremely lucky and they told him that constantly. Saying "I told you so" is always a pleasure.

However, his Grandpa remained quiet for a long time after the incident. Every time Grisha came to visit the village, Grandpa would just glance at his wounded head and turn away. This lasted until they took off the bandage and it became clear that Grisha would not be a pirate with an eyepatch. Grandpa laughed for the first time at seeing Grisha's two-colored face – white and pink – and invited him to come along fishing.

There were two fishing holes, one close by, the other far away. To get to the one further away, they had to walk for a few miles through the fields, then along a forest trail until they could catch a glimpse through the trees of the lake with the somehow shamanic name Shangema. Here, people went fishing for real, they set nets and the traps with a metal mesh that Karelians called a *katiska*. A fishing pole would be brought along, mainly just for fun. The nearest fishing hole was only about two hundred meters away. They only had to go around the neighboring house (there were only four houses in this hamlet) and then a big weir opened up on the stream. It had been made by hand using a great number of stones, large and small, and served for swimming and catching small perch. If they wanted, they could bring these fish back home for a good soup. The grownups rarely fished here as the place mainly attracted a bunch of village children, darting about just like the perch.

Grisha was amazed that Grandpa was bringing him here now. Grisha walked over the flimsy wooden bridge and unwound his fishing rod. Grandpa stood on the bank. Right in front of the little bridge a strong, angry current seethed. To the right of the bridge was a clean, sandy beach; to the left was a patch of swamp with sparse grass growing on it. The swamp was small but very unpleasant to the eye. A slight stink came off its surface, no one knew how deep it was and they never aimed to find out. Grisha cast his rod a few times. The fishing float was swiftly carried along the stream in front of him. The fish weren't biting. He, nonetheless, stood looking at the water carefully and didn't notice that his Grandpa had walked up next to him on the bridge. When Grisha saw what was happening, it was too late. Grandpa gave him a light push and the boy plunged into the filth. The swamp made a slurping sound and became cold, it greedily sucked Grisha in. Horror pushed down on his chest. He didn't dare shout but only gazed at his Grandpa with trepidation as he slowly sank. His feet sluggishly swept through the filth in search of support, but it was in vain. A bitter stench rose from the depths together with the bubbles and clenched at his throat. Grisha was drowning without saying a word. Grandpa also said nothing. Finally, the nasty slurry reached his chest and his feet touched the bottom. It was slimy but he could stand on it. Grandpa stood there for a moment, then stretched out his strong arm, grabbed Grisha by the collar and effortlessly pulled him out of the swamp.

On the clean, sandy bank the filthy little boy was wailing. He choked with tears at the fear he had experienced, at how hurt he felt, at how Grandpa had betrayed him. His old Grandpa sat next to him and talked. He talked for a long time, like never before:

"See, you were horsing around. You thought it was fun. I understand. But what happened? Fine, you got hurt yourself. But what if there was a fire? What if the children were burned? Huh, you didn't think of that, did you, little fish? You have to think. You always have to think. Life itself means you always have to be prepared. Always on guard."

Grandpa fell silent, then a grin appeared solely in his eyes. "Once you fall into the muck, you can't wash it off afterwards."

Grisha had already stopped crying. Grandpa was right. His feeling of being offended was mixed with shame. He wanted to offer some excuse but he couldn't, the words wouldn't come out of his throat. Grandpa looked at him again, this time right in the eye:

"Alright then, go wash off. I'll wash your clothes."

At first the river was calm, leisurely and we easily paddled against the current. So easily that we had time to look around and think about the journey. Because there is nothing sweeter and more exciting than to think about a journey, especially at the beginning of it. Only on the road are you truly free and honest before God and yourself. In any other circumstances, being dependent on human structures bends you down to earth. Only by taking upon yourself the whole joy of the burden of the road to life or death, by having only the sky over you and the earth or water under your feet, do you become the true master of yourself. The only thing that can help you is the cross you wear on your chest and the only thing that can hinder you are falsities from the past. Everything else is in your hands, your mind or your spirit. On the road you are pure and therefore strong and vulnerable. But that's a life worth experiencing.

The riverbank slowly swept past us. Thickets of dwarf birch trees were replaced by open expanses of mossy marsh. Sometimes sandbanks would suddenly appear and we could see on them signs of deer herds. It was quiet all around. Light rain drizzled. Fog came from our mouths. It was late June.

The riverbank slowly swept past and then stopped. Little by little, it started going backwards. At the same time, we heard a noise. I snapped out of my highfalutin' thoughts and saw that while I was daydreaming, the river had changed. It had become fast-flowing. We could hear the first rapids in front of us.

I was strongly counting on Volodya. He was still an athlete, albeit a retired one. Six liters of lungs and a bundle of heavy muscle. The two of us could get through a lot together. I had counted on several other people, too. They had intended to go with me, they had boats, guns, skills and courage. For six months I had been enticing them to visit the Ponoy, promising them golden hills, fish beyond number, natural beauty and great memories. They nodded in agreement, grabbed their guns and were ready for anything. Until the time to leave came. One after another, like buds on a tree that freeze off before they can blossom, these heroes and great fishermen fell away from the trip. The reasons differed: family, everyday obligations, whatever. I think that they were simply afraid of the journey. It really was a difficult one.

The last to fall away was my friend Konev. For six months he had been set on going, only to bail out on the day before our departure. "I've suddenly come down with an ulcer. I can't go," was all he said. No regret, no apology. Konev resigned from the trip womanishly, he disappeared just like that. It was down to Volodya and me. Now we were paddling with all our might and it was hard for two people, another person would have helped. The river was rushing along, it had sharply picked up speed and lost its quiet flow. Before you realized it would take you right back to the lake.

We barely managed to paddle ourselves to shore. Before the rapids was a quiet backwater, with a small whirlpool, so we headed for that. I hopped out onto the riverbank and pulled the canoe up. Volodya got out too. Somehow he had not been able to get used to things very quickly. But what do you expect if you put a man of the steppes into the conditions of the faraway North. In the same way, I would probably let some horse run loose like Volodya did with the canoe. Good thing a rope was tied to the canoe's nose. We barely managed to keep a grip on it as the canoe was ready to set off without us and continue sailing on alone. We would be left without food and gear right from the start.

But it was so beautiful, all around us, that our hands seemed to quickly do all the work themselves – a fire, the tent – while our heads were operating separately, taking in all this beauty through our eyes, ears and nostrils. The rapids roared; the forest was a pleasure to the eye with its fresh green. Only the high blue tundra mountains, decked with a creamy top of snow, hung bleakly over our heads. They seem to constantly observe you, as if you were a Communist –small and alone, but you have an enormous conscience.

I found it easy to get Volodya to go on this expedition. He's a good guy, but a funny one. He decided to go because the most interesting thing in the world for him were the ancient Indians. He developed some kind of obsession about them when he was a kid. He had Indians up to here: in his head, in his heart and in his eyes, that they were so large and perpetually astonished. The Aztecs, the Maya, Quetzalcoatl and all the other great stuff. He had even written a book about this, fantastical stories about the Indians, how they could foresee all and were capable of everything. So, it was enough to show him a photograph of the Ancestors, as the rocks in the Ponoy basin were known. These rocks really were magnificent, shaped like sitting giants, fantastical animals, hook-nosed profiles with features on their crowns – a real feast for a lover of fantasy. That is why Volodya agreed to go North on an expedition for the sake of southern knowledge. But this knowledge is outside any earthly geography. It is the geography of the human spirit, that's what it is.

In the morning we got up and were reluctant to take down our camp. A human being can take a strong liking to any place. Even a tent becomes a cherished home in just one night. How could it be otherwise, when outside it was raining and the temperature was just above freezing? Fog poured out of our mouths and our shoes were wet. Good thing there were still no mosquitoes or midges, it was still too cold for those. Plus, you shudder like a child at the horror of asking yourself where the hell you're going.

When I had still been at home and starting to get ready, I could never understand what was driving me here, whether it was divine providence or the goading of demons. I would look at photographs of the places here, so incredibly beautiful. I started to look for people for help – somehow everything came together easily. One person, then another, then a third; mutual friends were found, people out of nowhere on the internet – and everyone helped me, they were happy to give advice. I was very pleased at first. Then I got slightly worried. If everything was too good, then something was wrong. This is one of the basic things I know about life in my native land. A sixth sense of mine.

There is indeed a magical potion which turns fear into courage. It is called distilled grain alcohol. Volodya and I had some for breakfast along with canned meat and noodles, and we were again fine and heroic men ready for many things. We laid everything in the canoe neatly and tightly. Then we were off. Only now we had already completed the first stage of our journey. The one where you sit in your little boat and wave the paddles around while admiring the nature. The towing began. And the bushes.

Towing is easier than portaging. But not much easier. With portaging you would be carrying everything on your back. Here, everything is lying in the canoe. You just haul the canoe through the water with the rope attached to its nose. The canoe moves easily if the current is not too fast, and if the riverbank has a gentle slope and there is a clear path along it. Then you can just stroll along, smelling the flowers along the way. Here we were along rapids, where there was impenetrable vegetation and the river had become awfully brisk. The nose of the canoe would get caught in the bushes and you would have to pull it out with a rustling sound. Even if the birch trees here were dwarfish, two meters tall or less, they were all woven together, like a girl's curly hair after a night of full-on lovemaking.

We managed somehow. I went in front pulling the canoe and getting it through the birch trees. Volodya was in back with a paddle, pushing the canoe away from the riverbank before it could get stuck in the foliage. We made our way boldly at first, with an excess of energy. We did not care about the rain, or the cold, we were making process. We put up the tarp only when there was a downpour, otherwise we kept going over the drops and the bumps. Granted, when I heard a loud splash behind me for the first time, I got very scared, but I didn't show it, I just thought that it was a big fish. I turned around and it turned out that Volodya had gone completely overboard while rowing. It was not in vain that he was a swimming champion. That was the first time. By then I had already stopped turning around. Whether from weariness or from the horror of it, but Volodya kept falling into the water more and more often. His wading boots were full of water, he was wet all over, but he kept going, kept hanging on. We made a halt some three hours later when it was becoming unbearable to lift our legs up to the height of our arms in order to break through the thicket. You make a small fire under the tarp, you warm up some tea and add some liquor to it – a *punshik* the Pomors called it. Then back on the road.

At first we tried to make our way merrily. We remembered a song about the bush kangaroo Skippy, from a television series known from our distant childhood. So we went, sometimes almost squatting. "Skippy, Skippy," you sing. "Skippy the Bush Kangaroo-oo-oo." That is how the first day passed. We set up camp and made a fire. A tarp, a tent and no legs left. Volodya tried to dry his wet socks with hot stones from the fire, but it was in vain. The rain did not let up.

2003, PETROZAVODSK

Not very long ago, about twenty years ago, huge numbers of UFO believers roamed the earth. These were special creatures that believed that beings from other planets sometimes came and took people off with them, somewhere. Now you hardly find any believers in UFOs. Apparently they were all carried away somewhere by what they so fervently believed in. It is all so mysterious. Grandpa's fate held no fewer riddles, Grisha felt. A lot of time had passed now, already many people were no longer among the living, but questions remained, they ached like some metal fragment stuck in his flesh, the rusty hooks of painful memories. First of all, no one knew where his grandfather was originally from. Grandpa had never said anything about it. It seemed that he had come to Karelia from somewhere in the central strip of Russia, not far from the border with Belarus. He had some relatives there, sisters. But what was strange is that the last name of all those relatives was Grishayev. Only one child in that large family had a different last name. Grisha could not understand how that was possible and he found himself at a loss, like a bullfinch in the early days of spring. Grisha himself was a Nikolayev, his father was a Nikolayev, but with his grandfather everything broke off. Grandpa had been the first of the Nikolayevs, like the first man on earth, and before him was nothingness.

Grandpa had lived his whole life after his military service in a Karelian village. But he was completely different from his neighbors. In his appearance, there was nothing of the wide, cunning smile – "I know you're trying to fool me, so I'll be sneaky myself" – that is so powerfully cut across the faces of indigenous Karelians. He also did not fit the general stereotype that "a drunk Karelian is more fearsome than a tank," for he drank little, and when drinking he would become quiet and pensive; although when sober he could become terrible and raging, as if the pain in his soul tore at him so much that hurling it all out was the only way to survive. His way of speaking was also different – it was pure and correct, without any of the grammatical faults or the singsong quality and drawl with which the locals, russified long ago, differed from the pure Russians here and unwittingly revealed their secret Finno-Ugrian essence.

Certain words and sayings that his grandfather would throw out now and again, Grisha had never heard them anywhere, not in the south of the country, nor in the west or the east.

Thus he sometimes struggled to understand, as he did not know the meaning of the words, until one day he glanced at the Russian dictionary compiled by Vladimir Dal in the 19th century, where he found all of Grandpa's pearls with the note ("archaic") in parentheses after them.

Grandpa would remain silent, wheezing, coughing or dying. Grandma was also silent. While Grandpa had still been alive she was quiet, but after his death she started to love entertaining guests; she would finally sing songs in Karelian (a language that none of the children or grandchildren knew) and she loved a bit of vodka, too. She had no regrets about anything, and before she died of a terrible bone cancer, she told Grisha that she had at least managed to catch a little breath at the end of her life. But she said nothing about Grandpa then; nor why he had received a pension that was as small as a sparrow's tail; nor why some people came to the house without even waiting for the funeral and they took all of Grandpa's medals, one after another according to a list. "That's how we are, nest-robbing Nikolayevs." That was the last time Grisha saw her.

* * *

There is nothing in the world more beautiful than the shore of the White Sea. It is as if a slow, sweet poison trickles into the soul of anyone who sees the light-colored, whitish sky here, the water as clear as if it were from a spring. This stony gray cavity that meekly offers up its gently sloping body and gratefully accepts the gentle caress of the water. These rumbling beaches strewn with pebbles, these round stones that the sea rolls around incessantly, plays with them, and, as a result, this rumble does not cease, not even for a second, and you think to yourself involuntarily, "Don't joke like that, mother sea." These underwater kingdoms, a flickering paradise pierced by the sun, like the light calico of a woman's dress in spring is pierced by a man's gaze. This light wind with a scent of unearthly, watery freshness and boldness, and everyone knows now what freshness and boldness are. The lively noise of the pine forest, with a shy brown animal bolting away from the shore with the fat jelly on its rump bouncing. This joy of a boundless road, open towards life, happiness and death.

There is nothing more fearsome than the shore of the White Sea. The cold wind slaps you backhandedly and shamelessly in the face, carrying a malicious splash of reproach and failure. The turbid water roars in your eyes and soul about swift chaos and the futility of all things. A field of thick black mud stretches as far as the horizon – and if you step into this filth, it will be hard to survive it. Along the shore are huge gray crosses that serve as a reminder. The woods hold small, overgrown crosses that hide shyly in the damp ravines. A desolate region that the descendants of these people have forgotten. Turbid, gray, muddy pits. Only a plover bird cries its pleading, plaintive song as it goes on the wing, sounding like "leave, leave". This is how a child must cry, who does not yet know that someone else's anger can make life irreparable.

There is no greater border in the world than the shore of the White Sea. Here, all things are next to each other, close, inextricably linked with one another — white and black, drunkenness and honesty, fury and peace. Here is the main freedom of Russia, trampled by the promise of freedom. Here is a deadly beauty. Here is the joy of despair. Here is faith. Here is love.

Here too lives a rugged, bleak flower. On the stones, on the rocks, often against the very sea, it grasps its native soil with all its might. The four winds tear at this flower, but it knows that it will hold on, for it grows everywhere all the way to the Tersky Coast. It has stems like wires, leaves like thin metal foil – all so that it can live in this unkindly place. Sometimes a very high water comes and it will be hidden in a strange salty haze. Hours go by without air or light and it might seem that this will be the end for the flower. But the sea retreats, which means, once again, this living, tenacious and native flower will wave to the sky in the wind, whether praying or cursing. It will then delicately offer up to the sun a tiny yellow inflorescence and a fleeting sense of meaning will shine through in the gray meaninglessness of life. It does not have to believe, to hope or wait for something. It simply lives. It is called golden root because there, in the harsh and gloomy depths, it draws from all its hardships and misfortune a juice that is nectar for man and beast that will cure, save and help. For free, just like that. Because life is hard, death is easy and between them there is love.

1913, KERET VILLAGE

I remember a big village. On the slopes of a hill and on the other side the sea, with forest all around. On the other side of the sea there was forest too. Only not in the direction of the open sea but the bay. The open sea was hidden behind a big island. A wind blew from there, you couldn't see it, but you knew it was there. When it was totally calm, you knew all the same. But when it turns angry, you know to hide. A river flowed down into the bay. It was also big and turbulent. The last rapids were already called the sea rapids; there were high breakers right in the salt-water. That is where the village stood, right next to all of this. Rather, the village didn't stand but ran away from the water up the hill, like a smartly-dressed maiden. In the summer there were motley grasses. Flowering meadows all around – red, blue and yellow. There was little green, it was mostly flowers. The air was buzzing with heat. The grasshoppers chirped with a hollow sound, as if coming from under the earth. There were few mosquitoes or midges – the sea wind blew unceasingly. Only in the evenings would they appear, when the wind calmed before it slept and only blew in intermittent gusts. But they rarely came when the day had been without rain. There were always dark clouds in the sky, I remember, whether silent in times of drought, or suddenly splashing down drops from the sky, or pouring rain so heavy that you didn't even manage to run inside before you were all wet. Then too the village was like a maiden, laughing with its tiny windows at the patch of sunlight coming out from behind the clouds, wet grass flowing from it like hair, streams giggling on the stones as they rushed down towards the sea and leaped into it. Soon the summer rain ends, for the winds are strong and they bear away all the rain clouds in an instant. And in an instant they bring new rain clouds, so that the cycle of wet and dry happens several times each day. The nets are hung to dry in the sun, but under the rain they get wet again, then they again lay in the sun. Their colors quickly fade. They have to be painted often. But all of this happens in the summer. In late autumn and winter the village, like an old woman, hobbles down the mountain, bends down with its crooked houses under the heavy snow. Or it is silent, peering closely at its fate with its half-blind eyes under its furrowed brow, or when the storm comes and the sea, our father, is angry, it pulls the village about like a drunken son pushes his mother. It jabs her on one side, then on the other and then pulls her by her mossy hair shamelessly. With a harsh, rebuking sound the surrounding forest rustles, nearly screams, howls, but what can it do – such is life. Thus the old woman endures the evil attacks of the ill-taught and unloved as it rages with wind, water, waves and horrible crashes. It does so for many days, until it has exhausted its strength, until the storm over the sea falls quiet, until the tired wind soon falls asleep in the corner, and the ancient old woman, that is the village, catches her breath a little, puts her houses in order again and livens up a bit. She knows that after the beating there will be repentance and even tears, until the anger builds up again and a new storm comes from the sea.

We had a big church, a beautiful one. It stood high above the water, like a white swan that has spread out its wings: the church's porches. It was a church dedicated to Varlaam of Keret, the patron saint of our White Sea. From early childhood everyone knew who Fr. Varlaam was. On a winter evening some old man, a storyteller, would start singing his long song and we would sit slack jawed and listen:

Varlaam did not grow weary
Sitting at the helm.
Varlaam did not fall asleep
Looking upon his wife.
Varlaam did not fall silent
Singing his lullaby:
"Sleep, priest's wife,
Sleep, beauty beyond words."

It is a pity, now the days of old have been forgotten, no one remembers the words. It is not just a pity but a real misery without our grandfather teaching us that a person before a new life is naked, like some Arctic char.

Beyond the forest, not far along the road, is a big, flat glade. Here in the summer, the young ladies do circle dances. The songs are interrupted, you can't hold a tune long in the wind. Everyone dresses up: it was so lovely to watch. Their peasant headdresses, waistcoats, skirts – everything had pearls sewn into it. Their embroidery would feature a small pearl, while at their necks, in their ears, there would be a large pearl to admire. Light blue, white, pink, even black sometimes. This was for the rich. But the others were not lacking either. What was most important was beauty, love, true affection, things money cannot buy. A fine pearl can be bought, but it cannot help a girl without tenderness.

All of them got their pearls from my father. His brother traveled along the trading route. He did well trading fish, Pomor salt; then he built a sawmill. He did things for the people too: he built the school, the church. The door was always open to the needy at his home, to the Pomor widows and orphans. That is why everyone in Pomorye knew him and addressed him respectfully as "Merchant Savin".

My father learned what he knew from his forefathers. It was hard learning and difficult work. Sometimes he would cast everything aside and walk down to the sea in a huff, but he would quickly come back. "I'm ill-tempered," he would say to excuse himself, but we knew that he couldn't stand any authority over him. It didn't matter if it were an arrogant rich man, a spiteful pauper or some state official. If he didn't like something, he wouldn't do it. He would remain silent once or twice, he would keep it down for the sake of making profit, gaining something, but later he was no longer able to hold it inside and would rebuke a foolish authority so strongly that devils would be leaping out of the other's eyes. After all, within any man lies the demons of pride and swaggering. They are so afraid of criticism that they all huddle up and try to avoid it.

Thus, every time my father would return to his craft. It was just him, just his own mind, with the heavens and God above him, gleefully rushing water at his feet, and around him the freedom of the forest with its mosquitoes and berries. If you don't attract the devil, he won't bother you on his own. Nobody likes being cajoled, everyone wants things to be easy and simple.

His craft fascinated him so much that he never complained about his back, which had ached him all his life and by the time of his death was twisted like a northern pine in the frigid wind, nor about a life of poverty. A middleman would take the bulk of the profit, sell our northern pearls to foreign lands, and in turn – the goods having become exotic oriental ones – fools here in Russia would buy them again at exorbitant prices. But father loved the process of pearls: how, out of the underwater depths, through the secret of another lifeform, out of the flesh of a mollusk, beauty suddenly appears, so alive, warm, heavenly, that tears well at the miracle of it.

From a young age he began to teach me about his craft. At first he would often make me go down to our river and teach me about it. The salmon came to our lands to spawn, people caught many of them, but for my father such profit was not enough. He would scoop up a fistful of sand from the bottom and show me. "Do you see," he would say, "the little silver things?" Indeed, in the sand they glimmered like little stars, slightly bigger than grains of sand. In some years there would be quite a lot of them, in other years fewer. "I can tell beforehand, several years before, if there will be many pearls or few," my father said. "These little silver things are alive. They are the embryos of mussels, the shells that give pearls. As soon as they are born they swim in the water and look for salmon. They get into the salmon's skin and live there for two years. Silly people claim that the salmon tick spoils the fish. But after two years the little mussel will leave the fish when it comes out of the sea and into the river. Then the mussel will settle in a place below the rapids and become a shell. It will grow and get stronger. It isn't easy to create beauty, it has to mature first. You see, people think that it is bad, that it hurts the fish, but it knows what it's doing. The fish and the pearl don't care about people's silly ideas. They give themselves to us of their own free will, so that we don't slaughter each other. But we don't understand this gift. We really need to think about life, Good and evil are mixed in a complicated way, a person should not act thoughtlessly."

In this way he started to teach me, and I would always stare at the little silver things to see when they would start to crawl, for after all, they were alive. But they only glimmered through the sand and the water, those little but wise creatures.

When he started taking me fishing, it was a great joy. Father had a hut on the river far from the village. There was a secret channel there, narrow, but then it would widen before it reached the main river and it would fall into it with a roaring waterfall over the stones. The hut stood on this island. It looked small from the outside, but it could fit everything inside: a stove made from stonework, some wide bunks and various utensils. There was a chimney made from a hollowed log. He kept a little raft on the riverbank. In the morning I would set off fishing with him, we would push the raft into the water and push ourselves away from the shore with poles. Beneath us the river was two meters or so deep, no more. But we could not see anything, either the rays of the sun glared on the water or the wind was whipping up ripples, meaning the river itself was always in motion. We would sail to a place that was in no way remarkable, and there father would stop the raft and cast the anchor into the water. He would then take a pipe made from a hollowed-out beam and lower one end of it into the water. "You see," he would say, "they are lying there, the pretties." There really was an abundance of pearl mussels at the bottom. They lay there like little oval plates, like extinguished coals, black. Father would look at them for a long time and then point, "See this one, it looks humped. The big crooked one. It might have a pearl inside. And this one here to the left looks gap-toothed." He would look at a few in this way and then start to fetch them out. This could be done with a long stick that was toothed at the end, but that isn't ideal because the distance is far and it could hurt the mussels. So, father would undress and go into the water. He would be down there for a long time, but when he came up, he would be holding several mussels in his hands. I would take them and help him climb up onto the raft. Then we would go back to the shore.

Then father would take from his bag, made of birch bark, all the mussels that he had collected and spread them out in the shallow water. He would lie them down on the sand where they would be washed by the clear water and warmed by the sun – this was good for them. He would slowly begin to open them up, one after another. This was fascinating: they were nasty inside, slimy, but nonetheless alive. Take a closer look, and you see a kind of tenderness inside, a beauty, although it is of an alien sort: delicate fringes, jelly-like flesh, a play of orange and pearl colors. Father would gently take each of them in turn. The mussels would, of course, slam shut immediately. Here he had to apply force. He would gently press a knife between the mussel's valves and turn it so that there was enough of a gap. He would stick his finger inside and feel about, smoothing the folds. If it was empty, there was no pearl there, then he would neatly draw the blade out. The mussel would slam shut. He would put it back into the water. Myself, I found it disgusting at first to poke my finger into something unknown like that. However, father insisted, "You have to get used to everything in life." So, I gathered all my courage, even closed my eyes tightly, but I stuck my finger inside, though I didn't feel anything at first. Father even chided me, "More gently, you'll hurt everything." Then I proceeded more slowly, but rather ineptly. Until I realized, I could sense, how fragile everything was inside the mussel, how cool and slimy it was. Then I understood how it all had to be done. But when the veil was lifted and my finger pressed at something hard, I felt bliss and a thrill. The mussel had given me its treasure without resistance, in resignation, even affection. I took out the pearl and the mussel, for some reason, did not hurry to close shut. It was as if it was saying goodbye to me with its valves, like they were lips whispering something. However, I was ungrateful; I quickly put it back in the water and looked at the pearl. When I saw it for the first time, I gasped. I had come into a round piece of joy that was big, larger than a pea, lighter than the sky and more sparkling than a fish. There was a play of colors, as if the pearl was shuddering from fear. It tried to hide, but the light of its beauty was breaking out. I could not get enough of it, but now my father rushed me. "Put it in your mouth," he said, "and hold it against your cheek. You need to keep it there for at least half an hour. Pearls get harder that way, they take on a good color. Otherwise they fade quickly."

So, I walked around with my childhood joy against my cheek, always poking it with my tongue, as if I had grown a smooth new tooth, still new, but mine. I had a fine pearl, one without any flaws or cloudiness. I lost it quickly, my joy was taken from me.

* * *

I'm not going to the North for a long time now. It'll be a long time before I even think about filling up with a full tank of gas at the cheapest fuel stop, turning the music up and driving so fast that my foot would involuntarily hit the brake, because I was just about to fly from the feeling of happiness and the long road ahead. I'm not going, because on that route the rivers are lying in wait for me. The first will be the Yelgamka, gurgling merrily over rocks, then the dark waters of the Idel will flow along tranquilly, the gloomy beauty of the Tunguda will appear among the spruce trees and the fickle Pongoma will completely tear your soul apart. Then the time will come for the cool Keret itself to question you and judge you according to your deeds.

I used to go often. When I was in some remote, beautiful, foreign destination, I realized I was looking in the wrong place. It had suddenly come to me that only five hundred kilometers stood between me and places where you don't even need some frail canoe – you can drive your car right to the seashore, stop and immediately see the midnight sun shining a path of light on the smooth surface of the water. In your nostrils will be a smell that is fresh, pungent and thick, and deep within your soul you will feel a quiet and pure thrill. It is called the White Sea. Someone who lacks a heart will never understand it.

Last time it was at the end of winter. As I was approaching Chupa, I already knew how everything would go down. Whoever I drove there with, I would always say the same thing: let's just please not visit a local bar. "Why not?" my surprised companion would ask. Because we would pop in for only half an hour – the bar in Chupa is a funny, ramshackle place, almost like a simple eatery for village workers – and the place would be jam-packed with the Chupa girls, who would not take their eyes off you. You'll be amazed, thrilled, that in such a godforsaken place there are girls so beautiful. You won't even notice how unwittingly and unexpectedly a desperate hope to find happiness will come upon you, and you'll sit there all night long, dance, cha and just before the morning comes, the Pomor girls will fly off on their slender legs. You'll feel dreary and nauseous and you'll have to go God knows how far that morning, dozens of miles on the sea or across the snow. It would only take one tumble, you would barely survive your first day in the North. So, let's please not visit a bar this time.

I know a guy in Chupa, his name is Yura. He owns a company called Keret Tours. That is what I call him, "Yura from Keret Tours". He's a small guy and always smiling, like a bear cub, but he tries to put himself across as someone important, a big man. He gets into scrapes all the time. "Last autumn I was on my yacht," he would say, "my net got caught by the boat's screw and I had to land next to Cape Sharapov. Good thing I managed to jump out onto the sand." Everyone gasps and is impressed by Yura, until his mate talks about it and how they drank a lot of wine that day, so the experienced sailor ran the boat aground, though it's true he did it very skillfully, you can't deny that.

Yura came to meet me again this time. We greeted one another and thumped each other on the back. "Well then, shall we visit our bar?"

"Please no. You know it isn't a good idea, I've got a long way to go tomorrow, and it has been a long trip here. I'm tired. I really don't want to. Would it really only be for half an hour…?"

In the morning we set out early, as always. Yura's snowmobile, an old and rather ugly Buran, was already waiting. It had a trailer in the back on little skis. We threw our gear in there and I sat on top, then we glided along the snow-covered streets. As soon as we rounded a corner and left the cluster of houses, I caught a glimpse of something new. On a rocky hill, directly over Chupa's bay, was the new frame of a house, already five meters high and looking as fresh as newly-baked bread. Its happy yellow color immediately caught my eye, and it was almost as if the dark morning suddenly brightened up. "Yura, stop!" I shouted, barely heard over the motor. "Stop, I want to look!"

Yura stopped the snowmobile and looked unhappy about it. "What is it? We just got moving. We've still got sixty kilometers to Keret, it'll be fucking long."

"Just wait. What is that building? I haven't seen it before."

He turned around to see. "Oh, they are building a new chapel, to Varlaam of Keret. You haven't heard? A local saint, he lived back in the seventeenth century or something. It's a creepy story. But he was a real man, a genuine guy. Let's go, I'll tell you along the way."

The Buran rumbled into motion again. I continued to stare at the chapel, which was so bright among the dark buildings, so happy but at the same time severe, open to the wind and wise. "Varlaam", the old name, already forgotten and foreign-sounding, kept echoing in my mind.

The snowmobile sped along a well-compacted forest road, the trailer on skies waving from side to side in a way that left me breathless and my hands unconsciously gripping the high edges of the trailer. Then, when we had left the main road and were moving over untouched snow, our speed dropped and the rolling and shaking started, "Just hold on!" The skis were jumping as if they were going over tiny, sharp waves and my insides were shuddering in something that resembled horror. Outside, however, there was beauty. Little by little, very slowly, the sun appeared from its bed of clouds, cast them away beyond the horizon, and as if sweetly stretching, it spread its rays widely across the sky. The snow that lay in gloomy lumps immediately turned playful, shimmering in response like a stray kitten that had been unexpectedly petted. Once we had gone further from the road and crossed a viscous swamp with sad deadwood protruding from it, we immediately flew up the crest of a long, curved hill and continued along it, holding down with all our might the visceral delight that sought to burst out of us. To the right a wild forested valley stretched for miles with glimpses of clearings, traces of old logging and rocky slopes. All of this came together into a seemingly chaotic pattern that suddenly shone with such an imposing harmony, that only a proud raven with its abrupt "caw!" dared shoot down into this beauty and remain among the living. On the left, a few forest lakes began to gradually, shyly, peep out from among the dense rippling of the tree trunks. The lakes' shores were steep and high, their outlines complex and they seemed to be intertwined in some kind of rough, cramped ball. A few, rare twisted pines had managed to climb to the very top of these dark, primeval rocks and they had frozen there in fear of their own courage. The inlets to these lakes flashed here and there, everything seemed chaotic. "The Cross Lakes," Yura said proudly, as if taking credit for them, on seeing my incomprehension he stopped on a hillock. He slowly took out a map and unfolded it. On a green patch of forest were three little crosses in blue, just like the ones that infants have around their necks when they are baptized. They lay alongside one another, nearly touching, placed by some generous hand onto propitious land.

We drove on. The nature around us, as if it knew we had no guns with us, was teeming with life. A second before we arrived it froze and turned shy. Yet there was a lot of it around: the prints of hectic hares and deliberate foxes were tightly intertwined; I could see everywhere the scratching's of partridges, as if someone had scratched the snow with big claws on both sides of the birds' paths; the sparse prints of a careful wolf cut across the clearing; on top of all this a wolverine had trod abundantly and domineeringly. As soon as I had grown used to this abundance of tracks that had been left and had already frozen, black grouse began to bolt out from under the snowmobile. They were so close that I could have knocked one of them down had I been so inclined to catch one. About a dozen of them burst out like black blood gushing out of cut veins in the snow and settled on the nearby trees to curiously await what would be next: life or death. Even if I had a gun, I wouldn't dare shoot at these nobly carved, sun-drenched birds perched on the branches, looking like the translucent rooster lollipops I knew in childhood. They were too magnificent and trusting. Too innocent and too distant from the desire that was nibbling at my soul like a slippery fish. For six months it had been tormenting me. In order to heal it I had headed for these backwoods, away from people.

Besides the nickname that I had given him, Yura had another one in these parts. Everyone called him Thief. That was because he had lost all the fingers on his right hand in a sawmill accident. They had taken the big toe off his foot and sewn it on his hand where his index finger used to be. With two phalanges instead of three he readily managed – he could catch onto any opening, handle or grab a man's jacket in the heat of a drunken conversation. This strong finger, his toe, was rather scary for people, though it was his own. This is how awkward anyone looks who has got used to his profession and then suddenly ended up somewhere else, like a fireman in a PR rep's position. Yura was not offended by this nickname, nor was he ashamed of this finger, that is, he did not consider it a deformity. He even seemed to enjoy the frightened looks of his interlocutors when he grabbed a chunk of bread or scratched his nose.

In any event, Yura was an excellent guide. I have no idea what landmarks he used to orientate himself, or if he had just passed through this region of his so often that he did not need any landmarks, but we suddenly emerged from the forest exactly at the mouth of a river. It was still covered in ice, but here and there it broke out from under the ice exuberantly; it resembled in no way a sleeping beauty, rather it was more like a roguish girl who, even if she was covered in a blanket, still looked out from under it with mischievous eyes, giggled and fidgeted about, ready at any moment to jump up and start dancing.

"There it is, the Keret," Yura looked on it with fond eyes and took the hat from his wet head. Low, gently sloping cliffs rose on either side of the riverbanks, as if gently holding the river in their gray, work-worn hands. There were a few half-collapsed houses right along the sea and an abandoned cemetery. Further to the North stretched an endless frozen plain streaked with ice hummocks. In the distance we could see a narrow, dark strip of unfrozen sea and low clouds swirling around some island. The ice was white, glaring and right at the mouth of the Keret it turned a dark and dangerous blue with gaping holes. The silence was broken only by the wind, with its woolen rustling sound through the small, dry snowdrifts.

The sound of Thief's snowmobile disappeared in the distance and I was left alone among the snow. During all these days I tramped dozens of miles through the forest, among the lakes and along the seashore. My wide skis, padded with moose hide, allowed me to easily move over the snowdrifts, only sometimes, as I flew down a hill, I did not properly judge the height of the little spruces that were sneakily covered with powdery snow and tried to let them pass between my feet, but I was punished for my foolishness with unbearable pain.

I caught fish, did some hunting, but whatever I caught did not what really matter. I just had to wear myself out every day so that I could fall asleep at night, so I would stop shaking inside with a violent urge to gnash my teeth, lash out with my claws and get revenge. I tried to be reasonable and tell myself that was not necessary, that it was my own fault, that I knew that in this world love is impossible, and still I had confided in someone, opened myself completely, exposed my tender points. It served me right for being so stupid. I told myself that no one ought to suffer any more, that I should just try to forget it and move on, that I could get over it. But as soon as I was distracted from these thoughts, for even an instant, my mind would paint bloody pictures, and with a feeling of vengeance achieved I would stand in triumph, until I remembered that everything was still ahead of me.

Only running through the forest to the point of dull stupor, until I had terrible aches in my back and legs, helped me. In the evening, after I had eaten and I was falling asleep, I had a chance to argue with Thief, who had been keeping an eye on me all these days with a mixture of worry and understanding.

"You've got to try to have faith," he said with conviction. "Just have faith, without requiring any proof. Offer up your pain to God. Things will get easier, you'll see."

"That's really funny." I had never given up or ever been afraid of anyone so far. "You can't have any faith in this country. It doesn't make any sense. We're walking over the bones – all this country here – all the remains and dust to dust of people who also had faith and hope, and who waited. It doesn't make any sense, it's silly."

Thief sighed, but I did not fall asleep, no, I just died for a while, until morning came.

It was a bit far to the Cross Lakes, I could not get there on foot. I asked Thief to take me there and leave me for a day. For some reason, I felt I would have fantastic luck there – under the steep cliffs, along its shores, there was what seemed to be a dark abyss, full of mysterious fish. Thief said goodbye, and as he did he looked at me with some kind of pity. "If you need anything, ask Varlaam." I only chuckled in response.

I caught a few bass almost immediately, nearly as soon as I had sat down at the first hole in the ice and dropped my lure into the water. I rolled up my small weighted line and brought out a good one, with a thick line and a strong treble hook. When I put the tiny perch on the hook, it gave a pitiful squeak and I began to lower my pole into the water. As it turned out, it was about thirty meters to the bottom, the same height of the black rock whose shadow I perched. I sat there for quite a long time and started to get tired of it, when suddenly something pulled at the line. It was strong and confident, imperious. I waited a bit, then hooked it and started to pull it up. Something big was coming up from the abyss. It came without tugging, but it was so heavy that I shuddered within and my heart beat faster. I pulled the fish up to the hole – it seemed that the fish would not fit through it. A dark shadow appeared under the ice. I waved my mitten off and put my hand into the water, so that I might turn the fish head-up and pull it out into the light by its gills. I touched it and could barely keep from jerking my hand away. Bare, nasty flesh without scales, slippery and cold – it was a burbot. Huge, like I had never caught before. I did not like these fish at all. I was always creeped out by the sluggish swagger of those corpse-eaters. But I did not let the fish go. I moved my fingers towards its head and found its gills. Suddenly the fish darted powerfully to the side. I screamed from pain. One of the barbs on the treble hook had sunk deep into the flesh of my palm. I nearly jerked my hand out but realized a split-second later that I shouldn't.

The water was very cold. There was no pain, but there was no way out of this either. I tugged a little, but the hook only went deeper into my hand. Another one of the hook's barbs was caught in the huge, slippery fish. I was on top and the fish had frozen under me. It could wait a long time, but I could not wait at all. Already, I could not feel my hand. The ice under my cheek melted and immediately refroze, reminding me of the inevitable. I wanted to cry out but I did not – it would not make any sense. Thief would come by many hours later. I was cold and spooked. I wanted to live and I wanted everyone else to live too. I no longer wanted to kill. I felt very tired. I knew nothing of time. I started to drift off. My eyes closed of their own accord. Occasionally I seemed to hear the sound of an engine, but it was just the wind blowing through the pines. My lips twisted into a grotesque grin. With difficulty I parted them and hoarsely uttered, "Help me!" I whispered it almost inaudibly, then closed my eyes and gave in to my despair. I was awakened by a strong blow – next to my head a harpoon had driven deep into the ice.

THE MIRACLES OF THE RIGHTEOUS VARLAAM OF KERET, THE WONDER-WORKER

In the summer of the year 7172 (1664), on the first day of June, a man with the name Pyotr Vasiliev, who was known as Butorin, told this legend.

When I was young, eleven, my father was teaching me how to fish on the Sonostrov. I saw in a dream that my father and were sailing in a boat next to Cape Sharapov, and suddenly the sea raged with waves and our boat filled with water: I was very frightened. Then I saw another wave that was coming towards us, it was going to sweep over our boat. I looked behind me, and saw an old man with a gray beard in our boat, protecting us from that wave. Suddenly our boat lay in the calm sea behind the reef. After he had saved us from drowning, he said to us: "You would have drowned if it had not been for me, Varlaam of Keret," and he said that I should tell people about it. I woke up and began telling my father what I had seen. But he did not pay attention to me, for I was just a small boy.

In the morning we saw a ship going into the sea, it was close to us. A man came to us on another boat and said, "Our boat from Keret has passed here, but I did not dare approach it, for the waves on the sea are too strong."

My father thereupon spoke, "Let us go to the volost to trade." So, we went, suddenly there was a mighty wind. When we were near Cape Sharapov, a wave came and filled our boat with water. We were greatly bewildered and afraid. Then we saw another wave, even more ferocious than the first, and it too wanted to drown us. We feared for our lives. Then suddenly, our boat, without any man steering it, was behind the reef and close to the shore. We rejoiced greatly, bailed the water out of the boat and reached the volost. Five days later the same old man appeared in front of me in my sleep after my repast. He scolded me and would flail me with a whip, he said, "Why have thee not told everyone what I had done for thee?" And said that I must go and tell everyone.

2005, KERET

I finally quit smoking, and for several months after that I was glad. I hid my cravings. I told everyone who was carrying this heavy burden, "You see, I managed to do it, so can you." Yet on my tongue, in my head, my insides, in my stomach and on my salivary glands was one word: smoke. It is sweet and pleasant. It is there forever. Smoke is memory. Smoke is taste. The pain of recalling merry dancing and hopeless victories.

When you find yourself unconsciously rolling a tight cigarette, when small particles of tobacco sprinkle out of it despite all your effort of rolling and pressing, then it is placed on your tongue, you realize that you gave in again. Yet again.

With relief and a cheery despair you utter the words "The White Sea."

I love these first minutes that you wait all year for, trembling, worrying if they will ever come – it seems like there is no strong exaltation right away. Everything is perfectly ordinary. The sea, a wide vista of which is blocked by islands. The smell that is merely felt. It does not even smell like the sea, just the wet wood of the dock. A little bit of algae that has been thrown ashore. The smoke issuing from the gray bath houses. A bit like fish. And happiness. Thus, you stand on the dock staring unwittingly at the light water, into its depths. There too, everything is like it is usually: baby fish scurrying through the water, seaweed swaying. What is this here – a starfish. Suddenly you notice that out of the shadows, long from the low sun, a vivid burgundy jellyfish comes swimming, swaying majestically and in no hurry to get anywhere. Then, either from this fierce color, impossible in the North, or from the furtive smell, subtle, like the first female touch, you suddenly feel that your soul is already open to the horizons; that without even noticing how, you have already fallen into a tinder net, there are tears in your eyes and hollowness in your mind and only your heart is beating out a solemn march of "hello!"

At such moments it is best to pretend to be a hard, coarse man, eager for a drink and a big cigarette. That is why right there, on the forlorn dock, there are some slices of bread lying on top of a newspaper, some salted pork fat, a crunchy onion and a bottle. You feign an appearance of being famished, of being unable to live without vodka, that all else is unimportant. You need the strong smoke that burns your throat against all those smells, so that you do not get dunk, are not driven mad from them. But for some reason the conversation does not work, even if a phrase pops out, at the end there will be some restrained cry of suppressed enthusiasm. You want to laugh, too. You want to rejoice that you are alive, that everything around you is alive and that the salty blood in your veins is akin to the water under you.

At that very moment a local man in a padded jacket stepped onto the boat. One word after another, our group invited him to help himself, we had a drink, and on the way to Keret he said, "Find old Savvin. He knows about all of that."

"How do you spell that, Savvin or Savin?" I can rarely talk about smart things, most of the time it is only some unnecessary associations and half-sighs.

The man squints. "Two V's, I think. Why are you asking? You know him?"

"No, it's nothing really. Just a thought about something. Savin, Savvin, '*avva* father, take this cup from me'. And other silly things."

The man's name was Roma, he was a senior researcher at the bio-station on Cape Kartesh. He solemnly introduced himself as such. We drank some more. Then a bit more. We got so deep into our conversation that only later did we notice a lonely woman sitting on the next dock over – dressed all in black. She was still pretty young. She sat there completely immobile. I suddenly remember that when we had driven here, two hours ago, she had been sitting there in the same way, the same hunched position. Among the sighing and the excitement, we asked our new friend, "What's she sitting there like that for?"

He immediately turned serious. "The sea took her husband yesterday. He dived into it after coming out of the bath house and that was it for him. They still haven't found him."

A chill wind blew from the North. We started getting ready to go. We thanked Roma and said goodbye and then got into the car. We took a last glance behind us, at the woman in black and the White Sea.

Along a wide slope at the very mouth of the rushing Keret River, the uninhabited village also named Keret was spread out. It was spread out, yet supine. The remnants of houses lay on the earth, which could hardly be made out in the high, wild grass which was colored yellow, blue and white, with abandon by lush wildflowers. Old Pomor crosses lay over the graveyard and perennial lingonberry bushes had grown through the old white wood of the crosses. Also, lying there quietly, almost unnoticed, was the foundation of a large church, which had once been a proud white bird ready to take off and fill everything around it with joy. What had once been streets – an upper, a lower and one between them – lay there in indistinct, blurred terraces. Below the village, the White Sea, indifferent to all this, shone blue. On the other side of the bay, what had once been a shipyard, lay in a state of ruin. Swallows fluttered above it all.

My brother and I sit in the meadow right alongside the river. Nikolai Eliseyev is with us, a short guy with a sneaky smile and astonished eyes. Nikolai is a pure-blooded Karelian, and just from his features and from his witty sayings, proverbs and jokes, one could study the entire Karelian people, he was so characteristically representative of it. He was quite a complex Karelian, but where can you find simple ones? Nikolai had never seen the sea before and suddenly burned with a wish to go on a big trip. He ignored his wife's admonitions and plunged right into our difficult journey.

The rapids here had already emptied into the sea, and the sea itself, the water boils and roars so loud that we have to shout. We have a fire going, a tent, our bags lay scattered around – we would have time for everything. A grill is set up next to the fire and some meat on a skewer was sizzling nicely. Such a smell arose that everywhere around us, clouds of mosquitoes were going crazy. They were biting us. It was obvious why: living meat is sweeter to their narrow noses and grilled meat is hot.

We already had a drink. One cannot do without it. Otherwise the pain, which is joy, which is happiness, which is trouble, will tear you into bits. That is why we tighten hoops of alcohol around our heads and chests. The legs remain free and wander everywhere. But generally, not too far away – we are kept here by the smell. All around us, the place is desolate, cicadas sing. "Why don't you go fetch wood for us, cicada?"

Along the road leading to the little fishery hut which was not far off, two men are walking. One is younger and wearing camouflage, he has an independent look. The other is a shabby old man with thick spectacles and a leather cap tilted to one side. They are walking without any rush and look to be sniffling.

"Guys, come join us!" Our delight at being here is so overwhelming that we nearly wanted to hug someone.

The men are wary. "No thanks, fellows. We're in a hurry."

They are hurrying awfully slowly, in no rush.

"Oh, come on. You can tell us how to get to the Summer Lakes from here."

They come up to us. Very slowly. There is a struggle on their faces. Right next to the food squats a massive white canister filled almost to the brink with a crystal-clear liquid. "Ethyl alcohol for medicinal use" – the guys recognize the label and are pleased to see it. The female doctor had given us the canister as a gift, she knows guys, from the outside and from the inside. She is a dissector.

There is no dignity and honor left anywhere any more. Even the words are nearly forgotten now. In the cities muscled guys with swollen faces are digging through trash cans. On the television, people with anxious shifty eyes are careful to say the right words. Even poets are keen to get wasted on free drinks and only then will they read their poems. Even decent, respectable women have restless fingers, as if they are tapping the keys of an invisible calculator. There is no dignity and honor left anywhere. But here there is. Ever so slowly the men walk up to us. They resist our invitations and talk about how they just ate, but they do not leave. Finally they give in. "Where are you all from?"

"We're from Petrozavodsk, almost from around here," I answer for all of us.

"Oh, alright then. It's good that you're not from Moscow. They're rude folks, they demand fish right away. Fine that you're our people. We'll sit with you for a bit."

Half an hour later we are already good friends. Stepanych, the older of the two says, "I'm still strong! I'm seventy-five, but oh boy, I can still…! You know golden root? They also call it *rhodiola rosea*. I gather it and dry it. Then I can drink for a whole year straight. Me and the old gal, oh boy… Other girls see me, and oh boy…"

"Stepanych, is there a lot of fish in the river, salmon?"

"Not at all. Wild salmon is all gone now, they caught it all. Only the salmon raised at the fish farm is left. Old people used to say that you'd go down there and you could not even see the water, there were so many fish! They didn't have to catch them during the spawning season, up on the river. All along the sea there were *tonjas*," he used the old Karelian word for fishing huts, "but now, ugh."

His taciturn companion smoked a cigarette and nodded his manly head in agreement.

"That's great, Stepanych. But how can we get to the Summer Lakes from here? They say there's some kind of trail."

"There was a trail once, but it must be all grown over now. Better you find old Nefakin tomorrow, he knows. But he's a difficult man to deal with."

"Nefakin?" I asked, as I love all kinds of odd names. "What does that mean?"

"That, Grisha my friend, means that he's a *not far king*," the liquor had suddenly given the fellow a fondness for English. The others, with understanding, kept silent.

"But these lakes…" With all my might I felt responsible for our route and for us surviving this trip.

"What about the lakes? Now, golden root…" Then he turned serious. "Me, I'm from Sumsky Posad. Ever hear of that place?"

"I have. I've even been there. Church-desecrators, don't they say that about you all?"

Stepanych seemed thoughtful. "They say right. I was little then, around seven years old. Red Army soldiers came in a one-and-a-half-ton truck. They let us kids ride in the back. They put a rope around the church's dome and pulled it down. I thought it was fun back then, but now I'm ashamed of it…"

The sun was now half-hidden behind the jagged, spruce-covered edge of the nearby hill. The luminous twilight of the northern white nights setting in. The sky cast a heavy gold. The sea lay in darkness as the sun's rays did not reach it. In the air hung a clear, soul-wearying chill. Our friends got ready to go. They gradually took their leave and walked off. Stepanych was pretty much finished and his companion respectfully supported him by his elbow. They disappeared among the trees. For a long time still Stepanych's perpetual "And I can, oh boy… And also, oh boy…" carried from the forest.

We started getting ready to bunk down. We pitched our tent, made some tea and drank the rest of the diluted alcohol. While this was going on, an old woman dressed all in white quietly came from the graveyard and quickly passed along the black sea and towards the forest. After giving us a cool glance, she vanished in the direction our friends had gone.

"And Stepanych can, oh boy…," Elisyev said, and that was the last thing I heard before I fell asleep.

A great thing about mornings in the North, above all the other fine qualities, is that there are no hangovers. Or rather, there are, but among the pangs of fear, the horrible foreboding and the loveliness of the nature around you, who cares? Just a light, sullen shade among the stream of existence, so incredibly powerful, that you started living when you came here and it is as if you are unaware of anything before this place. It is as if in your carefree past life, in a city in the south, you were an egg: smooth, self-confident, uncomplicated. Only now does a fine web of cracks appear on your shell, from a distance they might be mistaken for wrinkles. You are wiser all around: your eyes, your legs, your nostrils. After a few days, when your shirt suddenly smells not like rank sweat but salty wind, then you will suddenly comprehend all the value of words, smells and sounds.

We got into the car and drove to the village to look for old Savvin. The road here had once been covered with muscovite, a jolly companion of mica. For that reason, it shone under the sun's rays with a glare so strong that it made your eyes hurt, and as soon as the sun set, it became unreal, an eerie yet affectionate pink color.

We drove up to two houses that were rickety, barely still standing. On a whim, we chose to walk up to the lower one, though it was further away and looked the more ramshackle. After we knocked on the door an old man came out. He had a bald, tanned head. His face was wrinkled, like Pomor rocks that had cracked under frosts and sun and been licked by the rough tongue of the sea. His eyes were keen and held a grin in them. He wore a faded pair of canvas trousers and an ancient boating shirt. It was clear that he was very old, yet also hale, like a tree tempered by the sea that spends years wandering through the saltwater and then finds itself a refuge somewhere on the shore. Moreover, when he turned around to close the door, I immediately noticed a pair of scars on his back, on his shoulders. They were round: bullet wounds. They made me remember our grandfather Fyodor – they were somehow similar.

I knew that our first words were very important, or rather our way of interacting with another, with people, with this particular person. If he senses even the tiniest bit of overconfidence, self-admiration or deceit, he will immediately clam up and will have already made his conclusions once and for all. I greeted him as respectfully as I possibly could, not because I knew this but because I liked the way he looked, the way he was dressed in a striped shirt and faded jacket, and his stooped but vigorous manner.

"Good day!"

"Hello there, if you mean that."

"Sorry for disturbing you. We would like to leave our car here. May we?"

"Why not? There's a lot of land. You from Moscow?"

"No, we're locals, from Petrozavodsk."

"The car can stay here, but where are you off to?"

"We've got a canoe. We want to get to the mouth of the Letnyaya and then up to the lakes. Think we'll make it?"

"It's doable, during daytime. You ain't scared?"

"A bit."

The man nodded to show he understood.

"So, we wanted to ask you if you could keep an eye on our car, in case anything happens to it?"

"Sure, I'll keep an eye on it. What could happen to it? You can park it here."

I stuck my hand into my pocket and took out a hundred-ruble bill. "Here."

"What, why? No, I don't need it."

"Come on, for the trouble. If the alarm goes off at night or something."

"You don't have to put the alarm on, there aren't any other people around here."

I rather insistently put the money into his dry palm. He stood up straighter, teetered a bit as he reflected on this and then went into the house. I realized he had done this to not waste time arguing. We started to unload the car, the bags with the canoe and our backpacks with food. The old man returned some five minutes later. In his hands was a large salted fish, a pink salmon.

"Take this. When you get to the place, you'll want to have a bite right away. So you don't have to cook anything."

Clearly he had made his conclusions about us. His eyes shone somehow more warmly. He took out a pack of cigarettes and offered everybody one. On the pack, a dark blue vein stretched across a pink map of the North of the country. Like a sharp blade it divided this meaty flesh into equal parts, two of them. Below, written in white letters, it read "White Sea Canal". Inside, the tightly rolled paper cartridges of cigarettes were squeezed against one another like bullets in a chamber. In our younger days it used to be easy to pack them with grass, as if they were specially made for it. It was unlikely that this old man knew that.

We began fussing over the canoe and this brought a man out of the other house next door. He came closer, with lameness in his step he supported himself on a curved stick. He watched us wordlessly like an overseer. His face seemed dusty. His smooth forehead was unpleasantly high due to large bald spot that reached almost to the back of his neck. What few pale hairs he still had were carefully smoothed, as if it was not a village home that the man was coming out of, but he was about to step up onto a stage. His small, dark eyes looked sternly under the bad color of his brows. So sternly that it was nearly creepy. It was as if those eyes were on the lookout for an enemy and perpetually so. His ancient plaid shirt had clearly been ironed. His trouser legs were tucked into his patent-leather boots. A pair of binoculars swung over the old man's wizened chest that was like a bird's breast. A narrow blade, curved like the claw of some animal, hung in a glossy sheath from his wide leather belt.

"Where are you heading to?" His voice, too, was bird-like, high. It was a good voice for asking unpleasant questions.

For some reason I did not feel like answering, but I had to, at least out of politeness or my timidity at being an outsider in these parts.

"Good day. We want to head down to those Summer Lakes."

"The Summer Lakes, then. Are you going hunting?"

"We don't have any nets," Eliseyev said coldly.

"Alright, then." The old man seemed to believe us.

"You wouldn't happen to be Nefakin?" I asked, trying not to notice the hostility that rang through in his gaze, in his voice and in his entire whip-like stance.

"Nefakin, that's me. How did you know?"

"They told me here."

"Who?"

I was starting to get tired of this unexpected interrogation. "Everyone said that you've lived here a long time, you know these parts very well."

"I do know these parts. And I know everyone here." The old man had slightly perked up, as if he had remembered something important. "We've had a lot of your kind here, hunters and fishermen. I know all about them." He suddenly turned and wandered back to his house without even a goodbye. In fact it was not goodbye, rather he sat on his porch and smoked a cigarette, his tough eyes hidden behind the smoke.

We finished putting the canoe together. We carried it along the steep, grassy slope down to the sea. We put it into the water, then loaded our things onto it.

"Guys, I hope you know what you're doing?" said Elisyev in a voice that was bold but unsteady.

"Don't worry, we'll make it. The sea loves us." It is nice to be an experienced Pomor. My trembling hands grabbed an oar.

The old man named Savvin came down to say goodbye. "Call me Nikolai. They used to nickname me Kolyamba." He laughed at some private thought. We also introduced ourselves and shook hands. "Did Nefakin come up to you, now? You be careful with him, he's a difficult man." His smile had disappeared as he said this.

"What's so difficult about him?" I was curious.

"He was the chief fish and game warden here for a long time, in the sixties. Back then they would sentence you to two years in prison for one fish. He put many people away, what a hero." Savvin suddenly broke off and slightly glanced around without saying anything. "Fine, you be careful, go along the shore. Our sea here is also difficult." He went into the water and held the canoe whilst we got into it and then gave it a push away from shore. We swung our oars, frantically at first, but then we caught a rhythm and started moving. Old Savvin watched us with an attentive and serious look, as did – from his high porch – old Nefakin.

We rowed out of sync at the beginning, but then we got the hang of it, and just when we gained strength and speed, right in our way was a dangerous reef, which we almost crashed into at full speed. We turned away from it with effort, waving our oars again and managed to make it out to the Uzkaya Salma strait, like an odd turtle. It was hard to paddle from lack of practice and we were out of breath. The waves had risen higher than at the mouth at the Keret, and had become more troublesome. Thus we rowed on, trying not to show our fear, rolling from one side of the canoe to the other. Some original knowledge awoke at once, muscle memory, a feeling for the sea and we began to keep the canoe's nose oriented properly towards the waves. Things had only started to calm down and everything seemed fine, when a massive humpback salmon leaped up out of the water two meters to our right. It flew past and squinted at us. After about a meter of flight it plunged back into the water with a splash. I gave a sudden jerk from fear and almost caused the boat to roll over. Only later did we start to laugh, but at first it was terrifying!

We made our way along the Uzkaya Salma strait, it is like a river, it's as if you could just reach out and touch the shore, so it wouldn't seem as scary. The movement of the water was also low and we seemed to have found a rhythm of sorts that allowed us to breathe. Things were good now, our initial fear had passed and we started to look around and admire the beauty. We saw an impenetrable forest, with cliffs plunging down the shoreline as if they wanted to bend down and drink the saltwater. There was a glade and a foaming river leaping down. Now we really felt like experienced sailors and I decided to cast my spinning rod. I put a new lure on the line that looked like a little silver fish and cast it out some twenty meters off. I stuck the rod between my feet and sat there fishing, while at the same time not forgetting to row.

Thus we went on, surprising even ourselves. Only now things started to not go so well. The headwind, formerly light, now picked up speed.

We looked up at the sky and saw a rain cloud that was all black. We frantically looked around and tried to find some way of avoiding the surprise looming in the distance. It was only two or three minutes away, but in the distance we heard a sound like a faraway train. It came closer still and began to rumble. We did not even have time to look back – a wall of rain was coming towards us; it was not just coming along but rolling vehemently, and it was not just rain but a downpour. It was already too late to make it to shore. In front of us the sky was dark, but above our heads there was still sun. Such a wild sense of excitement mingled with horror took hold of us, we started going much faster, so there was a wave of white water behind us, like it was from a motor boat. There was thunder and rain streaming down our faces, but the sun was still desperately beating at our backs, then suddenly my fishing pole started twitching madly. We didn't care about anything, the fervor was so strong that my hands began to dance. I threw my oar into the canoe, grabbed the pole and started reeling the line in as hard as I could without breaking it. I prayed that it would work and told my brother to help me. Suddenly, behind us a silver candle came out of the water and then disappeared again into the depths. Everyone was already soaking wet, the water was seething madly, with terrible weather above us, I pulled the fish in. I managed to get it to the side of the canoe, but I was afraid to lift in up into the air. I moved forward a little, closer to my brother, he grabbed the line and with a sudden jerking motion tossed our gorgeous catch into the boat.

We sat there looking like we had gone swimming in our clothes, with water streaming down our heads, shoulders and arms, we gazed at the fish and laughed out loud with joy. The fish lay at the bottom of the canoe, already dead – my brother had killed it at once – and as beautiful as a fish could be, even if it was just hauled up from the depths into the light of day. It had a sleek and slender body, a small, sharp head with a little mouth and scales the color of new, polished silver. There were splashes of rainbow over its entire body, with more towards its dark back, but fewer and paler towards its light-colored belly, where at the very bottom they already merged with silver. It was small, one kilo or slightly over that in weight. An Atlantic salmon.

The rain had stopped now. The dark cloud was rumbling off into the distance, while the sun's rays now playfully sparkled on the surface of the water. We decided that we would not bother heading for shore, that the effort of rowing would dry us off, so we continued on. Suddenly the coast parted and the wind blew powerfully as an endless expanse opened up: we were moving out into the open sea. We had calmed down a little but suddenly felt the ocean groundswell under us. Huge, long waves gently, but inescapably, lifted our fragile boat up and plunged it slowly and deeply back down, so that we felt a cold in our stomachs and a new sense of horror. A first wave, a second, a third, high and gently sloping like the hills of the prairies in books we read as children. Fortunately, human beings are adaptable creatures, we again took up our oars and gave in to this slow and heavy pleasure of the ocean groundswell.

It was not a long way to the Summer Lakes from the sea, around three kilometers. From Nizhny Letny flows a smaller river, also called Letnyaya, and then with a turbulent flow it plunges into a bay called, once again, Letnyaya. The lakes are connected by streams. There are three lakes: Lower, Middle and Upper. They are all a dark blue color that, like a bent sword, pierces deep into the dark-green Pomor taiga for thirty kilometers. This is a wild place, where swans, partridges, wood grouse and eagles live their lives without fearing anyone. They are just slightly scared. Everywhere there are signs of bears: two and a half meters up, the bark of trees have been clawed off, while on the moss, among the blueberries, we see black piles, the remains of their repasts. There are also countless signs of moose, but they evoke less fear as we walk past them. This wild nature seems primeval and untouched, but only at first glance. Then you start to notice that the life of human beings has teemed here, too. The level of all of the lakes has been artificially raised. On each river there are dams made from logs, the thickness of a man's embrace; while these dams already look half in ruin, they remain as strong as before. In the woods you constantly stumble upon roads laid with these same logs. The Letnyaya is followed along its entire course by a huge canal made from black wood of an incredible size. Sometimes this canal is laid high above the ground and the river actually runs along this viaduct. When you examine all of this carefully, it reveals the massive labors carried out here in days of yore. I initially thought that this was massive, forced labor, all to glorify certain bright and ultimately unrealizable ideals. Due to the myriad of nameless cemeteries that lay around us, and because of the barbed wire that our feet sometimes got tangled up in. But then I remembered that I had read long ago of the efforts of a Keret merchant who had dealt in fish and forestry and who had built a great deal. Everything had been built with good, honest labor – it was still visible a century later. What did they call him? He had such a simple family name, I remember reading. Then it came to me in a flash: Savin.

1973, PETROZAVODSK

Grisha, in general, had a very good life. At least, until he started thinking about it. Life was full of interesting things, quiet and predictable. Even in kindergarten he had noticed, about himself, an unusually acute attentiveness, something which only helped him enjoy various wonderful things all the more. He would run to kindergarten every morning so he could get there first and beat everyone else – for some reason, it was very important to be first. Yet, along the way, he still managed to delight in the first ice in the puddles, and did not just shatter the ice in the thin, whitish spots, he also became aware of the ice's wonderful flexibility and the disquieting moan over the deep, dark spots that chilled his soul and sounded like a warning – already the morning was proving not to be in vain. Or when he went down to the shop to get bread, and managed to catch sight of a mound of buttery, transparently orange caviar on the counter, abundantly heaped on the smooth, white surface of the tray. The caviar gave off a pungent and sickening smell, like the maws of a cheerful stray dog.

As the blackish end of the loaf of bread melted in his mouth, and his feet slowed their step, Grisha managed to eat half of the bread, and with a combination of anxiety and sweetness he readied himself for a scolding. During recess at kindergarten, if Grisha managed to evade the all-seeing eyes of the teachers, he would collect a handful of small rocks and begin to hammer apart a larger overturned stone – what beauty would be revealed in the fresh cracks, where the stone had never seen the sun.

Really, who said there exists such a thing as time; that it flows somewhere? We are born, grow up, live, get closer to death and die. If someone important says "I remember that time," don't believe him, he's lying. What one remembers, like anyone else, is only himself, his sensations, surging emotions, the harshness of insults and fear. Looking into the mirror at a tired, swollen, wrinkled face, you know that the mirror lies too, that in reality you have young eyes and a handsome smile, that the bald patches of an old man are just a silly joke being played by the darkness. After all, you feel how the fragrant summer wind plays in your hair, just as it does through strands of juicy grass that cling to the warm field, threaded with the buzzing of grasshoppers. After all, you know that if you do not have any hair, it is because you first shaved your head bald in search of some new sensation and now you are laughing at yourself, as you sweep water from the scratchy stubble with a wet hand after swimming. You know.

"Grisha, dear, wake up," came his mother's voice, carrying through into his sleep. He stretched so widely that his spine popped, which did not hurt but came unexpectedly and sounded funny. "Pop," he said to himself once, and then a second time just out of enjoyment at how sounds could be put into sequences, "Pop." Then he opened his eyes, sleep-covered after a night of good dreams, and through them he vaguely made out the window nearby. It was still covered in a patina of poplar fluff that had flown in overnight and stuck to the morning dew. "Fluff," he again said to himself as he breathed in the delicious air, "Good, we'll set it on fire." He reached out and groped for the matches that he had hidden in his trouser pockets the evening before. "Fluff burns good, like a safety fuse." He had asked his father about this fine, daring term the night before and was proud that today he would be able to impress his friends. "We'll set the fluff on fire."

"Grisha, get up. You asked me to wake you up earlier." His mother's voice that was simultaneously distant and close, now grew even closer, now he remembered. He kicked the blanket away onto the floor and leaped out of bed. "First. I've got to be first to kindergarten today! We argued yesterday about it," and he was already putting on his favorite pants that were like real trousers but did not have those awful straps. "No, no, today you're wearing shorts," his mother said, tending after him. She now handed him – oh, anything but those, but it really was them that she was holding, the yellow ones with creases and a pocket onto which that horrible disgusting donkey with its evil-looking muzzle was sewn. "Mama, I don't want to wear the ones with the donkey, I want the other ones, the black ones." He knew that his mother would be inflexible, but he whined, just in case some miracle might happen. "You'll go in these or you'll stay at home," she said, as if she knew, she could sense, that today he really had to go, that he had to run there fast. As always, she could sense this and she took advantage of it to make him do what she wanted. Just like that jabot he wore on that holiday. That word, jabot. His friends found out that the girlish frill he wore over his shirt was called a "jabot" and they started calling him Jabot, or just Jab. Granted, they did not call him that for long, because little Zhenya got too excited, he ran around all the time screaming "Jabojabojabojabo", until he got hit on the forehead with a shovel. It was a good shovel, a sharp one. Then Zhenya had to get stitches, he still had a scar, although he was now claiming that he got hit with a saber when he was off galloping with Vasily Chapayev: many people believed him because it was a very impressive scar. Very clever, Zhenya, good job. The two of them then quickly made up. But for a long time Grisha could not forgive his mother for that jabot, because she knew that Grisha was not supposed to put it on, he was supposed to give it to a girl as a present. He was torn, unable to decide who to give it to, Katya or Lena. Lena was a friend of his, of course, even much more than a friend. The word "fiancée" was too embarrassing, but "bride" was fine, not bad, beautiful even. Yes, it was really nice to talk to Lena and to send her love letters. Before the holiday he had written her a note "I love you" and gave it to one of her girlfriends to deliver it. Then he waited, and he saw how they were giggling on the other side of the classroom, whispering among themselves, his chest was beating strongly like a train going down the track. Then the note was brought back to him, and on the other side of the paper were the words "I love you too". Then it was decided, he had to give a present to Lena. On the other hand, Katya was nice too. A different kind of nice. It should have been embarrassing really, as their cots during quiet time were side by side. "You'll be a princess, OK? You fell asleep in your castle, and I came and saw everything." He said this with a sinking feeling, without any hope at all, just because it was impossible to keep the feelings inside, they burst out like air from a balloon. He felt relieved at once and not embarrassed, rather like a cosmonaut in fact, just like when, once, he had stood at the top of the slide and hesitated, trying to convince himself that he was Gagarin and that he had to go first. Then he did, he slid down to earth easily, without hesitation and felt a joyous freedom. True, he had bit through his lower lip when he hit his chin on his knee, but that had nothing to do with his flight. It was the same now: he said it and he was free. Then Katya suddenly agreed, "Come on". She immediately closed her eyes, just slightly peeping out from under her eyelids. Here he hit not his knees but hers. He could not catch his breath, his mouth became full of cotton wool, his tongue became so heavy, like a rhinoceros':

"Can I touch you?"

She did not get angry. "Yes, you can."

"Can I kiss you?"

She smiled. "Yes, you can."

And suddenly he said something unthinkable, not by his own will, but as if someone deep down inside him gave him a sharp, painful pinch: "Can I bite you? Gently?"

"No, no biting," and she turned away from him sternly. "I want to sleep."

Thus, how could he choose between the two girls when they were both good, but in different ways? He was wracked with uncertainty, but then he said seriously and solemnly, "Mama, I need two presents."

She smiled. "Why do you need two?"

"I'm going to give one to Lena and one to Katya. I need to."

Mama looked at him and laughed shrewdly. "You're my little Don Juan."

"I'm not Don Juan. It's just, you see…" But he could not explain it to her, or even to himself. At the holiday, when they had them lined up, the boys facing the girls, and ordered "Give your presents," he was the first to run to the girls and he opened his arms widely, because the girls were not standing right next to each other. He thrust his presents at them and then went back, realizing that he had done everything correctly, just the way he wanted things to be.

Grisha was remembering all of this as he brushed his teeth, rinsed his ears and combed his hair. When the neighbors knocked on the door of their communal apartment's bathroom, he leaped out into the hallway and shouted to his mother, "Ma, I'm leaving," and ran down the stairs. Before he emerged from the dark building entrance, he spent an agonizingly long time ripping the pocket with the donkey from his shorts. Set free, and with the same sense of his undeniable rightness, he slammed the heavy door shut.

Grisha ran skipping down Sotsialitichesky Street to Kindergarten No. 48. The wind gently whistled in his ears, because he ran quickly, without thinking of the distance, without measuring his strength like grown-ups would, but just dashing along without even being aware that one could get tired from running. He ran with loud, heavy footsteps on the new asphalt, with his sandals that smelled of leather. Poplar fluff had collected in cracks and crevices and promised the vivid satisfaction of a burst of flame. The yellow heads of dandelions flew from their stalks thanks to the whistling swing of a willow stick. He had just bit the willow stick off after not being able to tear it with his teeth, now his mouth was filled with the long and bitter aftertaste of living wood. Everything around him promised various joy and pleasure. Black patties lay next to the buildings, bitumen that had dripped off their roofs the day before when it had been hot. These patties could easily be stuck together to form heavy balls of a threateningly black color, plus, it was enough to stick the end of a rope into one to make it a fun and dangerous toy, which was great to spin around and make whir and then throw it over a power line so that it hung there like a monkey from its tail, or toss it at the window of a hated neighbor who had kicked a stray dog the day before – it was a complete delight. At the curb lay stones, ordinary cobblestones, only a few initiates knew that if you hit them with a hammer or another stone, often, a veritable cave of treasures would be revealed to you. Later, he would learn that the dazzling sparkles on the freshly cleaved stone were only mica, but for now he filled his pockets and boxes under his bed with these treasures. The wind blew candy wrappers along the street, sheets of gold and silver paper with abraded, chaotically wrinkled surfaces that were nice to smooth out with a fingernail, and then use with the other kids as a kind of currency. So, he ran and took in everything around him, he even managed to think of how complicated the street's name was, Sotsialisticheskaya, and how hard it had been to learn to pronounce it, as hard as learning to tie his shoes, besides, he still didn't know what this name meant. Nearby was another street named Pravda, meaning "truth", that was easy, he knew what truth was. But once the old lady that was selling ice cream there did not give him back his three kopecks in change and he wanted some fizzy water with syrup. Afterwards, he put the one kopeck he had into the machine, but it only gave him water without syrup.

When Grisha ran up to the entrance to the kindergarten, the morning sun seemed to immediately grow dimmer somehow. He was met at the door by that awful Zhenya, who had a smile on his face. They always competed to see which one was stronger, they even fought sometimes and shoved each other.

"Too late, too late!" Zhenya shouted merrily as soon as he caught sight of Grisha. "I'm first again."

"Fine then, but I've got something here." Grisha showed him the cork he had picked up from the street. It came from a bottle of juice imported from Bulgaria and had the outline of a woman's figure drawn on it. Corks like this were one in a million among the dull, colorless beer and lemonade caps and were therefore highly prized. Zhenya was jealous and fell silent, while Grisha enjoyed the already familiar sense of power that came when he could overturn, with just one word, defeat. He was upset, as he had tried so hard today, he had woken up early and ran as fast as he could. Zhenya would brag all day about how he was first. But how wonderful the word "but" is. It always works whenever you don't want to lose. You got lost in the forest, *but* you had some fresh air. You almost drowned, *but* you swam to your heart's content. You got punished for stealing candy, *but* your memories of the taste of chocolate make all the tears go away. A great word. But most importantly, Zhenya didn't notice, he did not even understand how Grisha had taken the victory away from him. So, it turned out that Zhenya was strong, of course, but at the same time weak, somehow dumb.

Grisha smiled at these thoughts of his and his disappointment vanished for good. "What are we going to do?" There was still almost an hour until breakfast, they had enough time to go on some little adventure. Zhenya thought for a brief moment, then said:

"Come on, I'll show you how spiders eat flies."

"OK, let's go." Grisha had already heard that some boys from their class had found a huge web with a garden-spider in it and they fed the spider flies, but Grisha himself had not yet taken part in this.

Zhenya led him to a deserted corner of the garden, to an old, two-story shed. On one side of the shed, in the yard, stood the slide that Grisha had once plunged down, there it was sunny and happy, but this side was mysteriously in half-darkness and felt a little creepy.

"There it is, look." Between the shed and the fence, in a narrow passage full of splintered wood, parts of toys and scraps of old books, the huge spider's web hung and trembled at the slightest breath. At its center, a fat spider with a cross on its back sat solemnly. It was scary big; Grisha felt a shiver at the thought that it might jump up at any moment and grab onto him.

"See how cool it is?" Zhenya said in a whisper that was reverent and even somewhat affectionate. "Now we'll feed it." He slid his hand along the top of the fence and then, with a deft and fast motion, like a sword's blow, he caught a small fly that had been dormant under the sun's rays. It was black and unremarkable. "It's better when you get green flies, you know, the ones that are fat and shiny. They like those more, but they only fly around here when it's very hot. No problem, this one will do." Zhenya pinched the fly with his fingers and then serenely tore off one wing, then the other. In the silence Grisha could hear how the wings tore off with a terrible sound and how the fly itself twitched violently and almost seemed to squeak. It was agitated now.

Grisha caught his breath with some difficulty and then asked Zhenya, "Hey, you don't feel sorry for it?"

The other boy only smiled. "Flies are bad. They told us so. Flies spread disease. So, we have to kill them. Mercilessly." He had also picked up a new word somewhere and relished repeating it: "Mercilessly." That meant without mercy.

He then gently tossed the fly into the web and it landed neatly near where the spider was. The fly twitched and tried to leap away, but it only got tangled in the web, spinning madly and getting more and more sticky threads around it. The spider was in no hurry. It carefully crept along the web up to the fly and touched it with its prickly legs. The fly twitched again, but it was clearly already exhausted and did not even have the strength to buzz. The spider determined that there was no threat and it began wrapping the fly carefully, even gently, in its web.

"It tucks it in. Like a baby." Zhenya was watching this whole process with wide eyes and holding his breath from excitement. "Now it's going to drink its blood."

The spider, as if it had heard this, suddenly ceased its tender work, froze for a second, then cruelly and intently, like an evil mechanical toy, stabbed the fly with short, black blades that had suddenly appeared on its head. The fly trembled, and Grisha trembled with it. He felt terrible, but together with that he felt a sweet shiver. Happy yet evil goosebumps ran down his arms and legs.

"That's it, it won't be so interesting now." Zhenya, possessing a knowledge of this business, pulled him away. "Now it'll hug the fly for a long time. Come on, I'll show you something else."

He led Grisha towards the other end of the garden, which was even more littered and unpleasant. Not far off was a large dustbin that constantly gave off the smell of something rotting, with a sticky sweetness that settled in one's nostrils. They came up to a small stone on the ground next to the dustbin. Zhenya knelt down and with some effort he moved the stone aside. Under it lay the crushed body of a dead rat… Of all this disgusting mess, Grisha was struck by the grinning teeth and the fat white maggots moving along the bits of shredded skin. He could not handle it and leaped away, then ran off as fast as he could.

"Scaredy-cat, scaredy-cat!" Zhenya shouted at his back, but Grisha ran faster and faster to get back to the light, away from the half-darkness and towards the loud cries of the nurses who were calling everyone to assemble. He ran and was afraid of being late – somehow his path seemed endless and grew longer the faster he ran. From a distance he saw how everyone was already lined up and going into the building in pairs, but he wouldn't make it, he would remain alone, with the spider and the rat, with Zhenya chortling behind him, with his morning feelings about Lena and Katya, with the anxiety that suddenly crept from his chest down into his stomach, with the smell of rotting trash, with the anxiety that was now spreading through his stomach, with the last couple of boys hiding outside the door, with fear that suddenly broke out with stunning sweetness, somewhere at the very bottom, where you must not touch, it pierced his back and continued to break out, so he ran faster and faster.

When Grisha entered the classroom, everyone was sitting on chairs around the nurse, who was reading aloud to them about Grandpa Lenin.

"Where have you been? Why are you late?" she asked, looking at him with a cold and suspicious gaze. Grisha said nothing. He knew that she did not like him for some reason. Could he really answer her and explain what had happened to him?

"Our little Grisha isn't saying anything. He's very clever, children." Grisha slightly smiled at her painstaking but futile powers of observation. "He's very naughty. But Grandpa Lenin was never naughty." The nurse realized that she would not get anything out of him so she continued reading: "Only once, when Vladimir's mother was washing apples in the garden, did he come up and say, 'Mama, give me some apple peels.' 'Why do you want the peels?' his mother asked. 'I want to eat them.' 'No, little Vladimir, you can't, you'll get a stomachache,' his mother answered and turned away. When she turned around again, she did not see Vladimir or the peels. That was the only time in his whole life."

What apples, thought Grisha, and what does Vladimir have to do with this? He sat in a chair not far from Lena, and to Katya's right; he was simultaneously the spider and the fly, then he thought about the dead rat and the stone under which it lay – would that stone be pretty, too, if he broke it apart? Then suddenly, for some reason he remembered his grandfather.

Each of the subsequent days were similar to one another. It was hard to get up in the morning, our whole bodies ached, then we would have a hurried breakfast and then we were on the road. The rain fell without stopping, only sometimes it reduced to a drizzle, but at other times it came down in cold showers, as if the sky had apportioned a certain amount of water that had to be poured down on the earth, burning with passion. Wet clothes, wet feet. Bushes. After a couple of days our cheerful singing about Skippy had turned into a cheerless ballad: "Don't tell me about bushes, don't. Better mix some alcohol with water. And don't let my new hat be lost, oh don't…" Things started to be lost with alarming frequency. A knife, our landing net, socks. Our gear dwindled, just like our food supplies. We were constantly getting lighter, throwing off our burdens and attachments. Our shoes were still holding to our feet, though cracks began to show in the rubber soles where they flexed, meaning water leaked in through them. During our brief halts, I tried not to look at Volodya's bare feet when he took his boots off in yet another vain attempt to dry them, or at least make them warmer. His feet were worn, swollen, lumps of flesh with a bluish tint. My own feet were in better condition, but I had managed to keep dry some woolen socks that I only wore at night, in the tent, and in the morning I would again carefully put them back into my waterproof backpack.

We sang songs along the way, not so much from happiness as from fear. Signs of human presence – the rare fire ring, footpaths, food tins – gradually dwindled and then vanished completely. In their place appeared the path of wild animals. On the sandy stretches free of bushes, we increasingly felt a primeval chill at seeing traces of wolverines and then bears. There started to be more and more of them. I had spotted the first remnants of bears' repasts on the second day of our expedition, but I did not tell Volodya. Later, they became so common that we could not *not* notice them. Sometimes there was nowhere to step on the path because of the black piles everywhere. When Volodya finally guessed what these were, he could not sleep and sat up half the night in the tent. Towards the morning, after he had finally fallen asleep, he cried out in a thin voice that startled me. He had dreamt that a bear came up to the tent and started pushing its paw under his back while breathing heavily and pressing against him with its warm side. Volodya moved aside docilely until he realized, with his partly lucid mind, what was going on.

We sang so that animals would hear us coming and get away from us in time. They say that this is the only thing that helps avoid attacks – a bear will only charge if it gets scared by an unexpected encounter. But that is all they say. As we approached a new thicket full of vegetation on the shore, we started bawling out classic songs about the eagle that soared higher than the sun, and about yesterday, when all my troubles seemed so far away. In terms of weapons, we only had a couple of knives and four firecrackers shaped like grenades. When these fireworks went off, they made a huge boom that should, theoretically, scare off any animal. At least, that is what we hoped. We did not have any guns – all the people who owned guns had done the smart thing and stayed at home.

Sometimes I tried to catch fish, but they would not bite. I cast the most enticing lures in the most wonderful fishing spots possible, but I still got no results. The pools, the lonely stones along the river's course, the rushing rapids – the river ought to be teeming with fish, yet every time I went fishing, I came back with nothing. My only trophy was a constant feeling that something was watching us from the forest. We had to sing even louder, but I was not certain that it was an animal, though my heart froze at seeing every black pile and at every little sound in the forest behind me.

It was generally very quiet for some reason. The birds weren't singing. Insects weren't buzzing. There was only the unceasing roar of the river and the sound of the never-ending rain. We got so used to this that we stopped noticing it. The silence seemed absolute.

Every time we lay in the tent in the evenings, we started to look back on things and talk just to overcome this silence. For some reason, we looked back mostly on women. We recalled the good ones and the bad ones, the fun and the evil, the sly and the innocent. There were quite a few of them. And each time, it turned out that every story was connected to pain, which could be quelled only with a stiff drink or cynical laughter.

"Just imagine, when I saw that all our potential companions had got scared of going, I started frantically posting on travel websites, saying that I was looking for partners for an expedition on the Ponoy. Immediately a girl answered, she wrote, 'I want to go with you. My name is Masha Izumrudova.'"

Volodya smiled for the first time in days. "Well you should have taken Masha along! Just imagine how we'd be strutting around here like turkey cocks. No journey could scare us. And the hours and the miles would just fly by as we competed for Masha." Then he thought for a moment and said, "That's a strange name, Izumrudova. Is she a gypsy or something? You know, it's good that we didn't take her along. Women, who needs them? We would have been beating each other up the whole way."

My inner sense stirred coldly within me.

You were sitting on my face at night. I used to love it before. I liked it now too, until I began to suffocate. I was running out of air and the hot joy that was life became suffocating, heavy, deadly. With effort I woke up, opened my eyes, and with disgust threw my wet woolen cap from my face.

That morning I heard some unusual sounds. After such a long and impressive silence, the sound of silver trumpets was now ringing down from the sky. Again and again. After first taking a wary look outside, I crawled out of the tent. The sounds were coming from the direction of the river. I pulled my damp boots onto my feet and went over to the shore. Below, over the slow-flowing water and like something out of a dream, three whooper swans were flying. Again and again they made their loud and clear calls, as if calling some unseen host to battle.

Volodya woke up in a thoroughly grim mood. "A cuckoo was calling."

"That wasn't a cuckoo. It was whooper swans, they are lovely creatures." I wanted to seem like I was in good spirits.

"You know, last night I dreamed of tombstones, yours and mine. Our names, dates of birth. But there weren't any dates of death yet."

I put on a brave face, though it was disquieting to hear of someone else's dreams in the morning. "Volodya, something's got you really down. Maybe we should turn back?"

"No. I'm afraid of Baba Lena," he said, dead serious.

He got out of the tent and started lighting the fire. I got down to reading the description of our route for the hundredth time: "At approximately the midpoint of the Ponoy is the abandoned village of Chalmny Vare. After it, the river changes sharply. The banks are higher. The sheer cliffs reach heights of 100 meters. The river grows narrower and is often winding. Sometimes it turns abruptly and there are dangerous sections. For over fifty kilometers there are eleven rapids. The last of these, Brevenny, is not navigable."

I was stunned that in spite of all my efforts, I had not managed to catch any fish. These wild, untouched places that held such promise should have been abundant in game. Yet it was as if some evil spell had been cast against us, creating even more obstacles in our way. I started to suspect something was up.

While I was away, Volodya, it seemed, went a little crazy. He would pace around our camp and constantly look behind him and dance. Singing became his only pastime. He would go through a repertoire of songs, sometimes he would just hum, but standing there in silence was unbearable for him. He held in his hands the little grenade-shaped fireworks, ready to pull the pin at any moment and cast this toy, his only weapon, into the broad daylight or at any shadow.

However, there were now countless birds. Each morning, and getting towards evening, we were followed by the melancholic cries of whooper swans. Enormous, fat geese flew past us, so low and close that we feared they might break our fishing pole. Now and again ducks emerged from the river at the most unexpected points and scared us with their sudden appearance from under the water. They all followed us closely.

On one of these days I decided to test my peculiar assumption. By this point many things that I would have never believed before, now seemed possible.

"Volodya, I'm going to fish," I said, "And I want you to watch me carefully. I know the name of a certain demon, a small but evil one. I'm going to ask it. You just keep your eyes open."

I went over to the shore. For some reason Volodya hid in the vegetation. The water was quietly gurgling through this small shallow part. I looked at the mountains above us. I cast my fishing reel.

"Katka, give me fish," I screamed, desperately and hopelessly, into the resonant void. I had not asked for anything for a long time. My hook fell far off, almost at the other bank of the river. I started reeling the line in, laughing deep down inside at my own weakness.

Suddenly my pole shuddered, bent and I pulled from the water a marvelous grayling. Before the fish could swing over to where Volodya was hiding, it tore itself from the hook and flopped around on the sandy riverbank. I quickly killed it by slamming its head against a nearby stone, then I cast my line again. A fish bit and a second grayling lay flopping around next to the motionless first. After that nothing more bit. The jokes and fun were over.

That evening, we ate fresh fish for the first time. But that night, in the tent, I was horribly awakened by a quiet, thin wail. It was Volodya, who lay motionless in his sleeping bag. His eyes were wide open. I gave him a strong push, several times, trying to make him snap out of it. Finally, he fell silent, he continued to lie there for a while and then heavily got out of his sleeping bag.

"Misha, a paralyzing sphere entered my head! I couldn't move. I could only lie there and call out to you. But you were sleeping. Then I got scared." Volodya's confused story was especially oppressive in the deathly silence surrounding the tent. Neither of us wanted to look outside.

"Volodya, that's all nonsense! You just imagined something crazy in your dreams again. There are no spheres or tombstones. There are bears, true, but they are keeping their distance. We're just traveling a normal Russian road." I tried to speak confidently to suppress the quiver in my own voice. My strong hands knew how to dilute the drink that would instill us with morning courage.

"What does that mean, a Russian road?" Volodya calmed down slightly and seemed curious.

"Our ancestors went into the unknown, the Pomors and pirates. So what if there were Lapp sorcerers and shamans all around? So what if there was Kuyva on the rock and the seidas around? Our guys had a cross hanging from their necks and axes in their hands. They baptized the Lapps – the only Lapps left, but they baptized them. But the demons are all inside us. There isn't anything outside, it's all on the inside."

This heroic tale and a shot of liquor, cheered Volodya up somewhat. "I'll put the coffee on." He carefully but resolutely got out of the tent, and the last thing I saw was a glimpse of his bare feet with bloody sores on them.

I stayed inside to think. I again took the map out. It was beautiful but somehow misleading in an elusive, feminine way. Some of the distances were wrong, we had been walking for seven days already, but there were no signs of the portage. One bend in the river was shown, but the next one was missing. We had not even noticed one stream, though it was big on the map. All the same, the region was beautiful. Green expanses of forests and swamps. The blue twisting of rivers. Geography. Any route today is simply following in the footsteps of people who went before you.

Inside was another story. Nothing was clear. It is blurry and never becomes clear. The human soul, evil and joy. Pain. And the path leading to pain. Love. Baba Lena. Blood that is always the color of a carrot. Cruel and empty eyes and the light of a smile. The map of the soul.

Apparently I had drifted off for a bit. I came to when I heard a puffing sound next to the fire: Volodya was fanning the flames.

The map lay nearby, with the description of our route on top of it. My glance fell on the last line: "The village of Chalmny Vare, meaning in Saami 'The Eyes of the Forest.'"

I then clenched myself into a fist. I clenched firmly. I said to Volodya, "Listen, aren't we tough guys? Let's not go crazy about finding a solution. Let's follow the Ponoy, through Svyatoy Nos, along the Tersky Coast all the way to the Keret. In the footsteps of Varlaam of Keret, so to speak."

Volodya had nearly lost everything, but not his curiosity. "Who's that?"

"He was a local saint. He went this way eleven times. With his wife's body on a boat. He rowed so much he got a hump."

"No, I don't want a hump. And we don't have a body."

"We're just doing this once. But let's just try. It'll be a bonding experience."

Volodya looked thoughtful and picked at the sores on his feet. "What the hell, let's go!"

2005, SUMMER LAKES

It was evening. The sun, tired and pale, hung low over the forest. The sky lay in the water like a large body spread-eagled. The forest, it seemed, had died – there was no cry from a bird, no rustling of foliage, nothing. For some reason, the murmur of the nearby river could not be heard.

"It's creepy." I wanted to say it in a cheerful tone, but my voice shook.

My brother smiled and nodded, then picked up the fishing rod. "I'm going to try throwing my line out a couple of times." He swung and sent the hook far off, all the way to the reeds. The line gently sang as it flew from the reel. The hook flew far away, then entered the water with a slight sound, like a pebble. My brother began to lazily reel it in. Everything was like it always was: the line cut through the water, forming ripples that were barely visible and the tip of the fishing line was shaking slightly. The lure was already nearly back at the boat now and was about to come to the surface. My brother began to raise his pole. Suddenly a dense, dark wave passed by us, quietly and powerfully. The wave missed us and it broke against the side of the boat. It left behind a whirlpool that swirled disappointingly.

"I saw it," my brother whispered. With fright the lure was pulled out of the water and dangled high above our heads. Then we immediately and grimly threw it back, into the depths. I held onto my own fishing rod with trembling hands.

A fish bit at my brother's rod immediately, as soon as the thin metal leaf of the lure hit the water. The fish seemed to know where it would fall and had been waiting for it. There was a loud splash and the whine of a line stretched taut. My brother raised his pole to hook the fish. The line was pulled to the side. He pulled and started to haul it in. The line drew a tight parabola in the deep water. Time slowed down and flowed like molasses. Several meters away from the boat the waters parted and up flew a bright torpedo half the size of an oar. Its white mouth was open. It had red gills that were splayed shamelessly. A green body with awesome curves. A taut belly the color of old butter. After the pike plunged back into the water, it tore away from the hook and swam away.

"That's not how it's supposed to happen!" my brother said, shaking. "Pikes aren't capable of shrugging off the hook like that! I've never seen that before! It doesn't happen!"

Time, like the water, became slow and viscous. The lure whirred, as if sparrows were flying over the water. Our fishing rods followed the ragged step of an ancient dance. A veritable feast of pike had begun.

I knew, believed, that such a thing would happen sometimes. For the sake of this, one could travel thousands of miles, make one's way through forests and swamps, scout, find and reach. One can take risks and jump on shortwaves. One could do these things, and we did. Now we received our reward.

We caught pikes, one after the other. We slowly moved along the bank and every twenty meters we confidently awaited a new tug on the line, held in palms that were sweating from the thrill. Half of the fish broke away. They simply opened their bony mouths and spat out the tiny, barbed deceit. It got quiet for a bit, after a minutes pause, we switched out the lures and began again. It wouldn't stop, it was simply strange to think that this incredible thrill might end. Yet, pikes bit at every lure we had: spinners, shakers, perch lures, pike lures, whether yellow, white, red, whatever. To them it didn't matter what they died for. After tearing away, a pike would again go for the spoon-bait so that it could kill this nimble creature. Three times it seemed that the hook had gotten snagged on something; my hands were stopped, in mid-motion, by some dark force that could not be living. I again made a ridiculous attempt to lift it to the surface, and the force seemed to be considering matters. I tried for a third time and this force, disappointed by the taste of iron, spat out the lure and retreated into the depths. Sweat and goose-bumps ran down my back.

Of the fish we pulled into the boat, we broke their spines by gripping the fish with one hand at the top, by its neck, and then with the other hand pressing hard on its nose. The fish's last spasms rolled along their flexible bodies, they lay at the bottom of the boat and seemed to freely sprawl there as life departed them. Blood boiled in their mouths and nostrils… It was as if death had come to them as an ecstasy.

When both we and the fish were exhausted, when the sun had begun to look ruefully through the trees at this slaughter, and when we ourselves realized that enough was enough – that we had had too much of death and life – we wound up our poles and slowly, without speaking, rowed to shore. We had no words. Our fatigue made the thrill we felt a quiet one. It made the emptiness bright. Our victory had a fishy smell and it had fish scales on its lips. Sky, forest, lake. My pole sat across the boat, with the hook swinging over the water. This silence was shattered a mere meter from the shore: one last pike leaped out of the water, the largest of them all. It caught on the hook and then fell into the water. I managed to grab ahold of the pole. My brother jumped out of the boat into the shallow water and pushed the boat to the shore. The oar I had cast aside floated slowly along. With effort, as if cutting through a thick cheese wheel, I guided my pole, bent so plaintively, and with the end of this heavy arc I swung and landed the pike on the bank. It flopped on the stones already without the hook, free. I jumped towards it and tried to break its spine with my feet. It wriggled out from under my boots, leaving scales behind on them and straining its bare side. I tried to grab its neck with my hands, but its neck was thick, so thick, it was as if I put my hands around my own neck. I fell on top of it and pressed my stomach to the ground, but it wriggled away, like a strong and spiteful woman. It mockingly beat the stones with its wounded tail and swam away through the water. Now my victory no longer had any taste.

In the clearing, where Nikolai Eliseyev had stayed behind and waited for us, everything was in ruins. The fire had gone out, Eliseyev's fishing rod was thrown down on the ground, and fishing lures and other small tackle were scattered about. Nikolai himself was nowhere to be seen. There were however traces of blood, violence. No one responded to our shouts, silence reigned over everything, just like it did an hour before.

"Let's go back to the sea," my brother said in a weak voice. "If he's not there, we'll look for him."

Where did our tiredness disappear to? Like spooked moose we rushed the three kilometers along the familiar path down to the sea. There, where the river flowed into the bay in a deafening stream, we suddenly smelt a familiar smoke coming from our campsite. At the barely burning fire sat our lost Eliseyev, looking morose.

"Are you crazy? Where did you disappear to?" It had become easier to breathe.

"I waited and waited for you guys. Then something ran by in the bushes. And I ran!"

We had cause to celebrate. We were down but happy. We did not have the strength for sharp movements or bold actions. We were in spirits that were tired but merry. In our net, as a farewell gift, a lumpish thing had landed. This is a rare and ancient fish with bumpy skin, magical violet–purple caviar and a mouth at the front part of its belly.

A little shoal of big herring highlighted the poignant singularity of this lumpfish. They all ended up in soup. The herring was delicious. The lumpfish's jelly-like flesh trembled in the pot.

"I'm already an elderly man," came the weak voice of Eliseyev, who had already been through a lot today. Even alcohol does not overpower me. My body can't even reject it anymore, like when I was a young man, it accepts any dose without complaining!"

As he said this, he was diluting liquor and river water to make a curative elixir. Aquatic insects scurried in his mug. His hand was shaking, more liquor splashed into the mug than was suitable for conversations on lofty subjects. The insects died. Nikolai bravely drank down this living mixture of dead water, ate a gelatinous bite of lumpfish, leaped to his old man's feet and boldly jumped into the bushes. We then heard the sounds of vomiting coming from the bushes.

"It's a magical place, the White Sea," I said to him when he had returned and seemed already a little less elderly. "Whatever you desire here, it comes true right away…"

Old Savvin was waiting on the shore, as if he had known the exact moment of our arrival. We noticed him only once we had come close; he was a living part of this great whole, his Keret. He stood there silent, gazing out at us from under a hand placed over his eyes, then he came into the water, took our canoe by the nose and neatly guided it to shore. We got out, already half-dead from everything: from the sea, the wind, the sun, joy, fatigue and sadness. On our lips was bitter salt; on our backs, heavy salt; in our lungs, a sweet, fresh salt and in our heads a clear salt.

After we caught our breaths, we rubbed our backs and backsides. I immediately began to trouble the old man with questions. He already trusted me:

"Our village was a lovely one. The streets were paved with boards. Keret people didn't want to walk through the mud. They kept the planks in front of their houses swept and polished. They didn't keep chickens or pigs, because those are foul creatures. Plus, any roosters would start crowing. No, things were quiet around here. A Pomor would come home and the roar of the ocean would still be there in his ears all the time. After winning bread for the family, the father would rest on a bed made from deer hide…"

"In the forest we saw some old construction. I read that a merchant named Savin lived here and worked in the forest. You wouldn't happen to be related?"

The old man tensed almost imperceptibly and his head jerked as if he had not heard me well. "Huh, me? No, we're not related. We came here later, from somewhere else, already after the war."

"Why did the salmon stocks dwindle? They say that before, it was impossible to overfish here, that the salmon were numberless."

"Our grandfathers thought it best not to fish here. They were careful about the fish, they were their breadbasket. They wouldn't even ring the bell in the church when the salmon were spawning. But in the thirties," he looked around, "They ordered that the entire river be lined with nets. After a few years the fish were gone."

"They say the village was big before? In the sixties it had eight hundred houses. Why isn't there anything left today, why was it abandoned? Did the young people leave for the city?"

The old man gave me a serious look. Even the wrinkles on his face seemed to straighten. He said in a harsh tone, "In '35 they arrested half of the men at once. Without a man around, a house won't stay up, weeds will take over the whole place. There you have it."

Around us, from the dark forest to the White Sea, along the pink-colored river and the shores of the bay, reigned a vast emptiness covered by various grasses.

We put our things into the car without speaking. Our packing was attentively followed by old Nefakin. "Well then, do enough fishing?" he asked.

We kept silent. We did not want to talk to him. He got offended. "Everyone is driving here these days!" He suddenly broke out into a scream, "You forgot everything! You forgot quickly! I'd show you now!" He then started scratching his right hip with his calloused hand.

We looked up, astonished. We were not afraid, only bewildered at first, and then sad.

"Forgot everything! Someone ought to remind you! Remind you!" He threw his stick down in anger and walked off towards his house, worn out from this rage.

Old Savvin came up when we were already sitting in the car. "Savin, the merchant that lived here, was a good man. Charitable." Then he held out his pack of White Sea Canal cigarettes.

1913–1931, KERET VILLAGE

Ask anyone whether he knows what happiness is. It's not a quiet pier, when there's no wind and that is already bliss. Rather, it's a sharp instant that comes like a bite, when your whole body is suddenly pierced by what feels like pain, but it's not pain, its joy. And your soul feels a bit lighter, as if the Mother of God up above was smiling, and you caught a glimpse of this smile and realized that it was meant for you and no one else. That tearful moment might be a kiss from your child. Or the sudden vastness of the sea, when you come from behind a rocky cape into the open sea. Or a young, inexperienced, wise night. But for me, happiness will forever be the first salmon that I ever saw, when it leaped out into the sunlight from the dark water, and froze for an instant in the rainbow of spray that flew up into the sky with it. It was nearly the first time that my mother had ever let me walk down to the river alone. I was crawling among the bushes and looking for different bugs and spiders to study them. Then I suddenly heard a splash so loud that it scared me. I looked out from the little promontory and there it was flying up. The day was dim, overcast, but there a heavenly light which shone right down on the fish from the clouds. Ever since then, whenever someone says that God does not exist, for me there is no question: I saw it, I know.

My father then started to teach me little by little. "Learn it, Kolyamba, while I'm still alive," he said. In our Keret River there were a lot of salmon. Our forefathers had caught them abundantly, but there was an endless number of them. Because our people respected fish. Everyone knew about them, all their habits, all their sneaky ways. They are sneaky, the mother fish, you wouldn't believe it if you haven't seen it for yourself. They won't go into ordinary nets, and if they happen to get caught, they will struggle until they work themselves free. At the fisheries they would create labyrinths of nets, so that if they did come in they would get confused in every direction and then they would get swept up. People would catch the fish quickly here; they couldn't be slow, because if you gave the fish a chance to think, they could escape from any labyrinth. Salmon didn't give themselves up to people easily. But when they were spawning, no one would touch them. We had a strict ban on that, something we had inherited from our forefathers. No one dared raise their hands. How the salmon would play in the river, like children at their games. After all, we had a lot of games back then. Tag and Rooster were our main ones. Tag was simple: you just ran after another person and would try to catch them. In Rooster you had to hide. You hid in some quiet, faraway spot – no one would ever find you. So, you had to crow like a rooster sometimes to help, otherwise the game would last until the next morning. The person who was searching would find you and you would run together to the gathering place to shout "*bak-balibak*". You would run along skipping, leaping over the big rocks like a horse, with your shirt fluttering and your hair thrown back. The salmon would leap out from the water in the same way as a child horsing around. Only the child would jump down from some height, but the fish jumps up in joy.

Then it falls back into the gentle water and you can see how glad it is to be alive. When it is spawning season salmon start to change their color to a bright red, they dress up. A few males chase after a female. They fight each other, these young lads, show off their daring and esteem. The female chooses one and begins to build a nest with him. Somewhere, in the shallows of the river, where there are pebbles and sand on the bottom and the sun can provide warmth, they make a large mound and there she lays her eggs. As flocks of salmon head upstream, they kill all the small fish, all the slippery hunters for salmon roe. The salmon don't eat these fish, but as our forefathers said, they "crash into them", kill them and throw them out of the way. After the female's pleasure, she swims back to the sea, eats her fill and waits for the next time. A portion of the males remain to guard the eggs, but the others also head out to the sea. They lose their colorful garb then and become awfully thin, skeletons with big heads. They are called *valchaki* then. The baby fish hatch from the eggs in three months. They have such lovely flanks and brown spots all over their bodies. Whole crowds of them sweep along the river's shallows, curious, like all little children. Where one goes, all the others go there too. They are so daring. When you go into the water and stay there, they are running all over the place, but after two minutes you look down and they have already gathered next to you and are touching your feet, the silly things. When an adult salmon goes from the sea to the river to spawn, it stops eating, so as to avoid hurting her little ones.

Six months or a year goes by and the speckled babies become youths. They are silver all over, impetuous and nimble. They scurry about and then suddenly freeze in ambush, not lying in wait for anyone, but just like that, to show that they are almost grownups now. They have a lot of strength but not much brains. Now they play their hunting games, chasing after other fish, but not after other salmon. They might try to catch a mosquito or some fly. This is all done in jest and it's very funny. Then they gradually start to swim towards the sea, that's why we called smolt "downstream swimmers". They get to the sea and disappear there, some for a year, some for two or at most three. What they do there, where they swim, no one knows. They only come back as full adults, after they have gained experience and put on weight. Again they go to their native river to spawn, so that the circle of life can begin again.

The ones who enter the river immediately after the ice breaks up and drifts downstream, we call ice-followers. They spend a lot of time around the river mouth, waiting for the ice to flow down the river. Only after the ice drifts have ended will the ice-follower make its way up the heavy, oily waves to its native spawning grounds. This was the most awaited salmon, because it was the first salmon we saw after a long absence. The female salmon is marvelously beautiful, white like a shy maiden who has spent all her life shrouded and now suddenly dares to bathe in a secluded glen. The salmon is just as fine. Desirable.

In her trail, after about a month, come the *zakroyka* salmon. Then the low-water salmon, the biggest kind. Close to August comes the grilse salmon, pipsqueaks, not even two kilo yet, but already mature spawners. Like big-city ruffians, mischievous boys and naughty girls. Behind them, already in the autumn, come the fall salmon. These are larger, but most importantly, all of them that have had their time in the sea, and they come back white and silver. That is what they are called, white salmon. There are also ones who stay in the river all the time, and you can tell those right away from their green-gray color.

I fell in love with them. Winters for me were dull because I did not see them. In spring things awakened again, life began with their first leaps when the ice-followers went through the heavy, oily water of the river. My heart warmed in my chest, like a little child that was running wild and not listening to his parents' call. Even when I caught and killed salmon, I loved them. I loved to lay their silvery bodies down on the stones at the riverbank and slowly, and carefully, gut them. Inside they were just as fine as they were on the outside. Their flesh was bright orange, with mother-of-pearl innards, always an empty stomach (when the salmon is spawning, it doesn't eat) – sometimes it seemed like all this was just some fine waxwork figure that clung to the highest spirit of beauty that the salmon bore within itself. I loved their smell – they smelled of themselves, alive, their leaps, their raging flights into the sky.

They smelled like cheating on the sea. I would breathe in this smell for a moment, and then for days to come I would walk around stunned, sick, healed by them. I couldn't sleep at night, a smile would never leave my face; I talked nonsense that turned out to be true – not a harsh truth but a tender one. I saw how people were drawn to me during these days. I could make them laugh, liven them up, save them – I was all imbued with the salmon's smell and spirit. Sometimes it even seemed to me that I was the fish. I dreamed of becoming one. Of frolicking as a carefree fry in the sunlit water. Of whipping along the fast-flowing streams as a smolt. Of hunting as an avid, voracious grilse in the ocean, discovering the dark life there, fighting, eating my fill, readying myself for the most important thing in life. Then returning to my native land as a shining ice-follower, to rejoice so much that sometimes you don't even notice the change of the elements, to look forward to what was to come, to desire, to love. Of loving almost to the point of death – otherwise it would not be love. Of not fearing either death or love. Of not being afraid. Of laughing with death and at it. Of scraping myself, my body and my soul, against the stones of the rapids, of breaking through and racing up against my own native current. Of loving so much that it is not clear whether it's your blood on your sides, or the wedding garment blooms with unbridled pain. Or it is everything together and there is no reason to divide the red tint. Of loving to the point of exhaustion, convulsions, despair. Of wearing myself out, nearly dying. Of exchanging my red color for dark gray. Of descending to the sea as a feeble *valchak*. Feeble and barely alive. Barely alive through the hope that maybe all of this will repeat again someday. Of surviving this and living.

1975, PETROZAVODSK

Once upon a time a boy's mother bought him an aquarium fish, a bull-head catfish. He had long dreamed of this kind, however unlovely it was, ugly even, but a very useful fish. A broad, flat head with long whiskers, a speckled body of an unpleasant greenish shade. But with a sucking mouth too, a powerful one with thick, avid lips. These lips were in constant motion; whether the bullhead sat on a leaf of an underwater plant or was darting up along the smooth glass of the aquarium, its lips were moving. At first the boy thought that the fish was silently mouthing one and the same thing, apparently something very important: "Look-there, watch-out." The boy would go into the pet store and spend hours watching this wonderful fish, straining to riddle out its sad and monotonous secret. Only after several days of this did the shop girl notice him. At first she gave him some long, hard scrutiny to see whether he was shoplifting, but then she went up to him and asked him.

"Look-there, watch-out", the boy, embarrassed, explained with some difficulty what he expected from the fish.

"That one," the older girl smiled, "he isn't saying anything. He's cleaning dirt off the glass. That's why this fish is very helpful."

She walked away, assured. But the boy did not believe her. He did not give up on this bullhead. Yes, it was helpful. Yes, it cleaned the tank. But it was also saying something important, the boy knew for certain, for he had seen it with his own eyes, he had felt the horror of communing with this mystery.

From that day on he tormented his mother, trying to convince her. He already knew that for her useful things were paramount, so he based his argument on this. He pointed out to her how clean their aquarium, with its silly little guppies, would be after the wonderful bullhead arrived in it. He strained and eventually won her over. She agreed with a friend that the latter would babysit Grisha's little brother Konstantin. They were set for a wonderful trip to buy the fish.

One weekend, one of the best days in Grisha's life, they went to the shop. They bought the bullhead from the same easygoing girl at the counter. They got a clear plastic bag with water and oxygen pumped into it. They put the melancholy bullhead into it and it immediately began cleaning the inside of the bag. This was for mama, so that she would like it. Then the three of them got onto the bus. Just then mama recognized an acquaintance of hers and began chatting with her, while the boy took from under his arm the bag with the water and the fish. The bullhead was cleaning it. Or rather, it was saying, mama isn't looking now. It whispered soundlessly, desperately, hopelessly, as if it wanted to warn Grisha about something, save him: "Look-there, watch-out."

"Mama, what are we going to name our fish?" Without a name things – fish, feelings – are only half of what they are. If love exists, it is a whole, while the half is called nothing at all.

"I don't know. Just wait a moment, don't bother me," said mama, absorbed in her discussion of important things.

"Fine." The boy was not upset, he was already used to it.

The bag with water trembled in his hands. The fish was in it whispering. "Next stop Schottmann Street," the bus driver announced. "Schottmann," whispered the boy. "You'll be Schottmann," and he carefully tucked the tireless fish back under his arm.

That day really had been a wonderful one. After Grisha neatly poured the water containing Schottmann into the aquarium, he wanted to spend some more time admiring the fish, but it got scared and hid under a branch. So Grisha went for a walk. His mother easily let him go out, while she stayed with his little brother. Grisha even got a little jealous, he felt that she already loved Konstantin much more than him.

Their yard and the neighborhood were quiet. Their yard lay directly on Sotsialisticheskaya Street. There was a big shop on it. A small crowd always swirled at the back entrance, they were giving empty bottles back. Bottles were not always accepted, therefore the line of people waited anxiously. It was generally orderly.

Along the street they were preparing for the holiday. On the lampposts, standing next to the big poplars, some special people were hanging red flags. A flatbed truck was driving past each post in turn. A man in a blue padded jacket stood in the back. He would take one flag from a pile of them and stick its staff into the iron pipe welded aslant on the lamppost. There were usually two such pipes slanted in different directions. Sometimes an entire bouquet would be sticking out from them. Grisha took great pleasure in watching this skillful and hardworking man. Generally, everything around was lovely and in perfect harmony. The light-blue sky and the worker's dark-blue jacket, the red flags and the slightly green leafy crowns of the poplars. Grisha knew that the wonderful celebration of May Day was approaching. During this time, the city streets and squares would be filled with columns of festive people with balloons, banners and portraits held up on sticks. Everyone would celebrate and when they were given the signal from the high tribune, they would loudly cry, "Hurrah!" He had already taken part in this march, which bore the complicated name "demonstration", and he too had shouted along with everyone else. There was a wonderful feeling that the entire crowd together, as if one person, was doing the same thing and rejoicing that everything turned out so perfectly: together as a team the crowd turned right, then left, but everyone together and smoothly. You did not even have to think about anything, such a thrill took hold of Grisha then, and all the adults too, he could see. "Hurrah, hurrah, hurrah," came the masses' jubilant cry in waves so powerful that sometimes you had to cover your ears. It seemed that an instant would pass and everyone would run together to the place they were told, towards some unknown, long-awaited happiness. This was spoiled only by the little gangs of boys darting among the feet of the adults. These boys would throw small shards from the bottles that they had saved in advance at the balloons; the balloons burst as if they were fireworks for the celebration. Sometimes a group of these boys, after they caught some solitary young child, would quickly punch him in the face and shake the coins out of his pocket. The adults were looking up at the tribune with red, tense faces and unusually did not notice these small scuffles. Only rarely would some elderly lady cast an incidental glance down at the ground, notice these little acts of injustice, and shout "Hey!" or "Don't!" But then the gang would quickly fly away in different directions, like gray ravens and there would remain among the jubilant adults one kid with a broken nose and red drops dripping on the pavement. The distracted crowd would immediately forget about him and again lift their eyes up, towards happiness. "Hurrah!" came the cry spilling over the columns.

Grisha was so lost in thought remembering this holiday, that he did not even notice that he had left his neighborhood. The poplars came to an end and the street was entering the few newly-built five-story buildings. These were gray, tall, smelling of some wonderful innovation in construction. They still had not made sidewalks, so everywhere puddles abutted on piles of sand and construction refuse. People jumped from pile to pile, trying not to get their feet wet. The face of each of them brightened once they looked up at this comfortable and convenient housing. It had been promised to everyone.

"Hey, kid, stop!" Grisha did not even notice where the two boys, already big, had appeared from. Only later did he guess that they had been following him, this solitary kid, for a long time already.

"You got any money?" They were quite grownup, with short hair and faces somehow grotesque. It was as if their souls within were so dulled that it appeared on the surface as a mask of mindlessness and misfortune.

"I do…" With hands that were suddenly sweating, Grisha took from his pocket the twenty kopecks that he had been carefully carrying for a long time now. Ice cream was sold around the corner.

"Give it here." One of the boys deftly snatched the coin.

You have to respect your elders, he had long been taught that. He did respect them. You have to fear your elders, he realized this in a split second. He suddenly saw how a person's eyes can be empty of color. He felt a cold, disgusted feeling in his stomach. He was paralyzed by a deathly fright. He saw himself look at everything that had happened from the side and could not make the slightest motion himself. It was like he was in a dream. The most horrible thing of all was the realization that this was no dream.

The boys seemed to scent the fear coming from him. "Scared? You like to stay at home with mom and dad? They bake you cakes?"

Grisha mechanically nodded to each question.

"You're coming with us, you little shit. You hear?"

Grisha again nodded. He realized that there was nothing he could do, only remain tense and vigilant. The air was twilit. In the distance red flags were being hung.

The three of them walked among the gray five-story buildings as if they were old friends, one younger and two older. The tallest of them even put his little hand on Grisha's shoulder in a brotherly fashion. So that Grisha could not run away. Through the thin fabric of his jacket Grisha felt the deathly grip of dirty fingers from which came a whiff of nicotine and something else, something so disgusting that Grisha could barely keep himself from gagging.

Grisha also took to heart the words of the second, thickset boy: "Look, I've got a blade." The boy opened his jacket pocket and showed Grisha a metal comb with a long, thin handle that had been sharpened to a stiletto. "You try to run, I'll stab this right through you."

They walked on, many people came walking in the opposite direction. One of them was a policeman and Grisha looked at him like a dog being dragged by the neck around a corner, further and further from people's gazes. But his shoulder was tightly gripped by the boy's fingers. It was as if they went into his skin, under his ribs, into his soul, so Grisha was unable to say anything, nor cry out, nor tear away.

It was a strange thing – he could understand everything that was going on, move, even sort of look at himself from the side at his terror, but any attempts to do something, change the situation, make an attempt to flee had been burnt out with acid and only a nauseating taste in his mouth was left from other feelings apart from fear.

"Alright, here we are." One of his new friends pushed the unlocked door of a cellar. It opened with a screech. They quickly entered the musty darkness that smelt of mold and wet sand.

It was dark in the cellar. Only a thin ray penetrated through a cat hole in the bricked-up basement window. It was an empty and enormous space, a huge empty cube with a sandy floor. A few pipes snaked through the middle of it, they were wrapped in half-rotten insulation that resembled decaying shreds of skin. Small specks of dust swept around the ray of sunlight, darting from side to side out of the horror. The smell of the place was so strong that it dulled his mind and the black abyss seemed to quench the very possibility of light.

What happened next would not fit in his head. It could not fit in anyone's head. He rose up to the ceiling and from there he watched with wide eyes that were now adapted to the darkness. It was not painful. He was somehow detached from it. He thought that it was bad that his trousers were getting dirty at the knees and mama would again scold him for being careless. For some reason, he remembered the whole time the fish Schottmann from that morning, who constantly made strange sucking movements with its mouth. It had whispered like it was warning Grisha about something: "Schott-mann, look-out, look-out."

So much time had passed that the world perished many times over, but he remained alive. Everyone got tired and breathed heavily. Grisha grew bored and sat by a cool, dank pipe. He could no longer smell the space. He nearly had no senses left at all. The boys shifted nearby, quietly talking to each other.

"Well, kid, do you want to live?" Grisha nodded with his heavy, aching neck. The boy who had asked was grinning. The other, standing slightly to the side, reluctantly picked up a piece of rusty pipe. Grisha felt how his eyes grew big then, taking up half his face, all of his face, where there was no longer a mouth or nose but just eyes. The one holding the pipe spat and was breathing heavily, excitedly. Grisha saw every slight movement and remained silent. The boy lightly shuffled the pipe in his hands, judging its weight. He made a first brief step.

The door to the cellar gave a loud creak. A sheaf of light violently burst into the space that widened. The two boys jerked, immediately jumped aside and silently dissolved into some dark opening without a trace.

A long time passed before Grisha stirred. With his hands chilled by the sudden draft he put on his dirty, soiled jacket and tried to stand up. Now he strongly and liberally vomited. He crawled away from the foul puddle and vomited again. No one entered through the door.

Grisha gathered all of his strength and crawled outside. The setting sun was looking him right in the face through the doorway of the cellar. Grisha warmed himself for a moment in its rays, then he was able to stand up and walk home. Sometimes he stopped and gagged again from the salty taste in his mouth. Along Sotsialisticheskaya Street, merry adults – already in a festive mood for the upcoming holiday – were rushing about. It was a long way to Schottmann Street.

O venerable father Varlaam, thou who art bold before the Creator, the Savior of us all, who is our true Christ, our Lord, venerated in the Holy Trinity, remember us in thy prayers, and accept and deliver all our prayers that we send to God. We pray to thee, save us from sorrow, and from the turbulent sea, and preserve us safe from drowning, and defend us from woes visible and invisible, because through your prayers, holy Varlaam, we shall be absolved from our sins, and we shall receive eternal blessings by the grace and benevolence of our Lord Jesus Christ, for to Him is due all glory with the Father and the Holy Spirit, now and ever and unto the ages of ages. Amen.

1932–1933, KERET VILLAGE

There will be men and villages that are verily untamed, like unto wild beasts…

St. Varlaam of Keret

How could you not believe him? He was a fine man, as I recall. We had never seen people like that before. He was a short, handsome man, like a child's toy. A black leather jacket, wide at the shoulders and narrow at the waist, sat on him like his own human skin, without any flaws or folds. He had clearly started going bald at a young age, but this was not noticeable, became he had shaved his head bald and it shined under the sun like a saint's halo. He had dark-brown eyes, shifty, sometimes funny, but they would gaze black and cold on one who dared to disobey him. He was overall quite dark with stubble – he usually walked around unshaven and he himself saw how men would look away from his wild appearance and the girls would blush excitedly. He was dark but shining, now that is a mystery. The shining came mostly from within him. When he began to speak, it sounded like a bird was singing. He always spoke quickly, so that you weren't able to object, or even think. He had answers to everything, he could even guess what the next question would be and he answered it in advance. This really amazed the men, it was as if he had some inhuman power. But gradually they began to believe, even though Pomors are slow to change their ways – the fickle sea has taught them not to believe in fast things. But he knew how to say special words that were music to your ears: about the overall misery in the land, about the tough lot of the poor, about what needed to be done to make everything good. The old men shook their heads in disbelief, but the younger ones, who were easier to rile up, were already rejoicing that a new life had come and they quarreled with the others.

Only the old men who had suffered through more than one winter on Novaya Zemlya or Grumant, who called death their sister because it always walked by their side, would talk about the sea mud called *nyasha* when the sea ebbs were in certain tough spots. If you get stuck in that mud, it'll be hard to get out and you'd need a long time to wash it off. But no one heeded their words any more. Who cares about things of old when there are new things around: we're building a whole new world of our own. The new ideas were invigorating, like the strong midnight wind.

But Fyodor – or Fedka, as people coarsely called the newcomer behind his back – could sense these attitudes like an animal. "Poverty is the most important thing of all," he said, "because there is more of it. Savin, the merchant there, he's got everything: boats and a big house, he sells wood and fish to England. He's got everything he needs. Is that really fair? You could be trading with England too, but you sell to him. You are busting your backs for that bloodsucker. You don't have enough to eat in the winter, so you get provisions from him on credit, then you slave away to pay it off. So what that he doesn't charge interest? It's still humiliating. It's unfair, things ought to be the same for everyone. We need to spread it around. If he won't give it up, then we'll take it. We're in charge now."

Savin was no fool. He heard these things and saw the evil in people's eyes and he gave away everything himself. But it didn't help him: a couple of years later he disappeared, as if the devil had licked him clean off the face of the earth. Then his house was burned down. Fedka sent his family off to somewhere with a convoy, like captured enemies who were not even aware that they were enemies. Savin's boats were handy though, and they began to be used as a collective fishery. It was normal to catch fish and give them to the state, which had become our own, and promised to take care of everyone. Everything was as it always had been. Before Savin had brought in provisions and sold them, but now a state shop appeared. There might have been less on offer there, but at least no one was profiteering. The red and white fish saw to themselves and the caviar was generous – the sea right next to us would feed us anyway.

Fedka became an important man, one of the authorities. But he was tireless. He got involved in every business, he was running around everywhere. Things were going fine on their own, these old professions laid down over centuries, but they didn't sit well with him.

"Men," he said, "there are too few fish. Too few salmon! The country needs more! The whole country is plagued by poverty, we need to catch more salmon!"

Where could you get more of them? However many the sea brings forth, that's how many there are. Plus, you need to spare some for spawning, and for their dancing because the world needs beauty, too.

"Too few fish," he kept harping on. "We need to catch more."

In May Fedka called a general meeting. Like the regional assembly, although now it was called something else. Our people got ready for this meeting like it was some holiday. The young girls put on their best clothes, for them it was one more occasion to show off their beauty. Married women gossiped and commented on them. The men were flattered too, they stood at call. Everyone came, there were as many children as the small fry in the river. Everyone was festive. They were happy too soon, for Fedka announced a bizarre idea. "In the river," he said, "there are a lot of fish. But we're always chasing after them in the sea. We need to set nets across the river, then we'll catch them."

After this was announced the people began to shout, the air shook: "Our forefathers never caught fish in the river. What will happen to us if we catch them all?" But Fyodor Trifonovich answered, "No problem, there will be new fish." But then he stopped arguing, he said that he had a decree in the name of the people. Whoever was against the general policy was against the people's government, so let them step forward one by one.

Everyone fell silent, their celebration had been in vain.

The next morning a company of soldiers came, Red Army men.

Two thirds of the men would not go out to set the nets. The ones who did go were glum, they wouldn't look each other in the eye. They set them quickly and skillfully. Just then the ice-followers were swimming upstream.

Along the riverbanks the grass had gently begun to turn green, but in the water awful things were being done. The water was rushing coldly, recklessly. Here and there bubbles appeared on the surface – the salmon were coming in droves. The red sides of the males and the silver of the females flashed, all so stupid, they didn't realize what they were jumping towards. The heavy lead in their native river should have warned them, but it didn't. They got caught in the nets senselessly, and sadly, without their usual shrewdness. Doing everything they could to reach the place where there would be love, life and light. They hauled them up into the daylight, clubbed over the head or dragged by the gills, by their mouths, their fins, their firm bellies, anywhere. They were thrown into boats, killed, and then it was time for another series of nets. They killed them on the riverbank too, their blood was mixed with a sad slime and formed puddles at their killers' feet. All that remained was a puzzled look at the strange sky and a barely visible flutter of their tails. Whilst from their anal opening, two drops of serous liquid appeared, sometimes a few eggs, a last effort made from pain, fear and the knowledge of what could not be rectified.

Men, old women and children hauled them in, forlornly carrying them in buckets and loading them onto carts. They were silent before the laughing red gang. Streams of blood poured down the carts and were soaked up by the ambivalent earth, by the grass which had been lush and greedy ever since. They brought the carts and put them next to one another. They were guarded by a convoy. The carts also carried away the men who had not come out to work, two by two. None of them ever came back. One season went by like this, then a second and a third. After that there were no more fish.

Fedka soared over everything like a black falcon at first. He loudly rejoiced. He put a stop to any dissent, not through persuasion but brusque prodding. Everyone looked away, stared down at the ground, but he did not forget anyone and on the next train of carts these men would be taken away two by two. The train trailed a streak of blood; during the day dogs, and at night animals, would come to lick it up. No one drove them off.

There were whispered rumors that the men had been sent to work on the White Sea Canal and that they would come back after their work was finished. Around the homes that had lost their men, weeds grew rampantly. The women couldn't see to everything. Four years later they took Fyodor Trifonovich away too, because suddenly the catch had shrunk significantly. When they came for him, he got aggressive and grabbed his pistol. But they quickly disarmed him and rolled him around in the dirt. He walked off with his eyes cast down and his leather jacket that had made half the girls sigh was smeared with thick, black earth. By the forest he turned and tried to shout something about the revolution, but they shut him up with a merciless blow. By that time half the village had been taken over by weeds. Fedka never came back either.

2005, KYUVIKANDA

"It's not a bad car, but don't expect it'll take you everywhere." Two men were avidly looking at Grisha's car. "But it's a good one, a good one!"

It really was a good car. Grisha had dreamt about it for several years. He did not even believe that he could have one like it. It was too expensive, it was too fine and too wonderful and truly functional, like a mighty animal that had been tamed. It had huge, splayed wheels with an aggressive, earth-rending tread; a high ground clearance so that he did not have to worry about stones on the forest paths; a body supporting a metric ton, where you could load a couple of moose or a dozen friends who had had too much to drink – and yet it had a pretty, smiling face, one made as if to evoke affection from its owner and passersby.

After Grisha had spent around a year searching for a car, a loan for it, repayment plans, he ended up quite disappointed in himself and the people around him. Yet as it often happens, in a moment of complete failure something will click in the universe, suddenly everything will come together: the friend whose car Grisha had stroked on more than one occasion, decided to sell it at only two years old and the price proved to be not too high; the bank, ordinarily the enemy of all living things, offered good terms for a loan. Thus, after just a week of running around like crazy, Grisha was already attracting the envious glances of men of all different ages.

He tried with all his might not to hang a thick gold chain around his neck, or worse yet, a tie made out of hundred-dollar bills; to not become a horrible clown hiding his empty eyes behind dark glasses, driving into the oncoming lane and cutting off drivers of lesser cars. It was just sometimes hard to keep the smile spreading across his face under control. He liked his new car too much. He would imagine, too vividly among his everyday hassles, how great it would be to drive it to his beloved North, how it would climb the mountains and tear across any swamp, how it would make him more free and independent of anyone; in yet another unrestrained attempt to understand, to breathe in the happiness, so difficult to explain, that he had grasped from his very first visit to the White Sea in the pearly twilight that blossomed over the treacherous caress of the northern sea's waters.

He could not remember when exactly that happened, or what the impetus for it was. The dull society in which he floundered, more from habit than any real need, had become completely unbearable. Everyone was cheating everyone else – in another, cruder way of wording it, it would sound much more erotic. "Oh, try this herring, what wonderful herring!" Yellow lips were pursed coyly over a plastic jar with its contents cut up and then industrially frozen, industrially salted, and for the delight of consumers, enriched with a drop of essence from a test tube labeled "dill substitute". "What tender, delicious herring!"

Not quite everything, but many things around him had suddenly become artificial, not real, somehow false. He could not understand how people could go against it and try to pretend that the lie was the truth – and since truth was unattainable, then let's mock it, we are all so wise and refined.

"Imagine, hahaha," one intellectual said, "they write in the newspaper that in the North a car killed a bear. Hahaha, how cute, there are still bears up there. It's so funny."

Grisha recalled how he had once come face to face in the dark northern forest with a pine that was oozing fresh sap. The deep scratches on its trunk, two and a half meters high, meant there was no doubt: the master of the forest had just been here. How Grisha's palm had sweated as he gripped the handle of his small knife, his only weapon. What a relief it was afterwards to realize that the master of the forest did not like to meet human beings. You only had to help it, so that it would not accidentally jump out onto the path as it was going about its business, so that it would not accidentally cross the line of getting scared and lashing out with an angry paw. Then all would be well. Just step and talk loudly and sing songs – the master of the forest is fed well in the summer, it likes cloudberries and blueberries. Let it stay calm, let it have somewhere to escape off to.

With everything here close, everything nearby – the water you drink from the stream without thinking about diseases, the air that you breathe in so deeply that your ribs ache, the sincere and simple emotions – fear, love, hate – are simply a simple set of seven truths, like colors of the rainbow. Just accept it for free, gratis, so you don't complain.

"Ugh, we're being bitten by mosquitoes…"

The road had immediately started to go through hills, large puddles lay across it. The water in them, dark-brown, the color of chifir, was thick and odorous, like a night somewhere in the southern extremes of the country. But this was the North, so it smelled of turf, St. John's wort and a desperate hope for better things. Every time they were scared of driving into one of those puddles. It turned out that under the dark surface was an unthinkable depth, a bog, and in such places the bright-green mossy marshlands extended as far as the horizon. Each time the car would make it past the deepest point, boldly, triumphantly break-ing free of the watery encumbrance, forming waves in front of it like a battleship. Still, although they felt a boldness within that had been awakened by the prospect of soon seeing the sea, the driver had been drinking – oh, the sweet impunity of forest roads – so they decided to be careful. Grisha's friend Nikolai and brother Konstantin got out of the car and walked quickly, almost running, in front of it. There were so many puddles that it never made sense to get back in the car. Thus, they walked along in front of it without tiring, as if they walked not on their feet but light, winged sandals. Before a puddle they would slow down, step into it, touch the bottom with their feet, make an encouraging ges-ture and then dash forward again, tirelessly. It was clear that this exer-cise was good for them, this air and their laughter; even the mosquitoes that hung in clouds over each of them were weak before the swinging of their strong arms. Grisha suddenly realized that he was looking at them not with forgotten memories but some forgotten tenderness. It flooded into him so suddenly and so strongly that he could not control himself and he allowed his eyes to tear up. "They are my guides, they are doing something to make it easier for me, they are helping me." He had grown so unaccustomed to doing things with other people, he had spent many years now in the terrible desperation of solitude, now things had become so nice and happy that he was embarrassed at himself. To rid his heart of this pathos of good spirits, he leaned out of the window and shouted to them, "I'll call you 'my merry Sherpas!'" But they would be offended by that, no, instead they laughed heartily and ran on further.

It might seem a trifle, fifty kilometers. Plus, the road had often let them speed up, and then everyone hopped into the car and merrily rushed through the forests towards their long-awaited goal. Nonetheless, time dragged on, there was no end to the obstacles and Grisha was starting to get tired. These fifteen hours at the wheel had been hard on him. His sherpas, who had slept while they were still on the highway, were also feeling low now and dragging their feet or occasionally stumbling over invisible rocks deep in the puddles. When everyone was secretly waiting to see who would weaken first and start talking about taking a break, the road was suddenly barred by a gigantic puddle. It was a small open pit with steep, sandy walls. There was no way for the water to flow out of it and it had become a pond nearly waist-deep. At first glance it was clear that the bottom of this puddle was clay and miry. There was no way around it, or apparently through it either. Grisha cut the engine. The car and the puddle stood face to face with a gloomy frown.

"Yep, the better the jeep, the farther you have to run behind the tractor," his brother said gloomily.

"Let's do it like this. We can think better in the morning. We spend the night here, then tomorrow we decide whether to maybe turn back and try somewhere else." As the driver, Grisha had the right to suggest their course of action.

"Alright then," everyone laughed in relief and, though it seemed like they were exhausted, they quickly got around to making a fire.

Grisha went off to get wood. He had no strength left in him. He dragged himself, hardly able to move his feet, along the puddle that barred their way. His head was empty and dark, without a single thought, a single feeling, except for a gray weariness, like a fog. He descended a small, sandy slope, feeling like a squeezed lemon and stopped. Right in front of him on the wet sand were the clear prints of a beer. Not a minute ago, not an hour, but sometime today the master of the forest had clearly been here. Grisha did not feel any tide of strength coming back into him, no, he suddenly became more alert and attentive. His former fatigue disappeared. He quickly looked around – it was an unpleasant little spot, low forest, swamp, a small lake behind the trees, but it offered the greatest freedom for wild animals. He listened carefully – nothing nearby rustled, no branches broke. He sniffed – many times he had been amazed at how his sense of smell grew more acute at such moments. The smell of a wild animal is strong and sinister, and once you recognize it you will never forget it. But here, now, everything was fine, it smelt of the evening, the leaves of the nearby aspens, calm. There was no fear in the air. "Ha ha, goddamn!" he shouted. His brother and his friend Nikolai came quickly running up, swinging their hatchets. They were in energetic spirits from their work and the expectation of dinner. Now they immediately became more subdued and looked around. But then like always, "Nah, he's been gone for a long time. Even if he was here, he would have smelt us and got scared. Plus, he would have heard the car coming for miles." After deftly reassuring themselves and each other, they went back to the fire.

There is a special story told during the white nights on the White Sea. A scary story. For you never know who laid this causeway in the swamp that you are walking along, slipping and stumbling. Where does it lead to, what awaits there at the end of the road? Something makes a plaintive cry in the middle of the night – it's just a bird, you reassure yourself. A branch snaps in the forest nearby – it just happened on its own. Even if someone roars not too far off, fifty meters or so, or even closer, then that must be local folks starting their boat engines, they are going fishing, you whisper to yourself through a cold sweat. Most importantly, it works, so you roll over a bit and fall asleep again, with the handle of your small folding knife in your hand. Every time before you turn in for the night, you carefully lay your hatchet down somewhere next to you. Just in case.

Therefore, one's first White Sea night is spent among such fears, doubts and an oppressive delirium. When you look around you, when the first shivers of your being stop, then you suddenly realize that there are no external threats. Nothing is going to attack you in these old forests that have seen everything. Another power reigns here, another whim. You start to think, to examine yourself. You listen closely and suddenly see that everything that is black, horrible and vile is within yourself. You feel how old grievances rise up inside of you in heavy waves, how you are unexpectedly overtaken by grief, then a desire for vengeance, for the hardships in life. You remember all who betrayed you and in a horrible way you want to get revenge on them. For an instant you lose control over yourself, you are blinded by a black sensation and an evil force enters your body – you run around, leap, burst out cursing like a man possessed. You lose the ability to look after yourself. You nearly die.

In moments like that, it is good when someone around you is calm. Someone who does not begin to argue but listens to all your groaning and watches all your writhing, then gently says, "Alright, then, let's go fishing." White Sea stories start out scary.

It was like that this time too. It came and then it went. They spent an hour telling each other some home truths. But then they calmed down and took a look around. Then they looked at each other with amazement. Then suddenly felt ashamed. This time Grisha – to his own surprise – was the wisest and most composed. He had not slept for two days and did not feel like sleeping. After everyone had calmed down, he took a look around at the homely beauty of the place and then at the nearby lake. "Are we going fishing or not? What else did we come here for?"

It was three o'clock in the morning. There was a soft, pearly, iridescent light. The sun was hiding somewhere nearby. There was no wind at all, not a single movement on the surface of the water. Surprisingly, there were few mosquitoes – they must have been sleeping, worn out after a long day. Only the most restless mosquitoes awkwardly tried to bite them and were either swept away with a weak flick of the wrist or were crushed into mere specks. Grisha's friend Nikolai could not handle all of this and from an excess of feelings, from the fatigue that followed this release of evil and misfortune, fell asleep in the tent. When Grisha and his brother grabbed their fishing rods and began heading for the lake, they heard the vigorous snoring of a good man.

After they had walked through a small grove of aspens and reached the lake, they went in different directions. His brother walked along the high rocky shore for some reason. Grisha, however, who was no longer able to think clearly due to his tiredness and the alcohol he had drunk, went along an inconvenient patch of swamp. He had to walk carefully, for everywhere there were holes with standing water, but the shore was more or less strong and gave firm footing, it only slightly shook as he walked. The fear and cloudiness had already left his soul, he just felt slightly dizzy and the calm that reigned serenely kept him on his feet.

Grisha was not a good fisherman. He had fished once upon a time in his childhood under the watch of his grandfather and uncles. Then he set the pastime aside, attracted to other, apparently more important things. Yet now, as he was almost exhausted by those important and, as it turned out, vacuous things, he turned again to fishing. At first nothing happened. He felt he was doing everything right, like other people, like his brother, but the fish seemed to mock him. Even his brother grew surprised at this. Konstantin himself, inveterate and persistent, never failed to catch something, but Grisha could not bear setting nets, nor spending hours sitting in one place, nor running for miles through different places. Everything was fruitless at first. But then something would happen. Some line would be crossed. Either old experience would finally come to him, or the fish would suddenly become grateful for all the attention he was giving them, but suddenly the fish would begin biting so much that he surpassed old hands at fishing, though he was only slowly becoming one himself.

However, this time, he saw that his brother was dragging something over on his shore. It was something small, but nevertheless a sense of daring quickly shot through Grisha's blood and blew the traces of alcohol from it. Grisha quickly set up his rod and cast his line across a small

bay overgrown with small reeds. He cast it without any especial hope –
he had already convinced himself that at three o'clock in the morning
they would not catch anything. They would just warm up, wave their
fishing rods back and forth. The second time he cast it right into the
lake. On the third try he was lucky.

He did not even have time to come to his senses, to think of anything. His hands did everything on their own. He only saw his pole arch
tightly over the water, his line whirred and the reel bent, then a toothy
beauty was flopping on the shore. Grisha managed to catch it with his
hands as it danced about and he quickly broke its spike. Then he sat on
a hillock to catch his breath. Everything had happened in the blink of an
eye: first he was sitting here, then the fish was lying there on the ground.
Suddenly an unrestrained, bright happiness poured into his soul. Maybe
it was adrenaline. Maybe he had finally breathed in a full chest of the
pure, sobering, yet intoxicating air of this place.

He sat for some time, cut off a flexible willow twig with a spear-
like protrusion at the end, pierced the pike's gills through with it, then
walked onward, fearlessly holding the twig at the pike's very maws. The
pike's tail dragged docilely over the grass.

Grisha stopped at the next creek. He lay his caught beauty down at
a distance so that it would not get in his way. He did not believe that he
could repeat his luck; too much happiness never comes at once for free.
He cast his lure across the creek. Then right into the lake. On the third
try he was lucky.

Everything happened as it had done before, right down to the second, to the fraction of a degree that he turned in place, to the slightest
ounce of effort from his hands. The tight arc over the water, the tug on
the line, a short and subtle Salome dancing on the grass, its head in his
hands, the crunch of its vertebrae and the release of death. The joy of
having done it. A short break.

It was a good thing that he had not smoked for three years now – he
would have smoked an entire pack now and the area around him would
have reeked. His hands calmed down on their own. After he had sat for
five minutes, he went on. Behind him he dragged two aquatic furies,
dangerous but wondrous, over the ground. They had been caught and
their bodies had surrendered to him, but their souls had slipped away.

He walked until he reached the next creek. Again, he sat down on
a hillock for a breather. He noticed how his brother was looking at him
from the other shore attentively, even slightly jealously. "He probably saw
everything," Grisha mused abstractly and he again carefully cast his line.

This time he was lucky right away, from the first casting. But it was an ill, nervous luck, he began to be in a rush and somewhere the precision of his movements and his composure were lost. Maybe he was getting greedy, he wanted too much right away. Maybe the leader on the fishing line was worn out. But the pike tore away from the lure and swam off.

Usually he would attach a new leader, add more lures. Granted, there was no chance now: the creature would be in pain from its torn maws and would hide underwater for a long time, while it expelled the iron fruit of its own greed from its mouth.

It is so strange, and it is always like that. He did not know pikes very well. He did not know this one very well, the most vicious he had ever seen. At his second casting it went for his line again. Someone once told him that if one pike tore away, another pike would come along in its place. Lies and foolishness, for when Grisha had dragged the fish to the very shore and its maws showed through the water, he saw the same bright-green lure that he had just lost. Grisha felt surprised, he even thought his hands worked on their own and tried to do the evil creature in with a swoop – and the line fell limp again. He slowly wound the reel in thinking that he had lost another lure. When the end of the line came, he could not believe his eyes: on the new lure hung the old one, it had been torn out of the mouth rich in teeth.

He cast his line a third time. Two previous times, he had caught nothing. The pike was resting. On the third time it bit again. He had no doubt now that it was the same fish. Were it a little bigger and him a little small, he would have wondered who was hunting whom. But the way things were here, he did not. It was just stubborn fervor, burnt out, then flaring up again, heavy and sweet. There was no longer any doubt. There could not be any mistake of it. He was fighting with the fish, it was fighting with him. Their strengths were unmatched, but it filled everything with its anger. It hoped that he would suddenly let up, stumble, lose control, fall into the water and drown. He stubbornly pulled. It leaped out of the water and tore at the hook. Then a second time, and a third. "It'll get away. Again it'll get away, the bastard!" His hands and his heart shook. Finally, it was lying on the shore. It had not resisted him too strongly. It was tired, it had given everything it had. He had won. He sat down next to it and looked at it with pity. A love was quickly kindled. His brother came running from a distance, dodging the swampy patches and holding a bunch of small perch on a string. "Give it to me! Give it to me!"

While they were hauling the fish back to their campsite, tiredness overcame them. Grisha breathed heavily, as the burden in his hands was a heavy one. Three sisters, alike in all ways except for their personalities – the last one's was downright wicked. But one more pike was added to the bunch – the lake had finally given his brother one so that he would not be upset. Plus, Konstantin had a bunch of perch, a lawful catch. They made their way back, taking the occasional breather; they had gone far off to fish. When they reached the tent, Nikolai Eliseyev came out of it half-asleep, remembering nothing of the previous day.

"Eliseyev, you remember how you shouted the whole way, 'How I love fish! How I love cleaning them!?' Well, take these now and clean them." Eliseyev did not object to this but smiled brightly in response.

Grisha loved his friend for that, for his kindness and caring. He always understood everything correctly, fairly. He might get into scraps with his brother, but never with Nikolai.

Meanwhile, now it was eight o'clock. Five hours had gone by. How had that happened, where had it all gone, was unclear. In his head, his memory and his body there were only three flashes, three moments of joy, three sisters hanging on a string.

He and his brother downed a drink quickly and happily, then they each ate a tin of stewed meat. Then it was off to sleep, on fully justified grounds. They had earned it.

Two hours later Grisha woke up from a feeling of happiness. The sun was gently warming his face through the windshield, on which sat a content mosquito, crimson after drinking blood. It was quiet. Grisha lay there for a while, still waking up, and then looked around. Eliseyev was at work at the fire without making a sound. Over the flame he had placed a pot with oil in it. He quickly grabbed some chunks of fish, pink in the morning sun, rubbed them in breading and threw them into the pot. Two minutes later, keeping a distance from the flickering flame, he would take the cooked fish out and lay it on the pot lid, then quickly throw a new batch in. It was fun to watch his hectic, jerky movements, but he managed to do everything and the pile of fried fish grew. Grisha opened the car door and then the smell hit his nose. That could only be the smell of freshly caught fish that two hours ago were swimming in their native waters and were now lying in boiling oil. The smell immediately woke him up for good and he hastened to the fire. He looked over at the tent, the color of the mossy stones surrounding them, and with a secret admiration he saw his brother hurrying out, drawn forth by the same smell. While his brother was still getting out of the tent, Grisha was already impatiently shifting next to the pot. Eliseyev had already grown bored, but now he was happy at their simultaneous arrival and filled their bowls with chunks of hot, greasy fish. Like a famished animal Grisha immediately wolfed the food down; he burnt himself. How delicious it was; it melted in his mouth like a piece of ice on his palm. The thin layers of meat came right off the bone and briefly shined in the sun like flower petals, before they disappeared, forever, into Grisha's insatiable stomach. His nostrils quivered, lusting after the smell, so he had to be careful not to bite his own tongue. His lips stretched into a smile from the deliciousness of the fish, the smell of it, the world around him, the men's friendship. All the darkness and resentment of the night before, the black seething inside him, disappeared, it fell to the ground and was swallowed up without a trace. Grisha suddenly felt pure and good, for the first time since he could remember. In just one night the White Sea had healed him, forced it all out of him, saved him yet again, and all before he had even caught sight of it – just the sea being near and the promise of it was already enough. Unexpectedly, tears came to his eyes, probably the next piece of fish had been too hot.

"Guys, guys, stop," Nikolai bustled about next to them. He had stressed everyone out the day before with his rambunctiousness and now felt a little guilty. Not too much – he knew that things were all good now, that the sea had also cleansed his soul of its grime. He now felt only slightly guilty, therefore he quickly diluted some medicinal alcohol in a big mug. "Here guys, morning exercise. Just a bit to get us to the sea."

Grisha was the first to take the mug from his friend's hand. He steeled himself for it and drank. Down his throat and in his stomach, then through his entire body to his fingertips, he felt a revolting, bitter, sweet, delicious wave. In spite of how he had tensed himself for it, he involuntarily and subconsciously shuddered, clenched his eyes shut to the point of tears and grunted.

"Alright, the morning workout is finished," said a cheery and forgiven Nikolai. "We've exercised all muscle groups. To the guns, my friends."

They suddenly felt so strong, so alert and in good humor, that all three of them suddenly realized that they could overcome anything. Their bodies were now ripe for great feats and their spirits were soaring through the heavens.

They got moving. They took down their camp in five minutes, then once more walked around the puddle from the day before. Grisha got into the car, started the engine, then turned on everything: four-wheel drive, low gear, diff lock. Slowly, in second gear, drove forward. Coming down from the hill he slightly gained speed and pressed the brake from time to time. Once he had already entered the puddle, he firmly gave the car a little gas. The seconds suddenly began to drag. The car did not roar but sullenly, like a workman or an animal, it moved inexorably forward. The water was up to the car's doors now, but Grisha did not doubt himself or the car. Like a battleship it cut through the yellow, muddy water and left powerful waves in its wake. Finally, without slipping, even once, without a single second of uncertainty, it flew up the hillock on the other side of the puddle and stopped there, purring contentedly.

"Hurrah!" he heard the men shouting from behind him, and again, like the day before, they ran along the edges of the hated swamp, slipping and sliding but moving boldly, his merry sherpas. Friends of merry days, companions on every journey. Without speaking and suppressing a boyish glee in his heart, Grisha stood there leaning on the front fender and watched them lovingly.

There was still more to overcome, ten hills, eight puddles and a stretch overgrown with foliage where the road could barely be made out. There was less and less forest along the hills, as if these hills were doffing their shaggy hats before people and exposing a green, mossy bald spot. There reigned, over everything, such a primitive simplicity that the human soul soared even higher, it seemed it would reach its limit, but no limit ever came. They drove along calmly and tried not to disrupt the splendor that surrounded them. The green color of the car merged with the early-summer tundra, its content purring only highlighted the silence, content with itself and the world that surrounded them. So what if several times its iron belly had caught on a bundle of roots or protruding stones – it was a reminder that one cannot be irresponsible, for even paradise is strict. But now, when they felt a good-spirited despair about whether the road would ever end, they slipped miraculously through the last swamp, a very scary one overgrown with green moss and with a stream murmuring under it; they sighed with relief. After this there was no more road. The car would be waiting for them here while they, who were going further and further from civilization and artificial existence, felt a nervous joy of entering amid the streams of the world. These high spirits were quickly lowered by mosquitoes, which flew in such numbers that they darkened the skies. But there was no time to think about them – they rushed to unload the car, to take the still-disassembled canoe and their backpacks onto their shoulders. Then it was down a barely identifiable path forward and downwards, towards where, through the trees, the Kyuvikanda was looking at them like a shy beauty.

There is nothing better in life than to quickly put a canoe together after a few days spent on foot and with hard effort, aided by goading, buzzing insects, to throw your things into it, to get into it yourself (still wary of the need to keep balance) and then push yourself away from the shore with an oar. To make a few oar strokes, then relax, sit still and listen to the silence. The light breeze will immediately sweep the hostile clouds of insects away and you can look around you, almost die of amazement at how noble and beautiful nature is. The blue lake (the color of Russian eyes) is surrounded by low, rocky hills that are sometimes forested and sometimes red-granite, as if the lake is lying snugly in the hollow of a strong, dependable palm, where the life mount and Venus mount rises around you and the narrow straits are leading you along the heart line and fate line. Whoever is not healthy, whoever is ill, the North heals their souls. We are northern people, we shield our eyes from the bright, southern illusions, we never try to forget that the outer wrapping is all there is and under it is emptiness. The Russian soul lies in the North, it would be stifled without it.

Soon the lake ends, though it is quite long. They went ten kilometers on what seemed a single breath. The wind was fair and the water smooth, with a light ripple that appeared and then immediately vanished. Traveling on water is better than bouncing around on the ground. It is happy, gentle. Any true cynic, any inhabitant of the capital, even their faces will get brighter and their hearts become softer. You don't have to rush anywhere, jump, hurry; you just have to know how to row and occasionally feel and do everything right so that your life is right at this moment, for another week and for another two weeks. No nagging doubts, no fussing about, only strength and joy around you.

Immediately the narrow river at the end of the lake runs lightly over small stones. Now they fearlessly hopped overboard to avoid scratching the canoe and waded through the gurgling water. Fifty meters, one hundred –suddenly an endless, boundless, calm expanse was revealed to them. They could see all the way to the horizon, the air was completely different here. The wind was different, hard and tenacious like a bird's claws when it tries to fly from your finger and it seems like it is trying to take you with it. On their left was a cape and on their right a cape, with a stony bay in the middle and before them the cloudless horizon. A quiet joy immediately surged inside them, a calm one like the sea bay. A strong joy. A heavy one.

Grisha could not fully understand why he was so painfully drawn to the North, to the White Sea. He had no particular reason for it, no relatives nor ancestors, or at least none that he knew. Nevertheless, it was as if a rope was suddenly pulling him there, not a conscious wish. Something boiled within him, his blood felt the call of another salty liquid. He resolved to go without knowing anything about it beforehand, without any idea of how things were there and what he was going for. When he saw the North, when he breathed the air for the first time, when he heard the local Russian language, he felt such a yearning, such a wrenching inside. As if he had known it long ago but had forgotten it, he had betrayed it at some time in the past and had erased this betrayal from his memory, but suddenly his heart recalled everything. For the first time in his life he heard words that his grandfather had always used, words that no one knew where they came from, what language they were related to. They were Russian words, it turned out, only ones that everyone had forgotten. They had been cast aside in the rush after ideals, then profit. Everything here was interwoven, joined into one: the sea wind, the gray stones, the golden sky and strong, meaningful, right words. He thought then, looked back, tried to figure out why he was so strongly drawn to the North, but there was no longer anyone to ask. All that remained was to trust his eyes and his hands when they would slowly, gently recall the shape of the oar, or the tender color of the moss, or the warmth of the stones.

Meanwhile, the temperature had risen to such a degree they had no need for a tropical vacation. The sun shone unbearably hot above, but the cool breeze from the sea blew the oppressive heat away as well as the flying insects. The rocks grew warm once the morning came and they could walk barefoot, but they did not freeze in the night, for the sun never lay down to sleep, its long rays shining at an angle caressed their steep brows even at midnight. The water splashed lightly against the shore, twice it would go out and twice it would come in. At high water there was not a single ripple on it from the shore to the horizon, while at low tide underwater rocks would emerge like moles on its clean face, they did not mar the sea they only made it more beautiful. Where they made camp it was shallow, but some two hundred meters further away there was a large reef with the roaring waves of the sea groundswell and behind the reef the sea immediately sunk to a great depth. Along the small river that they followed to the sea was a strong, well-kept fishing shack. The door was held shut with a stick but it was not locked. They did not stop there, however. It wasn't a place for them, it belonged to someone else, and so they pitched their tents at a distance on the rocks. They spent a couple of days looking at the place, at the sea, at the tourists sailing far off: it looked out of place here, celluloid. They always wondered if the fish and game warden would ever show up, so that they could either get permission right away or learn what rules there were. Yet, no one ever did come, and in the evening of the second day they decided to cast their nets wherever, for they already had a hankering for ocean fish. By that time the surf had grown strong, but they could risk it. They decided that Nikolai and Konstantin would go, while Grisha would stay behind on the shore. It was as if they had already distributed everything already, as if it was clear that it would be easier for the two of them, yet, when they got into the boat and set off from shore, Grisha was suddenly seized by an acute longing. Also a sense of worry, because the waves had already risen significantly and a bitterness, like a little child that they had not taken along with them on this daring job for grownups but rather left him alone on the shore, restless. This came over him so unexpectedly that it amazed him, he, who was a grown man and an older brother, but the feelings still remained there deep inside: the fear of being alone, of not being able to take part in some joint endeavor. He stood there watching as they maneuvered among the rocky islets, turned about looking for a way out through the reef. Then they found it and went along – now a big wave crashed into them and immediately flooded half of the canoe. They trembled, but it was nothing, they righted the boat, adapted to the waves and set a course for the open sea. He watched them wave their oars and head for the nearest cape so that they could drag their net through the sea. In this place the beluga whale had shown its white body the day before, it had been there for a reason: fish were present. For a time the two men could not be made out, they were either almost invisible from the distance, or sometimes completely obscured by the waves. Grisha felt troubled, worried about them and regretting that he was not there with them. Then they came back, feigning calm and severity. Without emotion they hopped out into the water in their long boots and gently brought the canoe to shore among the rocks. There was a happiness about them, drops of sea spray shone on their faces, and although they were all wet, they laughed. They recounted how they had set the net, how scared they were of the waves at first, but then got used to it. For a long time they could not find a way out through the reef, but then they figured it out: Nikolai Eliseyev pointed to the fishing shack. Next to it a tall pole jutted out with a white plastic anchor on it that could be seen from afar.

"I don't get it," Grisha said.

"Look here," Eliseyev smiled at his luck and his knowledge that had revealed itself at the last minute. Further away in the forest, on a high tree and at the same level as the first anchor was a second one, the same white color and visible from afar.

Grisha still did not understand. From the coast, it is hard to get a grip on matters of the sea.

"You're a greenhorn at this," they smiled, enjoying their superior knowledge. "Out at sea, if you line these two points up, the two anchors, then you find a way through the rocks. Good thing we figured it out in time, otherwise you'd be picking up the fragments of our boat on the shore."

Again Grisha felt like something had stung him, as if he had known this wisdom, this age-old experience, but he had forgotten it, which meant that he had betrayed it, now it came back on its own and had saved his friends.

A couple of hours later they went out to sea again, to haul back the net that had seven weights to sink it. These were good weights, each about a kilo and a half. Again it took them a long time to get out there and find the net. It had been swept from its place and twisted by the strong surf. What could be done – it was a straight shoreline with a constant open-sea wind, no islands or other shelter.

Now it was Grisha's job to clean the fish and cook soup. He did not seek to avoid this; he had already sharpened his knife beforehand. He sat on a stone and got to work with relish. A person who has only seen frozen fish in supermarkets has no idea what real fish is, fish from the sea. The smell, color and taste are completely different. It is even pleasant to clean them because they do not stink, but rather they have a strong, powerful, pleasant smell. He threw the guts to the seagulls but left the heads and the livers. Then, while his friends were resting, he got to cooking Pomor soup. One old man in the village of Keret had explained to Grisha how you should make real fish soup, *ukha* or *voyuksyanka* it was called. Grisha first threw the heads into the water after carefully removing the gills. Once he had seen tourists cook the salmon with the gills, so they spoiled the fish and the whole soup. Once the water was boiling, he took out the heads and threw them to the seagulls so they could have a treat too. He broke the fish up into large chunks and threw it into the broth. Naturally, he added salt, black pepper and bay leaves. But now came the trick to it: when the fish was ready, he brought some flat stones that were lying in the water, sprinkled them abundantly with salt and laid the fish on them. Then he added the fish fat to the broth and called his friends. While they were coming from the tent, the *voyuksyanka* was ready. True, the Pomors sometimes add sorrel to it, which it makes a really thick stock, but there were no salad leaves nearby and Grisha did not go looking for them. The men sat by the pot. They made a toast first to their fish soup, then they got down to eating. They scooped the broth into their mugs and sipped the hot liquid. They then took the fish from the stones; it had slightly cooled already and it smelt of the sea, seaweed, of free freshness. You will never find a taste like that in the world of frozen or canned fish. It is not only a feast for one's stomach but it also brings gladness to one's heart. Because this pure taste is also one of those few truths. Thus, they had each drunk a mug of *voyuksyanka* and eaten the fish, and that was it, they did not have room for anything else. Pomor food is filling. Sleep now tugged at them. Grisha put the leftover fish back into the pot and the men trudged off towards their tents.

Sleeping too much means a wasted day. Grisha woke up in the evening. Granted, during summers on the White Sea it was hard to tell evening from daytime, but everything had become slightly darker, gloomier. The sun was now closer to the horizon. The easterly wind had brought clouds in. Grisha looked at the sky – he rubbed his eyes, no, he wasn't dreaming. He had never seen such beauty before in his life. Purple clouds in a flat, tight bunch were moving along, as if they were paradisaical birds in flight. Before him was a blue sky with a tender golden tinge, like the eyes of a newborn child. The edge of the cluster of clouds shined gold from the sun, so bright it hurt his eyes, as if someone had knocked over a church dome in the heavens. Further from the edge, the gold faded away and now the clouds were streaked with red, first scarlet and then an ever bloodier share. The clouds became darker, no longer purple but a heavy, raw blue. The bloody red streaks grew thinner and then disappeared completely. To the east it was dark, a foreboding blackness, lightning flashed here and there without sound. All of this happened above the mirror surface of the water which reflected everything faithfully. The surface of the sea was still but the east wind blew above it. Heaven and hell had come together in one place. Before the battle, calm and silence reigned. There was nothing to lose. Everything was so clear – truth is truth, a lie is lie. Whoever proves victorious, that one will have the right to change the top and the bottom, truth will be called golden, or it will put on scarlet garb.

Watching this majesty all alone was unbearable. Grisha went to wake up his companions. Nikolai refused to get up, but his brother did. They admired things for a while. They each drank a cup to this beauty and to the imminent battle. Then his brother looked over and saw that the sea was at low water, like it had never been before. Rocky islets were sticking out of the water and it was shallow all the way to the reef, no more than waist deep. "Let's go put the net out now, on foot," Konstantin said, having quickly got enough of the beauty in the sky. For him fish were the real beauty in life, everything else was secondary. It would be interesting to try this. They put their wading boots on and went to put out the net. They tied it to the rocks right near their campsite and spread it across the shallow water towards the reef. In front of him, his brother took the fishing net off the stick and lowered it into the water. Grisha held the net behind him so that it lay evenly. Within five minutes they had unwound everything, set it up and hung the end on a floater so that they could find it when the tide came back in. They came back without even making their legs above their boots wet. What made Grisha shake the net that they had just lowered? He almost let the upper cord slip from his hands – a healthy-looking flounder, about the size of a frying pan, was sitting in the net. It was a good thing his brother had brought a landing net with him. Two meters over another, smaller flounder were fluttering. Further on a third, also big, burst out of the net, hit Grisha's leg, then jumped back into the net. Wonder of wonders, not even fifteen minutes had gone by and they already had seven kilo of the best-quality fish flopping in their hand net. They sweated in excitement and had neglected to take a look around them. When they raised their eyes, they saw a boat coming along the rocky shoals. The men on it were rowing, so it had come up without a sound, unnoticed.

All they could think was, well, that's it, we've been caught by the fish and game warden. They couldn't just drop the fish into the water, it was already clear what they had been up to. On the other hand, it was just some flounder, they only had one net and they had caught the fish to eat it, not sell it. What could they do? As usual, they went to talk about it.

Meanwhile, the men on the boat had come up beside them and were looking at them warily. They did not seem to be in uniform, but they were wearing long waterproof cloaks and who knew what they had on underneath them. Nor could they immediately tell from the men's faces, which lacked the grin of someone with authority, but sometimes among wardens you could encounter people with ordinary faces too. The boat reached the shore near the fishing shack. The men jumped out of it. They then bent with effort, they started to haul the boat in. Grisha and his brother went up to them with a guilty look.

"Can we help, fellows?"

"Sure, if you want."

They all took hold of the boat together, gathered their strength and tugged with all their might, then once more and the boat started to move over the logs. It was heavy, but it moved. With each meter their tendons strained with effort, but they managed to move the boat some ten meters from the surf. Sweat was running down their faces, they were all breathing heavily. They sat down. Grisha's brother took out a pack of cigarettes and offered the men one. They lit up. Grisha shook the hand of the younger one first, who had piercing eyes.

"Grisha."

"Mikhail," the other man answered.

The elder of the two, battered but strong, introduced himself. "Pyotr."

Konstantin entered the conversation. "Guys, we set out a net here, is that alright?"

"What do we care? You go ahead and set it out," Mikhail responded with a mysterious grin.

"So you're not the fish and game warden?"

"No, we work here at the fishing shack."

"Oh, great. Then come to our fire for a while, have a bite to eat."

The men exchanged glances.

"We can drink something," Grisha's brother jumped in. "Have a chat."

"Alright, then. We'll bring our things in and then come join you." Mikhail and Pyotr livened up slightly. "We've been on that boat for about four hours, we're tired."

"Come on, guys, it'll be no problem," Grisha began to merrily bustle about. It is always nice when, instead of being ambushed, everything works out well. It rarely happens, but it is good.

Half an hour later the newcomers were already sitting at the fire and slurping the fish soup from that morning. They had not come empty-handed either; they offered a fine humpback salmon.

"Alright, guys, don't you mind, but give me something to drink," Pyotr said in a guilty voice. "I just finished a bender, it's hard to come back out of it."

"Sure," said Grisha. He diluted a big mug of pure alcohol and handed it over. Pyotr drank down half of it and his face brightened.

"Alright, then, I'll take some too," Mikhail said, and finished his cup. Grisha and his brother drank too. Then they had more to eat. They ate. Then they drank again.

"Winters I dig graves, make some money," Pyotr explained. "But when fishing season starts, I'm here. We'll stay here until the snow comes." He was a battered man, worn down by life, but still strong. His heavy hands rested on his knees, they were like crabs, with fingers that were thick and splayed and bent only with effort.

"So, we're going along and we see someone poking around in the shallows," Mikhail recounted with a sarcastic smile. "We think they're catching worms or something. Then we see that they're setting a net. We never set nets here. We always do it over there, behind the shore gates." He waved a hand towards the reef. "Did you catch anything?"

"Yes, we got a lot of flounder, and fast."

"Oh, flounder. We don't catch that."

"What do you aim to catch?"

"Now the humpback salmon are coming in, we catch them for the time being. Then maybe the Atlantic salmon will come in." Mikhail had a striking foreign look, as if some southern blood had mixed with northern. But both were badly dressed: they wore threadbare sweatshirts and old waterproof jackets. But why should they dress up to go fishing?

"Are you from around here?"

"Yeah, we're from here. Lived here all our lives."

"Pomors?"

"Of course we're Pomors. The sea is our farm," Mikhail grinned again as he looked at our bright fishing poles and tackle. "What else are you going to catch here?"

"We want to catch some cod and pike in the lake. Is there brown trout around here?"

"There used to be. Try in the river."

"There's no problem with the fish and game warden?"

"We'll talk with Rumyantsev, tell him you're good guys. You're helping us with the boat – we're catching humpback salmon."

"Yes, yes," Grisha's brother stirred to life. "I hear you have to put the net at an angle to catch those."

"A *gavra*," Pyotr used the Pomor word for the net and seemed unafraid of revealing their secrets, "is always at an angle. The fish always goes against the sun. It gets caught in the corner of the *gavra*, it turns around, then it gets caught in the wing."

"Interesting. Of course we'll help you, just take us along."

"Are there bears around here?" Grisha asked, concerned about his own constant obsession.

"There are, how couldn't there be." Mikhail again was clearly mocking them. Or perhaps not. "Not long ago I'm walking through the forest and I see this brown thing running. I think it might be a moose, but I look and see it has short legs."

"Me, I was walking through the swamp last month," Pyotr could not resist either. "It was overcast, a light drizzle. I look and see it lying there. I think, it must have died. I've got to get that fur off it. I run to fetch my knife. Then I go up to it and nudge it with my foot and it jumps up and runs away. It was sleeping," Pyotr ended the story with a sigh.

"Two guys came here before you, last year. Also with a canoe," Mikhail continued to tell tales. "They had rowed here all the way from the Kola Peninsula. From Lovozero, they went down the Ponoy and along the Tersky. Thin, dirty, hungry-looking guys. Their canoe was beaten up. How they had survived, I have no idea. One of them was called Volodya, the other one, I don't remember his name. They had decided to travel the way of St. Varlaam of Keret, the fools. They were lucky they made it out. Without some sense and God's help it's easy to row far – and end up in no place at all…"

It thundered suddenly close by. Grisha and his brother jumped up and set up their tarp. Everyone sat underneath it. Big drops of rain drummed on the stretched fabric. The wind howled madly and whipped up foam on the water. It thundered above their heads. A first flash of lightning, then a second and then a third. They went into the sea, bifurcated. Then came a single one, then another double one. It got a bit scary, but the newcomers did not seem afraid.

"It's so loud!" Mikhail's face lit up as he watched the raging of the water and wind. "You wouldn't head for the *golomya* now. You know what the *golomya* is?"

Grisha was pleased that he did. "The open sea. My Grandpa used that word."

"Where was your granddad from?"

"No one really knows. But I remember some of the words he used."

Mikhail looked at Grisha, this time in a slightly different way than before.

Soon, after half an hour had passed, the thunder over their heads abated. Again the clouds were swept away. Then, something they would not have believed just a minute before, the sun started shining.

"Everything happens fast hereabouts, the storms and the calm take turns," Pyotr said with a mysterious sigh.

But Grisha was no longer listening to him. Right in front of them, in the sea that had turned calm, in the water, right on its blue surface, was a rainbow. Not in the sky, not vertically, but flat, taking in the bay and going further into the open sea. It lay there bright, pure, as if it had come out of the water, washed by the depths and birthed by the sun.

"Amazing," Grisha whispered. "Look! It's the first time in my life I've ever seen it, it's lying right over the water. A flame out at sea, that's what Grandpa used to call it. I never understood what he meant before!"

Again Mikhail gave him a strange look. "Did you ever hear a story about a barge?"

You loved all kinds of words, Ivan, my friend. It was just how our language was, we all talked like that, but you suddenly started to think about how it might disappear if nobody wrote it down. Because people are alive, but then the language becomes lost with them. Old lame Fyodora has died, so now no one can repeat all her shouting and crying. It's good that you wrote it down on paper. All that old crying proved useful later on, in the new times.

You taught me everything, remember? "What's with you, Kolyamba? You've only got one thing on your mind, that salmon of yours. Now, words are more interesting than anything material. You might think there's nothing to them, but they carry a spirit, they keep it, like the memory of whole generations of people."

You and me together, when we were young, would travel the coasts and the surrounding villages.

"Do you know how many old names there are for salmon?"

"Of course I do," I said. I didn't want to seem ignorant. "I'll count them now on my fingers for you: *zalyodka, zakroya, mezhen, tinda, listopadka.*"

"What, you only know five? And you call yourself a salmon lover!" You laughed at me, I was so arrogant then. "Old people had sixteen names. What about the winds, do you know their names in our talk, in the old Russian?"

Well, when it comes to the winds, any Pomor can list them just like that. Your life often depends on them, you have to be able to tell in time what's coming. Now I really tried my best. "*Vstok, polunoshnik, siver, poberezhnik, russky, obednik, shelonnik.*"

"My Grandpa Ivan once told me something, an old saying: the *shelonnik* wind has a beautiful wife, overnight he goes to sleep with her." You were so happy then, like a child the very first time he caught a fish. But it was as if you filled your cellar with the catch of words.

"There are twelve names for snow, depending on the season, the place, its composition – thick, loose, blue, pink. Ice has ten names."

"What about the names of our coasts and islands?" I too had caught his excitement. "Letny, Zimny, Karelsky, Onezhsky, Tersky."

"Serebryanka-Ostov, Pudinka, Parus-Kamen, Skovorodny, Vodokh-lebikha."

"Vilovataya Luda, Sugryobny, Syrovatka, Bolshoy Robyak, Maly Robyak, Bolshaya Varbulda, Nakhkonitsa."

It became a sort of game, who could remember more names. Things where we lived sounded so lovely, so funny: "Odinchazhny Mys, Luda Skotekonskaya, Karbas Luda, Sonostrov, Golomyanye Yuzmengi, Pezhostrov, Kishkin." This was already close to our Keret.

But like always, you beat me here, too. "Grandpa Ivan told me. Remember Sidorov Island, there is a pool there, a shallow and dirty one?"

"Of course I remember. It's always full of cormorants. They sit on the small rocks that stick out and wait for food to come by, like dirty little beggars."

"He said that old people used to call it the Sidorasovo Pool."

Then we fell on the grass laughing, this name seemed so funny. We rolled around laughing, but then caught our breaths and looked up at the sky, at how the clouds were sailing along, so light and impossible, as if our lives would go on so happily.

Your father, a famed seaman, had gone from cabin boy to captain, but he appreciated your word-collecting. "It's a good thing you've started on this," he said. "I'd have preferred you went for the sea, but the sea of words is no less important. We've got to remember the old ways and the old words, they've saved us from many troubles and temptations. You go on doing that, and may God help you."

You were so happy to give it a try. First you learned on your own – self-taught – how they had compiled dictionaries before you. There was nothing to it, it seemed, an inquisitive mind could figure everything out. That is exactly how it turned out. You made progress with it. Old people in the village liked the attention and you were one of their own, not an outsider, so they had no secrets to keep from you. Again, your family cherished their old ways. Your dictionary grew fuller, I even got jealous at how you were beaming when you made your first book. You bound it yourself, you had taught yourself how to do that too. It's easy to learn something if you have a passion for it. Then you got an answer to your package from the Cultural Institute, "You're doing important work, young comrade. You have great talent." You really lit up then, like a gilded samovar. But no, you weren't arrogant about it, you were just happy.

You shared it all with me. "Look," you said, "isn't there so much beauty, so many stories, in our language? Learned people call it 'folklore." You would talk about it for hours and from your notebooks you would read off words that had already been forgotten:

zasidka – a woman who likes to come visiting for a long time
zasidok – an old maid
zyuzya – an awful, dirty trollop
zymza – cornice under the window inside a house
kryazh – 1) a smooth meadow without any bumps; 2) a short log; 3) a thickset, stocky man
kuliga – clearing in a grassy forest
kulpakha – fever (used when wishing illness on another)
kugat – drunkenness
kurvishchyo – girl of low morals, "Oh, Olga, you're such a *kurvishchyo*"
kurva zagovenye – silly fun, fooling around

Everyone was so happy for you and they readily told you what they knew. Only your mother felt uneasy. She was a sort of clairvoyant, she would see something and then it would happen. She was a beauty in her youth, with looks that a man couldn't get enough of. I remember staring at the photograph in your home. She was sitting there in it like a lovely Virgin Mary, with a shining face, clear eyes and a barely noticeable smile on her lips. In her face there was some pain, foreboding. You sat on her knees, three years old, wearing a canvas shirt with an embroidered collar and sleeves. You were looking at the camera curiously; you also knew the beauty of the world – and its pain. Your hands are folded crosswise. Your legs are thick little things and your heels are visible. Your legs are placed together, one over the other. I liked that photograph at your home, it hung like an icon on the wall. As your father was walking by he joked, "Look, it's the Virgin Mary and her Son." But your mother got angry at this, she did not like that joke, it scared her. "You just move along," she said. "Don't invite disaster."

She could already sense it, your work frightened her. "Ivan," she said, "You shouldn't do something too fancy like this. You shouldn't stick out. If you get too noticeable, then it'll be easier for an animal to get you. A big black, iron, leathery animal will come and it'll notice you right away."

"Oh, leave me alone, mama," you would always answer with a smile. "I'm writing about people, about things from the past, nice things. Who could that hurt? It'll only be something useful for everyone." You had already gathered up twelve little books of material with words, proverbs and charms.

They played well at your wedding, everything according to the old ways. The old rite of engagement and so forth.

How happy you were when your little Anna was born! The first time they showed her to you, you completely froze, you didn't even dare to breathe. They gave you a little wrapped bundle and you didn't even know how to hold it. Awkwardly, cautiously, you took your little treasure who was so fragile, soft and defenseless. Your proud wife was lying on the bed, she was a strong woman. "What are you being so yellow-bellied for?" she said. "Look at your daughter."

You didn't know how to fold back the edge of the blanket, to open this little envelope with the blessed letter that God had sent you and everyone. But then you managed to press her to your chest with one hand and unfold her little burrow with your other hand, holding your breath. All of a sudden two big blue eyes were staring at you and you were completely stupefied, your heart ached, tears stung your eyes – your own native blood, given to you to preserve and keep, was looking at you trustingly. It was too much for you, you felt a twinge in your nose from the emotions welling up inside you and your wife laughed, "Why are you so moved, you big hero. You made her yourself, so there you go. You just think now how you are going to feed us. You're taking care of two people now."

But how to feed them? The Institute promised to pay you for your books real soon. They really liked your work and praised it to the heavens. "We'll hire you, Ivan, as an employee with a steady salary!" What new times we were living in! A peasant, a Pomor would be on the staff of a research institute. You stood tall and proud as you thought about it, taking care of your daughter, raising her up. She was so smart, she took after you that way and with her beauty she took after her mother. Both of you were very fond of her. She was a healthy little thing, perky and affectionate. Russian children are the best in the world, you can never love them enough, rock them enough, they are so sweet.

That institute of yours let you down, they kept stalling on paying you. You trusted in everything, waited, picked up some work where you could, but you never stopped writing and gathering material on your native tongue. You lived hand to mouth, but with hope. So, one year went, a happy one. Another year passed. They came for you when your daughter had just turned three.

It was a good thing that the sea had already taken your father by that time; he never came back from his last wintering. You grieved bitterly over him, but you got through it. But he wouldn't have let you go, he would have fought against the authorities, a hopeless cause. It was three men who came for you, on horseback. Three riders. In their black leather jackets they looked demonic. They came in without knocking, like they owned the place. Your mother told me later that you were ill then, lying in bed, after you had walked in snow through the neighboring villages. They lifted you up from the bed all wet, like a drowning man from the sea, you were breathing heavily. While they took a perfunctory look through your papers, your mother and wife stood silently. Then they finished and the old woman asked what her son was guilty of. "Of anti-Soviet agitation, old lady," they said. "Your son isn't interested in the new life we have. He's always screwing around with old words. Not without reason: over at the Institute they've buried a whole gang of wreckers. He was involved with them. Local historians, damn them."

At that moment little Anna ran into the room and climbed onto your knees. She sat there like a frightened little mouse, only her heart was pounding, you could feel it. "Daddy, who am I going to live with now?" she asked quietly. "With mama, my little darling," you answered. You were carried off by three men in black and behind you were three women in white watching you go without a word. They didn't shout or object, it is not the Pomor women's custom to yell at outsiders.

They arrested your wife six months later.

ANOTHER MIRACLE
OF THE VENERABLE SAINT

Certain men, merchants of the town of Kargopol, told this story. The name of one of them was Iakov, called Posnov. The other's name was Euphimius Bolnishchev. We were going on a boat in the spring from the mouth of the river Onega to trade. And when we had passed Solovetsky Island and we were on the open sea, we encountered a great amount of ice, and the ice surrounded our boat from every side, so that we could not pass through it. And the ice was coming towards the boat and sought to destroy us, and we labored hard but could do nothing, we were all afraid for our lives. And the aforementioned Euphimius was standing in the stern and was leaning on the broadside, and from his great sorrow he fell asleep. And then an old man appeared in front of him on a boat and asked him, "Are you traveling far, brothers?" And Euphimius spake, "We go to Pomorye for trade, but the ice blocks our passage and we are all going to die." The old man said to him: "Do not be afraid, brother. Go to Keret and God will clear the way for you." The old man then went to the bow of the boat and began to push the ice apart.

Euphimius awoke and he did not see anyone there any more, only his companions that were with him on the boat. And he began telling them what he had seen in his dream. And suddenly it was as if a path had appeared through the ice, and they rejoiced. They began to carefully follow this path, and then a tailwind blew and we went out into the sea safely.

And they arrived into Keret and they told everyone of the appearance of St. Varlaam, and how God had saved them from death thanks to his prayers. And to commemorate this miracle, that man Euphimius made a shrine over the grave of the venerable Varlaam, and from then on he kept his faith in the great saint.

For me, there is nothing better in life than to go along the White Sea coast in a canoe when the weather is fine. The beauty of this border region is capable of driving you mad if you are weak in spirit. That is why the road leading here is so difficult; so that a person can grow stronger before they reach here. But once you are on the water, you move along without fearing anything. Just look carefully at the sky, the wind, the clouds, it makes your soul open wide. You admire, drink in and absorb the grace of this place – it will later serve you as a reserve to draw on after countless years of a gray existence. The coasts here are rocky, red granite – that is if you are going towards the North, towards Chupa and Keret. But if you are going south, there are fewer bare stones, the coast is even lower, and only rarely, among the swamps, will a smooth opening or a steep promontory stick out. In both places two colors dominate the coasts: red and green. They are not bright colors but saturated, thick, somewhat muted yet strong, speaking directly to one's soul and lending a sense of calm to the eyes. The sea, if it is blocked by islands, is like a wide, slow-moving and static river that flows off towards an endless distance from which nothing returns. If the islands are far away, they seem to hang in the air, merging with the clouds and confirming their beauty with their lightness. It seems like it would be enough to blow and they would be swept away like a merry procession. But if it is open sea, then this is a feast for the soul. I do not know, I cannot understand why that open, blue, flat expanse awakens all the best emotions in a person. You feel the joy of freedom and pity for those who cannot share that joy with you, as well as a primitive sense of bravery, when you can trust only in God and your own courage. Within you an otherworldly strength awakens, a watery kind of strength when every stroke of the paddle sends your boat ten meters forward and only your back catches this swift movement and struggles to keep balance, but your arms know neither restraint nor limits. That sweetness of the air in your lungs, only here do your lungs feel so light, when before they were heavy, strained. You rejoice at that sound of the sea, not just a single splash but the whole roar of the surf on the glacier-formed beaches, when it rolls pebbles back and forth and the little seagulls screech imperiously and the rustling noise of the forests sometimes comes through. Suddenly your eyes hurt – a beluga whale is shining in the sun like a great lump of snow-white sugar, one, two, three and fear comes over you. It is a big one, twice as big as your boat and you tell yourself that it is a peaceful creature, peaceful.

But how can you describe the feeling of your heels, your hips, your buttocks, which rest firmly on the thin layer of rubber and can feel all the bottomless life of the sea under you, all its secret rocking and movement. Through your heels you are directly linked to this living water, tied to it, pinned down, nailed to it. You cannot go anywhere, you are a part of it, its calmness and wisdom enters through your heels. But there is a sense of kinship, of love towards all who row, either those passing you in the opposite direction or coming up from behind – you wave to them and smile so widely that your jaw cramps and you see the distant twinkle of their smiles in response. I said that and now I suddenly wonder if the white flanks of the beluga whale are the sea's smile to seafarers.

Whatever senses a person has, just tell me and in the finest details I will describe how rich they are on the White Sea. Smell: the scent of the sea's freshness, ocean-going fish, the sea sun. The sun has a smell when its blinding glare dances on a little ripple. This smell is sizzling, fizzy, merry. Your nose itches from it, your mouth desires the bitterness of vodka. There is a charm here: you are a charming rower and your friends are charming, you love one another for your agility and unity and how inseparable you are from the sea, which you also love so greatly that you must remember it constantly, so that you are not completely overwhelmed by affection. "Keep further away from the shore, further away!" your friend shouts with a nasal twang, and just in time – a wave has hit you in the side of your face, and due to the feelings welling up you have suddenly got distracted and lost the rhythm of the boat's rocking. "Maintain straight for shore," he says again after he has caught sight of the way into the bay, he who is so delectably tired and already anticipating a meal. You suddenly feel that your entire body, all your flesh, is heavy and you again remember that you have experienced one more unforgettable wonder – the tiredness of being at sea.

2005, KYUVIKANDA

That morning turned out to be one where, even as Grisha was still crawling out of the tent and pulling on his damp boots which had not dried overnight, he already felt a sense of happiness. His swollen, sleep-filled eyes opened wider. Together with the fresh air in his chest he had a feeling of hope and bold readiness for whatever life might bring. There could no longer be anything bad in it – all around him, as far as the distant horizons, was paradise. The sea and the sky competed with their blue colors, like two mischievous girls who had just learned to flirt and were proud of their new skill. They did not even suspect that their main charm lay not in the beauty of their youth but in their liveliness, the gaiety of their young smiles, their laughter and the openness of their ways. Thus, these two dressed-up beauties of the morning giggled at one another and at the whole world with the brilliance of bright reflected light on their fresh palms outstretched to one another, they whispered with the clear murmuring of foam over the gay multicolored rocks, flirtatiously waved their white kerchiefs of the clouds reflected in the water, then the light breath of the fresh breeze reached Grisha's sleepy face and smoothed out all past and future sorrows. He stood there for a long time, unable to move, admiring it all and breathing in deeply. Tears came unbidden to his eyes. In his heart a quickening faith in providence stirred.

Then he got ahold of himself and went to the fire. Fires on the White Sea are good in that they almost never go out, they are perpetually ready to burn unless they are deliberately flooded by human action. The thick pieces of driftwood, bleached to a wise gray by their wanderings in the sea, dried out right in the fire, and when the end of one piece is lit with the flame, the other end is constantly producing outbursts of steam. The wind, which rarely subsides here, bears away the ashes and blows the coals, like a restless child who gets bored without a boisterous flame. The campfire's flame sweeps back and forth, leaping in different directions, so it is hard to find a place where smoke will not eventually blow into your face and bring tears to your (already emotional) eyes. At any hour of a campfire that has laid there since yesterday without any sign of life, you are sure to find a hot coal. You only need to turn the burnt wood over and throw a couple of new pieces on top and within a minute a new flame will devotedly lick at the wood, enticing it and convincing it that the bright rage of burning is better than the calm of a slow, unhurried life.

Now he lightly turned over what remained of the huge piece of wood from the day before, which apparently had been a part of some ship — old-fashioned nails stuck out of it in a long-forgotten order –he did not even wait for the result of his efforts. Instead he took the kettle and went to fetch some water from a nearby gully in the rocks. He had not taken a couple of steps before he heard the resurgent fire erupting behind him and gently whispering hot, eternal dreams to the ignited wood.

The water came quickly to a rolling boil. Grisha took the kettle off with a long, smoky stick and then, on a pair of stones in the campfire, set the frying pan with the leftover fried flounder. He threw a good handful of ground coffee into the water. The smell began to float across the surrounding area and immediately a large stone began to stir not far from the campfire. For the tenth time he was slightly startled and then recognized his brother's tent, painted the same color as the sur-rounding mossy stones. With the pleasure of one who had missed any interaction with another person over the night, Grisha listened to the sound of the opening zipper, the hungry grunt of his brother and the first swear of the morning, inevitable when one's warm body comes into contact with wet clothes. The tent opened up and like a gnome popping out of the rocks, his sleepy brother sprouted from the tent. Nikolai came rapidly forth from his shelter and like each morning, a fresh new friendship arose.

They had not yet managed to have breakfast before Pyotr came from the fishing shack.

"Well, guys, are you going to help us launch the boat?"

"Of course we will," Konstantin jumped to his feet first. "Just take me along too, I want to watch."

"Fine, just two of you, otherwise we won't come back." Whether it was their chat of the evening before or their drinking together, but now they spoke normally, with a secret fondness for one another. This was surprising for Grisha – life in the city quickly weans a person from nor-mal human interaction – but how could it be otherwise when you had the sea, the wind and work to do.

They got up and without saying anything further walked behind Pyotr. It was high tide, the rocks in the shallows were hidden under it as the sea merely roared on the barely visible reef. With white foam it erupted and then washed away.

Either it was due to yesterday's fear and excitement or today's excessive grandeur of the beauty around them, but the boat proved heavier than they thought. Mikhail came up and the five of them put all their strength into it, but the boat did not want to budge. The wet, crumbling logs on which the boat lay seemed to suck it down and hold it fast.

"Again and… push! Push! And push…" Finally the boat moved from its place and freely, under its own weight, slid right down to the water, only lightly supported by the men running alongside it. It flew along with its keel, cutting through the sand, at times it seemed it would sink down, but no, the boat immediately rose up on a light wave that had come in and floated along the shore, what a beauty.

"Do you have the tamer with you?" Mikhail was clearly the senior of the two.

"Oh, I forgot it," Pyotr said and made a quick run to the shack. All of them were feeling excited before the fun, dangerous work ahead.

"What's a tamer?" Grisha asked.

"What, you don't know? It's to tame the fish," Mikhail laughed, just then Pyotr ran up waving a heavy stick.

"But guys, where are the nets?" Grisha's brother asked with surprise as he looked over the boat.

"We already set them yesterday, while you were hunting for worms here," Mikhail laughed, everyone smiled – it must have looked funny when Grisha and Konstantin, without noticing anything around them, had walked through the water and hunted for fish in the shallows with a net.

"Alright then, now we'll see what the sea has given us." They took turns getting into the boat from the water by jumping over its sides. A sad Nikolai Eliseyev was left standing alone on the shore.

They did not start the engine along the shore. Pyotr sat rowing while Mikhail took a position at the nose with a pole and watched out for stones.

"Further away from the shore, further away!" Mikhail would cry to Pyotr now and again, but Pyotr skillfully oriented with the guiding marks on the shore and sent the boat straight towards the surging reef. Things got a bit scary, it seemed that they were about to hear the sound of hitting something, a crash, then they would have to think about how to survive. However, as if by magic, the boat passed through the breakers without even grazing a stone.

"It all went so well!" Grisha was amazed, as was his brother.

"Of course it did. Our forefathers knew the sea here, they set up markers everywhere. We've learned a thing or two." Mikhail took pleasure in their admiration, but he was trying not to show it.

They moved past the reef and now the surf started to rock them, not violently, but calmly and powerfully. It lifted the heavy boat like a child's plaything and it made them involuntarily think about their canoe, that it would have been like a mere splinter in this sea and the playing child would have crushed it. But this time it did not want to crush them, it let them pass through the reef.

They went another ten or twenty meters from the reef into the open sea, then suddenly Mikhail gave the order to stop. With an iron hook he grabbed onto the cable around a fishing float and pulled the boat in.

"Well, time to get to work. You can help us now." He started to lift the net, straining his hands, red with cold. The net was a tall one, six meters or so, and heavy. It had been woven from thick strands that were almost like ropes.

"Yep, this is no amateur net," Grisha's brother said. The two of them started to help hauling the net up, pulling the boat closer and lifting the exposed portions up over the stern. Pyotr carefully kept the boat steady with an oar.

"Aha, they're here, a nice catch," Mikhail deftly untangled from the net the first silvery beauty, hit it over the head with the tamer and dropped it on the bottom of the boat. It was a fine fish, just raised from the depths of the sea, with the slender shape of a body that had swam quickly not long before.

"What's that, an Atlantic salmon?" Grisha asked, somewhat embarrassed at his ignorance.

"This? No. It's a humpback," Mikhail said with contempt. "Scientists introduced them here, in the White Sea. They aren't bad fish, but there are much fewer of those Atlantic salmon around today."

"What, they don't share the same spawning grounds?"

"No. Humpback salmon are stupid fish, like sheep. They aren't like Atlantic salmon at all in how the act or how they spawn. They do go up the same rivers as Atlantic salmon, but they die there after they spawn. Atlantic salmon know the water in their own river, it can smell it; often it can sense its native stream hundreds of miles from shore. It so happens that Atlantic salmon get to the river, but they can tell that these lousy humpbacks are there. So, the entire school of Atlantic salmon will just up and leave – I've seen it myself many times, it's a really sad sight.

Where they go off to, no one knows. Only there are just a lot less Atlantic salmon now, nothing like the old days."

"The Norwegians get angry at us," Pyotr took the subject up. "'What are you doing with those humpback salmon of yours?!' They get into the Norwegian rivers, too. But here, like usual, everything is screwed up. Now the Norwegians have to clean their rivers of humpbacks after they spawn. Who is going to clean our rivers? No one cares."

"Enough talking, let's do better here," Mikhail said and suddenly began taking the fish from the net one by one. All of the fish were alike, as if made to standard measurements and they weighed around two kilo's each.

They quickly and without speaking emptied the net. The constant leaning over made them tired and their backs ached unbearably. The cold saltwater stung their hands mercilessly, especially Grisha's brother – he had never had good skin on his hands, it easily came off due to eczema. Now blood flowed down his hands, both his own blood from cuts and scrapes and from the fish. The bottom of the boat had become slippery and it was hard to find a safe place to step on the slimy boards among the piles of fish.

"Aha, we got an Atlantic salmon, look," Mikhail looked happy, as he took from the net a wonderful silver fish. It was about twice as big as the humpback salmon, they could readily tell which species was the nobler and which was of lower birth. Mikhail "tamed" it just as quickly as the others, but he set it aside separately from them. It lay there like a dead princess among the vulgar masses.

"Caviar," Pyotr nodded at it. The men then noticed the fish's swollen, oval belly. "The Atlantic salmon is the fish of kings, especially the wild ones. The Norwegians raise it artificially now, but no, it's not the same kind of fish at all. The meat looks different, tastes different. It doesn't even have the same scales, the farmed salmon has these small, dim-looking scales. Mankind doesn't know all of nature's secrets yet. But there are so few of them now. Old folk used to say that before, Atlantic salmon would come up the river like a huge wave out of the sea. You would be thrilled but a bit scared to see such a force. It used to be that way in the Keret, but now there are only farmed ones that they release themselves. There are no wild ones left at all. They caught all the wild ones."

They worked until the net was completely empty. The net was not set straight but had an angle to it, one wing of it sharply turned back. The bulk of the fish had ended up in this part of the net.

"The fish constantly go according to the sun. So, you set this corner of the net this way. Then the fish get caught here," the successful fishing trip had made Mikhail loquacious. There were around fifty fish lying in the boat.

"What is the biggest one you've caught?" Grisha asked, who also felt happy and excited.

"Pyotr and I once got one that weighed twenty kilo. It was impossible for a single person to haul up. We had to stick something through its side or under its gills and then turn it over into the boat. It started fighting us then, it almost capsized our boat. Pyotr jumped on top of it, but it hit him so hard with its tail that his shoes flew off." Mikhail laughed.

"My father once told me," Pyotr said, also wanting to be part of this conversation, "that in the twenties and thirties they came up to a *gavra*..."

"What's a *gavra*?" Grisha's brother asked at once.

"What have you just hauled up and cleared?" Mikhail said, laughing. "That's a *gavra*, a net for salmon."

"So, they came up to a *gavra* and started hauling it up. They saw this huge white thing. Then they got scared and dropped it back into the water. It was a dead man in the net. There were a lot of bodies in the sea, in the twenties. They dropped the net and sailed away, shaking in fright. What could they do? They still had to get the net up. So, they crossed themselves and went back."

"What happened then?" Asked Grisha, astounded.

"It turned out to be thirty-three kilo of Atlantic salmon!"

They paused, reflecting on what they had heard. Then Grisha could not resist asking, "Where did the dead bodies come from?"

"People were arrested... Sometimes they were being sent to Solovka but they would try to make a run for it. Different people."

They fell silent. Pyotr took to the oars and headed for shore. Konstantin was looking at his hands. "Look, a miracle! All my sores got washed away in just a couple of hours. The sea washed them away!"

ANOTHER MIRACLE

The same man told us this. There was once one of the tsar's noblemen who ruled in Kolsky Ostrog and was a voievod during the reign of the most devout sovereign Mikhail Fyodorovich of all Russia, after the Lithuanian War. His name was Guriy Ivanov, son of Volyntsov. He had the falling sickness, and he did not know how to be saved from this illness.

And Saint Varlaam came to him when he was having a seizure. He was garbed in the clothes of a monk and he spake thus, "Do not be in distress, God will release thee from this illness." The man then said to him, "Who art thou, master, and where didst thou come from?" Varlaam answered, "I am Varlaam of Keret." The man woke up from his illness like from a dream, and began to tell other what he had seen and he asked who this Varlaam was. And men of the city told him, "In days of old there was such man who served in Kolsky Ostrog and later he lived in Keret as a monk, and there he died."

The same nobleman sent men to find if there were anyone from that village living in this city. And he found such a one who had lived in the Keret country, whose name was Vasily, called Mukhin, and he asked him about St. Varlaam, how and where his venerable body was buried. That same Vasily told him in detail about the saint, and that he lay in neglect, and that he rested in the same place in which he was laid.

The aforementioned Guriy undertook with Vasily that a canopy be placed over Saint Varlaam's grave and a cross put there. And he gave Vasily some silver for the works. Vasily took the silver and came to Keret, and like the nobleman had ordered, he made a tomb over the saint's grave. And the nobleman was free from the evil spirit by the prayers of the venerable Varlaam.

* * *

In late winter 2001 I went to the White Sea, to settle into an old, abandoned hunter's cabin in the forest for several weeks. I had long been drawn to these places. I had already made a few journeys along the coast, but those were all summer trips. I had never been here in the winter.

In earlier expeditions I had often been overwhelmed by the beauty here, by the culture and folk wisdom of the local old timers, as well as the great Pomor language that was still alive – many words that were unknown to Russians in other regions and were marked in Vladimir Dal's old dictionary as "archaic". Here – and this impressed me – these words were still in common use and had an amazing ancient air around them, as if they had come from the dawn of Russian civilization. Here, I had also heard legends, old tales and songs. All this, along with the severe and beautiful nature, the free spirits of the locals (the Pomors had never been under serfdom and they told Tsar Peter their opinions right to his face) and the difficult history of this region that started from the Russians' colonization of the North, continued through the horrors of the Church schism, which ended in the gulag horrors of the twenties and thirties, touched my heart so much that I could not imagine a life without traveling in the North. But a man whose heart is touched is always the victim of temptation. I had always been an unbeliever, brought up among the strict atheist propaganda for the first half of my life. Here, on the White Sea, I met a woman whom I loved with all my strength. I thought she was my hope and the answer to all the questions in life. As I was already experienced in matters of relationships with the female sex, I nonetheless gave in to temptation, like a blind puppy that stretches its mouth to the teat of its long-desired, blessed mother. Our story, which lasted three years, became a delight and a torment. Minutes of mutual understanding and passion would give way to the hellish torments of envy and feeling used, which were completely founded. Once those three years were up, that charming woman who had got from me everything she needed, began coldly preparing to split. The violent foreboding that this would happen had drawn me to the North, where, in the harsh winter conditions, I was hoping to recover from the delusions that I had originally come down with here.

Something interesting happened: while I was heading to the Cross Lakes where the hunter's cabin was located, I briefly caught sight of the church that had been built in the village of Chupa and the chapel in Keret. After I had asked locals about them, I learned that they had been dedicated to St. Varlaam of Keret. I learned some brief facts about his life from these people. Later I found a biography.

THE BRIEF LEGEND

OF THE VENERABLE VARLAAM OF KERET

The venerable father Varlaam lived during the reign of the Tsar and Great Prince Ioan Vasilievich of all Russia, the despot. He was born and raised in the Keret volost, *on the sea. He learned letters and by God's will was made to be a priest in the city of Kola, in the Church of Saint Nicholas the Wonderworker, and there he did well, battling the evil deeds of the unseen enemy, and teaching the people the law of the Lord, as a true shepherd, and he was pleasant before God and men.*

The devil saw that Varlaam was full of righteousness and that his own wretched powers were weak and just like a spider's web were torn apart by the priest. The devil set his net to capture the righteous man, like he had once done with Adam and he led Varlaam to kill his wife.

Varlaam, after committing the sin, understood that the devil had envied him, and he wept greatly and thought himself to be unworthy of priestly service, and he wished instead to wander and suffer for his sin. And so he began to sail over the depths with the dead body of his wife from place to place, until that dead body would smolder.

And the efforts of the sole righteous man could be seen, how he traveled the sea in a small boat with the dead body, from Kola, near Svyatoy Nos, and even all the way to Keret.

Unlike other men who waited for good weather for sailing, he sailed through the turbulent sea and the oars never slipped from his hands, but he labored very hard while singing the Psalms of David, because that was his nourishment. During the day he labored on the sea, and at night he did not sleep but prayed to God with tears in his eyes that God might grant him absolution.

And because he had labored a sufficient amount of time, he wanted to receive a calling. He reached the aforementioned Svyaty Nos. Until then it was an impassable place because of the multitude of sea worms there, which caused many woes to sailors. They did not harm Varlaam, but he wished to make this way safe for others. So he stood up to pray, and he raised his arms to the heavens, and his prayer was heard, and he worms disappeared. Thus he made the way near the Svyaty Nos clear for sailors, and it remains such even today.

And because the venerable Varlaam had received a calling from God, he soon left the world and became a monk, and he went to live in the deserted places, and with God's help he defeated many demon, and he departed to our Lord in peace at the Chupa Inlet. After that his venerable body was moved to Keret and was buried next to the Church of the Holy Martyr Saint George, on the eastern side, behind the altar.

After some time the Lord wished to shew forth the efforts of His saint, the venerable Varlaam. A merchant named Euphimius, from Kargopol, sailed on the sea and his boat was sinking because of the turbulent sea, and he was full of grief and he expected to perish. And then the saint appeared before him and saved him from sinking, and he told him who he was. Euphimius and those who were with him, saw how the venerable saint had helped everyone and Euphimius returned to Keret, where and told everyone about how with the intercession of St. Varlaam of Keret, God had saved them from perishing in the sea. Euphimius ordered that a canopy be placed, in his name, over the tomb of the saint, and that candles be burnt in front of the holy icon. And he set off on his way rejoicing, and thanking God and His saint, our venerable father Varlaam of Keret.

My several days in that distant cabin near the White Sea, among the snowy forests, were perhaps the most harrowing of my life. No, it was not the solitude, the savage nature or the animals and birds that scared me. It was myself. Now, after several years have passed, I can calmly look back on it. But at the time, I was like a wild animal, like a raging demon, I thrashed around the small space, the log cabin's sole room. The weak light of a candle cast wild shadows on the walls. It was like the devil was in me, I was truly scared in those brief moments when I could look at myself from the outside. A hellish pain rent my soul, a devilish jealously burned away what remnants of humanity I had left. I howled and rolled around on the floor, on the bed, sank my teeth into my own arm and scratched the crude table with my nails so hard that deep furrows were left on it. Vague, but no less bloody, images filled my head. I thought up plans for revenge, each more horrible than the last, and they were truly horrible in how feasible they were to carry out – I am not a stupid man, nor a weak one. I drank, but the alcohol never took hold. It was as if the liquor turned to water as soon as I put my lips to the bottle. I could never get drunk, the hatred and grievance I felt burned the vodka away, as well as my heart and my mind. Several times, when I was brought to despair and I sought to prevent the terrible, inevitable things to come, I put the cold barrel of my gun into my mouth and reached for the trigger. But the thick metallic taste of the barrel briefly snapped me out of it, it was like the cold neck of another bottle and I set the gun aside.

Finally, I could not stand it anymore and I fled from the forest, from the White Sea. I ran to the city, where everything was supposed to happen. A sense of inevitability drove me on like a whip and for the first time in my life, on the road to death, I flew over the icy ground at a speed of 150 kph. I completed the five hundred kilometers of winter road in three hours.

But then I got my strength back somehow. Not my composure, no, but rather the strength to stand there on the edge. To hold on. To bear it all. To leave things as they were. I do not know how it was even possible. How could it be explained by ordinary, earthly life? Perhaps it was one more miracle of St. Varlaam of Keret. Then, years later, I found out that his feast day was celebrated at precisely that time of year.

ANOTHER MIRACLE
OF THE VENERABLE VARLAAM OF KERET

In the winter of 2001 one Karelian was of ill mind and in the grip of the demons of jealousy and pride. Because of the evil one and his own weakness, he directed the thoughts of his empty soul towards the destruction of his own soul and his life, and also the destruction of certain other unrighteous but living souls. He was led by dark thoughts to despair, he was blinded by jealously, which encircles like a serpent the eyes and hearts of those who experience it, and he was nearly ready to put his bloody designs into practice. But now an elder appeared to him [it was not an elder but a small birch tree, covered by drops of snow that had melted over the winter and then refroze, which gleamed in the light of the electric lamp like an otherworldly crystalline wonder, its beauty standing against the surrounding night] *and spake in words that could not be heard, "I am Varlaam of Keret. Take control of yourself, man. Does my example not suffice for you so that you see the vanity of revenge and your pride? Draw strength from the ancient story, gird yourself with courage and patience. A man must learn to forgive so that his own soul will not perish." Then the Karelian could renounce his evil thoughts, and though he drank bitterly and deeply for many a year, he burned his former love from his heart through alcohol and found peace with time. Thus Varlaam of Keret showed his intercession before God for those drowning in their passions.*

1935, KERET, CAPE SHARAPOV

> Three little pale clouds
> Tremble on the gray sky.
> A black barge
> Sails around the White Sea.
> There's a little church on the hill,
> Its dome shot through.
> And under the hill there is grass,
> With bloody dew…
>
> Alexei Zhidkov

I wanted so much to be a fish. A Salmon. To be strong and independent. Free. So that it would be clear who were my enemies and who were my friends. So that I wouldn't see such incomprehensible meanness. So that I would not hear lies.

The sunset was red and foreboding. The village had known well beforehand that a large detachment of soldiers was coming. But they thought that it was for fish again. At first they would take away the fish, then they would carry on their propaganda. For a better life. But where was that better life? Something had gone wrong with the rule of the people. It didn't work out. There were many promises, but few of them were ever met. The old ways had been wiped out, the new ones were reluctant to come along, only with effort, by force. Everything was done as if in defiance of divine providence. Strength had crushed truth. Rumors came from Saint-Petersburg that the merchant Savin had been shot. "For what?" the people asked. They remembered how not long ago he would rescue the entire village from hunger, he would loan out provisions without charging interest. That's how it was. How his wife had built the church. Look, the church is standing there, it rises over the river and the sea and could stand for long centuries. Only now it's closed. The new authorities closed it. They took the priest away for "resettlement", a strange word. Then everyone found out what resettlement meant. Well, fine, the merchant and the priest are marginal in the community, many people thought. The new regime doesn't need them. But we are the working classes. Fedka had told us that back when everything started. Everything was being done for us, for the common man.

They started the arrests the next morning. They came into people's homes without wiping their feet, without taking their boots off, like they were walking into a cowshed. They gathered people up like cattle. Everyone who had refused to take part in the extermination of the fish. Everyone who protested. Everyone who was unafraid to state the truth. Fedka was no longer among us, but it turned out that they needed his papers. Then everyone learned what kind of lists he had drawn up.

The men walked off silently. As if it had all come down on them from above, on these helmsmen in icy waters, who feared neither the sea nor the dry land. As if they immediately saw, they knew that it would be a long winter ahead, that they wouldn't survive it. The younger ones put on a brave face, saying that everything would be figured out, that they would be released, because we are native Russians, Pomor workers. The old men already knew what lay ahead and rebuked the stupid ones, telling them to be quiet and to be patient, for perhaps God would show mercy; that everyone should pray towards the closed church. They made the sign of the cross, with two fingers according to the old custom. It was no time to act like a hero.

Both my father and I were arrested. My father had greatly disliked Fedka, he had told him everything that was right and dependable according to the old ways, what he had experienced. He was a talkative man, he couldn't keep the truth inside. They took me along, saying the apple doesn't fall far from the tree. My mother only had time to say a brief prayer for us.

The women were silent, they did not cry. Pomors' pride will not let them shed tears in front of outsiders. They only stood there watching, huddled together in a crowd, one up against another, it helped them keep their spirits up. They held the children so they would not run, not cry. It seemed that the little ones knew too and remained silent.

They drove about a hundred men together into a crowd. The most skilled hunters, the proudest, the most successful. The fruit of the northern lands, men who appreciated the White Sea. The ones who were left were completely unremarkable. But they stood around these captive men like around a herd of cattle and drove them down the road to some foreign place. As soon as the straggled crowd disappeared from view, behind the closest rocky hill, the deathly keening of the women, almost like howling animals, rose over the village.

We walked all day without a break, without food. Twice we were allowed to drink water from a swamp. We trudged all the way to Chupa. The barge was already there waiting. It was old, barely still afloat. In the hold the water was up to our knees. They drove us in there for the night. There were already men sitting there, from other Pomor villages. Some people were known to us, others we had heard of. Everyone was restless and started asking questions. But nothing was clear, it had been the same in every village. Someone had specifically watched the village, listened to people, and if someone said something that sounded unhappy, he went on a list. Every place had its own Fedka. That is how things were. Now sitting in the hold, waiting to see how things turn out. Some said that they were taking us to the Solovestsky Islands, to repair the citadel. Others said we were going to some canal, we would be building it from the White Sea to Lake Onega. A third group of men simply remained silent.

To avoid sitting there idle in the wet conditions, we asked the guards for a few buckets. We made caulking from boards, and over that night, we filled in all the leaks and began bailing out the water. Things got much better by morning. At dawn, we were already sleeping on a dry surface.

It wasn't so dark that night, but the next morning it was still easier to see who was where in the hold. We found Fedka there too. Without the swagger he used to have and looking beaten. Although he still tried to order people around and hold forth. My father asked him why he had stayed silent that night when the others were bailing out the boat. Fedka answered that everyone had their job to do, that we had all shown a lack of faith in our government, now we had to set things right, help out. Big construction projects were starting, great things. But as for me, he said, there must be some mistake, once we get to our destination everything would become clear. You just keep on saying that, my father told him. People believed him once, he actually thought they would do it again? Nonetheless, even a black sheep has its uses: Fyodor managed to learn from the sentry that we were headed for the Solovestsky Islands to repair the citadel.

When it was completely bright, they started the engine and the barge set off. There were holes in the barge so wide you could see everything through them. There was some kind of commanding officer on the deck, a guard of five men and two machine guns at the fore and aft. There were two hundred men sitting in the hold.

As we set out from the mouth of the Chupa, the barge began to rock quite heavily. You could see that terrible weather was coming. There were blue skies, but to the northwest there was such a black storm cloud, a small one far away. There was a wind too, the one called *polunoshnik*, untypical for this time of year and blowing hard. The seagulls disappeared from view; it is a rare thing that they didn't meet a passing ship and accompany it. Things weren't looking good; a storm was on its way. The men might have been torn from their homes, but they knew the sea and they were troubled. They shouted to the men above us, hey, Red Army, we need to turn aside, bad weather is coming. But what did the soldiers, a rowdy bunch of men used to dry land, care about the yelling coming from below? Their superior office was conceited, he didn't answer us. We could hear him giving orders, he just wanted to get to where we were going before dark. That fool didn't know that the last thing to do on the sea was to plan ahead. You could pray to God, but they had no god, they had driven Him from the churches and knocked down the crosses. They had no sense either, for as soon as we had left Glubokaya Salma and went around Pezhostrov Island, the sea began to swell drastically. The barge shook, creaked, rolled from one wave to the other like a clumsy behemoth. Waves started to slowly whip over the broadside and again flooded the hold. We tried to bail it out and again tell the foolish representative of the new regime that we needed to turn aside before it was too late. He seemed to slightly consider it, the sea will make anyone think twice, but then he was emptyheaded. We'll get through, he shouted, we've seen worse stuff during the war and revolution. In the name of the working class, he said, forward!

We were cast into darkness. The old men prayed, but the younger ones seemed to have already forgotten and only some of them made the sign of the cross with two fingers. Others tried to make jokes and laugh. But the sea is no place for laughing. Brutal waves came in and hammered the barge's hull like a woodpecker. The wind flew in gusts. We looked and saw that the men steering the barge had completely lost their minds, whether from fear or demonic possession. We somehow went past Sosnovets Island and was heading along the coast for Cape Sharapov. Now fear gripped us entirely, because Cape Sharapov was a bad place. Even during calm weather we tried to keep our distance from it, but this time the sea had gone completely crazy.

At Cape Sharapov there are shallows where the current lifts up big waves. If there is a wind, then it whips up other wave and the two crash against one another. The sea is seething here, it dances chaotically, in mad fits. Waves that are twice as big rise up, from all sides, with foam and wind – such is our Pomor hell, a *suvoy* it is called. We could see those spawn of Satan steering us right for the *suvoy*, they wanted to go right through it as if they couldn't see anything at all. How could they see anything if their eyes and ears were so full of the revolution? After all, they didn't need to think or look, they only needed to know how to shout and destroy. They had thrown the old knowledge overboard and hadn't found any new knowledge.

My father beat his fists on the hatch of the hold. Don't worry about us, he shouted, worry about yourselves, you fools. Steer for the open sea, you need to get out to the open sea. But it was too late. Right in the middle of the Sharapov *suvoy* is a reef, Sibirka it's called. Even in the shallowest water the sea does not reveal it, so it lies there as a vicious hard obstacle under the smooth surface of the sea. In a storm it cannot be made out among the raging waves. Meaning that we had to pray to St. Varlaam of Keret to make it through this, since we had wandered so foolishly into this whirlpool.

But it was too late. The haughty commander was directing the barge towards the Sibirka reef. Right at Sibirka.

It was five hundred meters from the reef to the shore. Everyone has a sacred right to fight for their own lives, though a submissive man might be unaware of it. Once we heard the first grinding over the rocks and then a loud roar below, we knew immediately. The barge rose up as it came to rest on the wall of rocks, like on a pedestal. Waves began to batter the barge like a merciless crow that would swoop down on a random forest bird. Water rushed into the hole like precious moisture down a dry throat. Up on the deck they were running around like silly pups, scared, screaming and sobbing. But we banded together and tore the hold's hatch away as if with steam power, though we did it with our own bare hands, as if God had helped us. On the deck the guards were huddling in the corners, half-dead from shock. The sea roared and rumbled all around us, a cruel father but better with him than with crazy fools. We crossed ourselves and began to jump into the water, the sea took us in its icy embrace around our chests like steel hoops. It held us fast, but then it let us go and we were able to swim among the heavy dancing of the waves.

Many would have made it to shore. Not everyone – the sea would have taken its share. But I took a look around, through the water and the wind that I had inhaled. When everyone had run up to the deck and to the sides of the barge, Fedka had shouted something about treason, about running away, about how the country would not forgive us. It was silly, who would have listened to him at a moment like that! But he was rushing frantically around the deck and probably felt like he was in charge again, always right. He hadn't learned from the previous officer, who could no longer be seen. A wave must have washed him away. What a demonic force was in those people, those monsters – Fyodor tightly grabbed the machine gun positioned at the stern. I couldn't believe my eyes, I couldn't accept it deep down – God turned away at that moment from us, from everyone and from him.

The White Sea was black. An austere, mourning color. The frequent waves shone white, tipped with foam. The backs of the men swimming shone. They wore white canvas shirts that their wives had managed to get for them so that they would not be ashamed when they were taken away, perhaps for the last time. The fair Russian heads shone. Then the machine gun from the barge rang out with its stuttering sound. It barked, it spouted flame, like it had some dark authority, as if someone had granted him, that liar, the right to violate life without hesitation, without fear, without reproach.

Bullets spread over the water like a fan. The water turned red. The setting sun appeared and illuminated everything. One by one these men, who had been bold sailors on icy waters, now sank into the depths. One by one our northern people disappeared, Russia's men of steel. Like fish that flash white in the depths, they disappeared into the sea. Like a flock of salmon that has left its native shores forever, tortured by an incomprehensible, evil force, it settles only as a wide arc of red, pink, white, boiling blood and bullets and dissolves in the sea. A bright, sinking, heavenly rainbow lay itself over the sea, it was parting now along with life and hope, following after the tribe of fish, which not so long ago had been people, they had left because of human evil.

Everything dragged on slowly and painfully, like in a dream. I was scared, but the water took away my fear. I turned and swam on, with my last bit of strength. It hit me in the back then; it wasn't painful but it was loud. I saw the sun through the transparent glass of the mother-of-pearl water.

I was pulled to shore by a man from a neighboring village, from Letnerechensky. I didn't know him. His name was Varlaam. Only five men made it to the shore, out of two hundred. They carried me dozens of miles home. I never saw my father again.

* * *

It is nice to go swimming in the White Sea, but risky. There are days when the sun shines so hot that it is no longer gentle but full-on baking. It burns your face like a frying pan in the sky. Then you go along red-faced, happy, like you just came in from the prairie. Your nose starts to peel right away, then the skin on your forehead and cheeks comes off, for after all, if the weather is fine the sun is there burning you for twenty hours a day and sometimes you can even be sunburned at midnight. Plus, you are spending the whole day out in the open, you are not hiding from the sea wind and the light of the North. This will happen whether you like it or not, but you will survive and your first sunburn will fade after a few more days spent in the northern summer. Then the real magic begins: the glow from the sky heats you up until you sweat, it dries you up with a salty air, the sea breeze smooths and caresses you — and you take on a color of a unique, distinct beauty. Especially if you are a woman. Old women of the White Sea who walk around all summer with a kerchief tied under their chin to evade the mosquitoes, look funny when they take their kerchiefs off. Their faces are dark-brown but around their face is a strip of white. You admire them, these swarthy women, you stare at their funny faces which quickly become sad, and back again. But that is only as long as they do not start singing or telling stories – then you do not even see them any longer but simply listen to the words that ring like music, flow into your ears like honey. If you are fortunate to meet one who remembers tales from olden times, you cannot break away, you cannot get enough. You just want to stay there forever, so that you are never far from this native dialect.

However, if you are a city girl and you have time to tan properly, then you will become a legendary beauty, even if you are homely in your everyday life. The sun along with the northern summer wind caresses you so that you turn olive all over and you make your girlfriends in the city jealous. When you come home from your challenging but enjoyable trip, everyone will ask you what unknown southern regions you were traveling in. You will only laugh in response, satisfied, because they already told you that a northern tan lasts for a long time, it will not wash off with a sponge and water, unlike the fleeting sunburns of the south.

One is really drawn to swim in the White Sea on those hot days. It seems as if there is no water in the world more blue and gentle. You walk barefoot over the rocks, heated to an unbearable degree. You look out to the sea and sniff, testing with your foot to see whether the water is too cold. Then you decide to do it, you undress and jump into the gentle waters. Now something takes hold of you lightly, to the point of stupor. The half-meter of water at the top is warm, but under it is chilly. No wonder they say that the White Sea is, not just along its shores but also in its depths, two different beings. At the top, for about a dozen meters there is one water that can heat up and cool down, depending on the weather and the season. But at the bottom there is water that flows in and out from the Arctic Ocean and does not mix with the water above, remaining minus three degrees Celsius all year long. There dwell different fish and animals. While swimming, you quickly feel the breath of the Arctic and your heart is chilled by a light terror. Then you crawl back out onto the rocks, shaking all over. Five minutes pass and you warm up again. Then such a feeling of strength arises in your body, such an unbridled vigor, that you feel like you could pick up the nearest bolder, half the size of a house and hurl it far into the sea to create a new island.

You sit like that, warm up, admire your inner strength and go over to the fire to drink tea. You walk barefoot and unafraid. There are snakes around, but on the smooth stones you would see them from far away. In fact, you will not notice them at all, for they are shy and do not creep out when people are around. They remain quietly secluded and dream of being alone again with nature. The old Pomors had a custom: if they saw a snake, they would immediately catch it and put it into a glass bottle. They would then close the bottle with a cork and put it on the roof or in some other sunlit place. After a month had passed they would look at the bottle again and there would be nothing in it but some light-colored liquid with a few small bones swimming in it – the snake had dissolved in its own poison. There is no better remedy than this liquid for a sore back, sciatica or other muscle and bone aches.

You sit by the fire, throw a handful of tea leaves in the kettle and set it on the flame. The water boils in five minutes. If you know your herbs, then you throw in some rosemary or cowberry leaves, or some black crowberries – you will not taste a finer tea anywhere. You pour it in your mug and do not skimp on the sugar – during your long journey you can permit yourself everything and both the sugar and the thick slice of pork fat will, along with everything else, be burned by hard work. You blow on the dark amber liquid in the mug, take a sip, cringing a bit as your lips touch the hot mug. Such a taste, such a smell comes over you as if some tart freedom has finally been granted to you. If you have some salted red fish, freshly caught the same day, you cut off a slice of it, only slightly salt it and put it on some black bread. You bite into a sandwich that melts in your mouth and on top of it you drink the hot, sweet tea. You like feel like an otherworldly happiness flows through your veins along with the swirling flavors, like you are merging with the earth and the sea by tasting the salt and the sweetness. The wind will instantly sweep away the tears that have come to your eyes – for the umpteenth time you feel that this is home, this is the Russian North.

2005, KYUVIKANDA

Grisha remembered how in childhood, before fear came, he loved to go with his father to the grocery store. There, hung over the counter, were multicolored glass bottles of conical shape. They hung with the narrower part pointing down, also the glass bottles were not themselves in different colors, but rather, life-giving juices of different sorts floated in them. There were usually three such conical bottles, with apple, tomato and some kind of pumpkin juice. But back then, among the grayness of Soviet life, how bright, how unusual and wonderful these had seemed to him. He did not really like the apple juice, especially as it came with a disgusting pulp that would stick in his throat. As for the pumpkin, he had never even considered it juice, rather it served as some kind of decoration apart. But the tomato juice, yes! The juice was bright red, triumphant, like the nation's flag (granted, mama always said, for us fools it could have been a little redder) and it lived its own quiet life within the conical bottle until Grisha's father paid at the counter and the grave-faced woman at the counter set a glass below the little valve at the bottom, then a thick, full stream issued from the bottle and filled the glass. The juice in the conical bottle also decreased, but much slower than the glass was filled, and Grisha, fascinated, observed these different rates and tried to understand why they should be different. Next to the counter was a container of salt with bitter white salt; a sloppy person had already spilled a few drops of red into it. Next to the salt was a glass of water in which aluminum teaspoons idly lay. Grisha had to take one, scrape at the salt which had hardened and throw a little heap of it into his glass of juice. The salt sank slowly, not right away but with a kind of reluctance – white inside red, then he had to push the salt on top down with the spoon and stir it for a long time, with the spoon ringing against the glass walls. For some reason this was fun to do. After all this, the spoon was put back into the glass filled with water. The water was already opaque, red and there was something unpleasant about this, as if it was trying to ape the noble tomato juice.

When the juice was ready to drink, Grisha's father would take from a paper bag a sweet roll that he had bought beforehand. The roll had powdered sugar sprinkled on it and was already wonderful in itself. But if Grisha washed it down with the salty tomato juice, it was delectable. At various times in his life, Grisha often looked back on these trips to the shop with his father, on the juice and the roll, and could never understand why he remembered this, what was so special about those things. Suddenly and quite unexpectedly it came to him: perhaps this was the main Russian sentiment: when things turn sweet, but they are followed immediately afterwards by salt. To ensure that you don't enjoy things much, you don't grow weak by allowing yourself too much, so that you keep sober. This sentiment, this constant readiness for the salt that follows on sweetness, is instilled in a person starting from childhood. Yet, at the same time, it is so much sharper, more delicious than the two tastes alone, for then they would lose much more than simply being divided in half. Salt and sweetness together, at the same time, one right after the other, inseparable. Plus, the knowledge that it would always be that way – salt following on sweetness – makes you not just stronger and faster, not just twice as much, but far more. It enables you to stand ready, to survive. Salt in turn after sweetness. Salt for sweetness.

While Grisha, sitting by the campfire, became lost in his thoughts, Mikhail came up. He held a large aluminum bowl with caviar in it. "Well then, care for some caviar?" He was pleased to know already what the answer would be.

"Sure," Grisha said gladly. "Is it salted?"

"No, I haven't managed to salt it yet. Now we'll make some fast caviar. You know how to do it?" Mikhail seemed to be testing Grisha again.

"No, I don't."

"I know, I know!" Eliseyev said, excitedly. "I love to make caviar!"

"Well, you said that about cleaning fish too," Grisha mocked him. "How much you love it. Then you ran away after three fish." Grisha was in fact jealous that Nikolai really did know how to do more things than him.

"No, this time I'll do it." Nikolai Eliseyev had not noticed their grins, he never thought about how he seemed to others. The important thing was not to seem but to do. "Now we'll clean it a little." Nikolai, as if he had already known, had kept a piece of white gauze aside and was now taking it out of his backpack. "Hold this!" He thrust two corners of the gauze square towards Grisha's outstretched hands and grabbed the other two corners, then poured the caviar onto the gauze. "Now roll it!"

Carefully and trying not to drop the gauze, the two began to lift up one end of the square and then the other. The lump of fish roe gently rolled over the surface. All the tiny motes, needles and what seemed like peels stuck to the gauze and the caviar suddenly shone with a new, mother-of-pearl, deep-red color. Mikhail watched them with satisfaction.

"That's enough of that. Now I'll make some brine for it." Nikolai poured some vigorously boiling water into a large mug and then threw a good handful of salt in.

"Isn't that too much?" Grisha asked.

"Fish and caviar will take what salt they need. They know how much," Mikhail answered for Eliseyev. The latter was focusing on stirring the mug with a spoon to dissolve the salt. Nikolai then took the mug and poured the boiling water right into the bowl with the caviar.

Grisha gasped. "What are you doing? You're going to cook it!"

"Don't worry," Eliseyev was confident and businesslike. "Let's keep an eye on the time."

Indeed, five minutes later he drained the brine from the bowl. The fish roe remained as they were, red, translucent and magnificent. The taste of the caviar proved to be just as magnificent, impossible to describe as life itself. Caviar in fact is life itself, an ideal life without any flaws, not yet begun and therefore perfect.

"This calls for a drink, too," Mikhail said in time, Grisha readily poured some alcohol from the canister and added cold water to it.

"Let's dig in!" Mikhail said, and once again two flavors, two absolutes, swirled playfully around Grisha's tongue, the warm taste of eternal life and the crystalline taste of eternal death. They merged and remained inseparable.

With fish soup, alcohol does not take hold of you, and if you are eating caviar, then alcohol retreats completely, the green serpent hides. They did think that they were drinking pretty heavily, but none of them felt that their wits were dulled nor did they have a headache – only a quiet sadness, like the evening itself was quiet, calm. They sat around the campfire as it crackled quietly to itself as if it was all happening a hundred years ago, maybe two hundred, or even in time immemorial. Grisha sat looking at the map of the northern coast, the White Sea and the Barents. It was a fascinating map, the names on it were wonderful Russian names but also Saami ones, as if from ancient tales: Norinyok, Everveyvr, Kolbinyavr. But those were towards the North, while to the south one found more and more Russian and Karelian names.

Mikhail looked over his shoulder at the map. "You see, all the rivers and bays are covered by islands. Kola Bay is covered by Kildin Island,

Chupa Bay by Keret, Sidorov and Kiskin Island. All the small and big rivers too."

"What does that mean?" Grisha asked, amazed.

"Old folks used to say that when the Russians came to the North, the Lapps were very upset. They lived in a sort of peace, but still, sometimes, our people did bad things to them, they took their salmon grounds or rustled some of their reindeer. So, they complained to their greatest witch. She cast a spell and islands came floating in from the ocean, each to its own river or bay. They floated and closed it all up, so that the Russians had no outlet to the sea."

"What happened then?"

"St. Varlaam of Keret prayed and the curse was removed. The islands had moved in, but they stopped before they blocked the rivers. Otherwise the Russian tribes couldn't have lived here." Mikhail smiled.

A smile came to Grisha's face too. "Well, the Russians can find a hole everywhere."

"You might think so, but not everywhere. Now there aren't many Pomors left. The ones who are left are drinking themselves to death."

"What, the young people are leaving for the city? Urbanization?"

"Urbanization." Mikhail knew that word too. "Just look at Norway. People lived there for centuries in their villages on the coast, they still do. They work in fishing, or if not, they entertain tourists. But in our country, everything has been destroyed and people no longer have the strength to go back."

"But why not? They have already restored some villages that were burnt, some monasteries that were destroyed. They rebuilt them."

"Look here," Mikhail scooped up a spoonful of caviar. "Think about salmon. When you appreciate and respect them, you get as much of them as you need. But they overfished the salmon, they killed them mercilessly – and now it's like the salmon have lost all their strength. Now they're raising farmed salmon at the fishery in Keret, they get millions of salmon eggs and fry, but it seems like the salmon just don't want to thrive. The schools don't grow. The ones they release keep coming back and the wild salmon are completely gone. The fish don't have any strength left after they were basically wiped out. The same goes for people: they destroyed the old way of life, raised everyone's hopes without anything ever coming of it and wiped out the strongest men right at the root. Many years have gone by, but you look and where are the people? They don't come back, just like the fish. It's a hard job, not a simple one. When there's no love, nothing will result from science and force alone. Plus, I heard that the Church recently admitted that the schism was unnecessary. There was no justification for it. So, many people were burned just like that without any reason for it. Four hundred years have gone by and they admit it now. But those simple folk aren't going to come back now. They won't believe either, or have any desire to. When are they maybe going to admit the Revolution was unnecessary? It'll take three hundred years."

Mikhail sighed and threw a bunch of caviar back in the bowl. It stayed there, transparent, scarlet, but no longer living, like a pearl that turns gray and dies quickly without love and care. Fish roe are not the same once they are salted and killed, if you leave it until the next day, it has to be thrown away completely. In its depths no life beats any more. Nature dies without love. Man might be master over nature, but it is nonetheless a part of the whole. Everything is one, the same laws and the same feelings. You look along the northern coasts and you see only a wasteland devoid of people. Where are the people here? There are none.

1935, KERET

When they carried me back to the village, my mother understood everything at once. She hid me in the hayloft, where we kept hay for the sheep. Not a word was said about my father, she did not cry any tears for me. She just seemed all dried out, her face seemed like it was carved from black wood. I can't remember anything about how it was at first – about how she bandaged me and changed the bandages every day, or how she rolled me over so that I wouldn't lie with my bones pressing on my flesh, or how she rubbed my arms and legs so that I wouldn't weaken. There was a good nurse in the village who showed her how to do everything and helped.

They looked for more survivors, but not too hard; they realized that the men wouldn't have survived a whirlpool like that. They felt less enthusiasm, life went on and each person was told how to act. Now in Fedka's place was another man, a local, but he only pretended to order everyone around. They did keep coming to the village, to the houses and asking questions. But now who would tell them anything? The men who had been arrested along with me and then carried me home, did not stick around. God may have to teach a stupid man something many times, but for a smart man once is enough. They scattered through the forests and kept away from settlements; they already knew that the government of the people doesn't forgive its people. They didn't even leave any footprints behind.

They didn't find me either. My mother hid me in the hay in time. They didn't look for me especially – a feeling of horror came over the village after the black news the men had carried here, along with me. The old women wailed, but not for very long – you can't live like that forever, you have work to see to. There are children to raise, you can't neglect them. They started going out to sea in the men's place, the ones who were strong enough. The collective farm was then organizing the fishing, using the boats that had been taken from merchant Savin. They would come in from the sea to the dock, all along the banks of the Keret and start to gut the fish, immediately those who couldn't work or were hungry would come across the river in a little boat. It was obvious that the fishers would help their own first. But then they had to give up all the fish they had. They could keep the heads and the offal though, they divided this up with the neighbors. The roe and cod livers also went to the offal. So, they managed somehow.

The village shop began operating again, in the same house that had belonged to my uncle Savin. Fewer wares, true, but that was alright as long as there was always bread. But then they started selling eggs and butter. The government had such ridiculous ideas, it decreed that villagers all over the country should produce eggs, butter and milk. We Pomors had never kept chickens or cows as far back as anyone remembered, we traded fish for everything. So, people were forced to be sneaky: they bought from the shop eggs of poor quality and milk too, then they handed that over to the state to meet the quotas. We had never seen such idiocy before, but what could you do? We had to learn and be cunning too.

Gradually life seemed to resume. The women had wailed and cried enough over their own. It was just hard. Without a man around you can't cope with everything. So, the simple folk began to quietly scatter in different directions, some to the mica mine, and some all the way to the city. Grass grew in high walls through the village. In every house they were struggling. People were still living there, but the weeds began creeping like a snake and they suffocated everything. It was as if the earth had grown fat on the blood of the fish and the people, as if it didn't want human beings to live on it anymore, so the earth began to drive them away with grass. It would all grow so fast that people were amazed: just yesterday there was a lane where people danced or ran to swim, today there's a wall so high you can't get through it. Snakes came too, though the village had never had them before.

Then the church burnt down.

It was strange and horrifying. Many years the church had stood there unharmed, now it had burnt down. At night. There was no thunder, no lightning. Granted, there hadn't been a priest there for a few years now, he was the first person to be arrested. The church had stood closed, but by habit people looked at it and crossed themselves before they went out to sea or in other situations. They would still bury everyone there too, in the graveyard.

Now it went up in flames. Not from one side but from several. As if an inexhaustible candle stood there in the darkness of the night. The light from the fire reflected in the sea so bright that it hurt our eyes. People came running up, but what could they do? They didn't have anything to put the fire out with and it was impossible to approach the flames. All they could do was pour water on the walls of the nearby houses. They formed a bucket brigade starting from the sea and passed the water along. Just like they had passed the fish along when they got the order to wipe it all out. It was the same thing now, only this time it was our turn for such misfortune. In the graveyard the crosses closest to the church also burnt down. The old Pomor wood, washed by the sea and whitened by the rain, now went up in angry flames, as if our forefathers had sent us a curse from beyond the grave, something that they couldn't tell us while they were alive. Pomors are a quiet people, they aren't keen on shouting. They keep everything inside and bear things as long as they can. But now there was a crash, shouting, an uproar from the villagers, sparks flying and a blaze of heat, as if the gates of hell had opened on a spot that was previously holy. The crosses were burning madly, like loyal people going to the slaughter.

Then the bell tower collapsed. The steel cross that had stood atop it plummeted like a slain bird. It fell with its arms spread to the sides, like a person. When it had stood there, it was proud. As it fell, it was in despair. It fell and hit the ground so hard that the boom passed through the entire area. Like a message resounding from under the earth: "Here I co-o-o-me!"

Everyone froze like statues. They stopped trying to extinguish the flames and gave into despair. The cross bent when it hit the ground and it lay like an arch, like an eternal bridge from one thing to another, from white to black, from God to the devil.

They stood there until morning and waited. The church burnt completely to the ground. A black square remained on the earth. Wild, unkempt grass surrounded it.

Only later did my mother tell me that the cross had bent but it did not break. When fate strikes a blow on the Russian people, the Russians sometimes bend, like a pine tree under the north wind. But they are not broken. Pomor steel is strong. Bad times had come, but there was one thing to do: hold your ground and be patient. Bend, but not break. The darkness will pass all the same, then the sun will come out. Morning will still come.

The village grew over with weeds, but I recovered. As if the earth, the sea and the fresh wind had given me their last strength. The wounds on my back healed, though few had believed that I would make it. Only my mother believed and acted. When I was already strong again, when

I could already walk upright around the house (though I never showed myself in the street), she sat me down for a difficult talk. My mother was wise. Once an animal has caught your scent, it won't let you go. Days would pass, years, but it would remember its victim's smell and catch it again if the victim was near. You too must go, Kolyamba. Go far away, to other regions, there, maybe, it will lose your scent. Be meek and learn to pretend, to be unnoticeable, then it won't smell you. The Russian lands are big, in the past people came here to save their lives, but now they must leave here. Don't worry, don't cry, it is not so scary. You just have to live and have faith, then all will be well. We Pomors are not slaves. We are fish. We just need to beat with our tails and go into the sea, then see where the wind is blowing and where the current is leading us to. We can be caught when there is love and we turn completely stupid. Or we might believe when we hear the words of another, then we might come together and swim towards the sweet call. But know this: you won't catch a Pomor like that: the freedom of the sea is human beings' strength. Whoever lives free fears nothing; you won't catch him with empty hands, he'll see your net from far away. Swim away, like an ice-follower, swim away. Don't wait for the approaching beast to arrive.

She quickly gathered up some things for me. She put some provisions in a bag, some clothes. Before I went out she said a quick prayer for me. Then she quietly said farewell and pushed me out the door. I walked on, holding tears back, only I heard her gentle voice the whole way: "Swim away, like an ice-follower, swim away."

I never saw her again.

So, I left as an exile, through my own native land. Good people took me in, fed me and sent me onward. They asked me nothing about why I was on the road, nor what my destination was; they all understood everything. Such are our wise northern Russian people. I have always remembered one piece of advice I got from a hunched old lady. She told it to me after a meager but good dinner, which she had made for me with her last bit of strength: "Farewell, Christian, dear guest! May St. Nicholas and Varlaam of Keret speed you on! You are bound for a distant place, you will encounter all kinds of woes. May you who are traveling return alive and gladden us. We won't forget you in our prayers, though we are sinners. Look out for the bad things that are inside you: either when you have no wind behind you or when fear overcomes you in a storm, or when you face great doubt and despair – direct a prayer to Varlaam of Keret. This is why he, that saint, chose to have his earthly abode in our country. If you pray to him, he will help you."

However much Grisha tried to understand his own people, he simply could not. He could not understand himself either, apparently he was a part of this society that cannot calm down, make peace with one another and with their own selves and begin to peacefully create a good world, not just say empty words.

Everyone was evil to one another, like wild animals. They did not even need a reason to be like that, everyone would find his own reason in any circumstance. But a furious rage is boiling inside, ready to burst out at any moment, either as hot hatred or cold, calculating envy. The worst you are among this pack, the weaker you are, the better it is for the people around you, the more surely the sharp hook will catch you under your rib. "In return for the good things we do, we get a knife in the side," the Russian people know well.

There was a time when Grisha drank heavily. There are points in a person's life when neither science nor medication help – he writhes like an earthworm torn in two. Spins round and round, overwhelmed by grief. In such times it happens that alcohol is the only means of salvation. A dangerous means, but you have no choice – it is either sudden death, or a tough battle with a tender snake which squeezes its coils around you tighter and tighter, while at the same time it whispers tender words into your ear. It is hard, but you cannot do anything about it. Grisha drank for three years, every single day. A bottle and a half on average. Once he read that with that rate of drinking, a person could develop cirrhosis in three months. But no symptoms appeared. The only good thing was that he was able, by some miracle, to avoid resuming his drinking right away the next morning. But eventually, he could no longer hold back; at one point he began drinking in the mornings, too, right away he noticed how a beautiful blue funnel with smooth walls would arise and spin around him, shining brightly. It was wonderful and sparkling, Grisha found it fun to be carried along its vortex, with his arms, legs and soul sliding through the mist that obscured everything. There was only one downside: though this sliding proceeded in a spiral motion, it led him ever down into a fantastic depth, it was such a force that one day he could look at himself from the outside, up close though blurry and it scared him. In literally just a couple of months his clothes had begun to turn to rags and a smell appeared that would not go away. It seemed as if his soul was rotting and giving off the smell, a miasma that issued from every pore on his body. His shame was gone – it began to be fun to think that this is how things should be. That the only right thing, true freedom, is to stop thinking of others, to stop caring for yourself and consequently for anyone else, too. Before this point Grisha had considered his concern for others to be one of the main traits that he had been brought up with and fostered, the right thing. Now that he had lost it, he suddenly got scared. He realized that without that feeling, life was truly empty. If it is empty, then it can easily fly away at any second, with a gust from the passing breeze. Compassion is the anchor that holds us firm to life, it does not let us fly away like a meaningless dragonfly into a poor and frivolous nonexistence.

He got scared and was able to stop his morning experiments. But he could not abandon alcohol entirely. Nor could he lower his intake. Lunchtime and evening drinking allowed him to maintain a decent appearance, to not plunge into a labyrinth of contradictions that was invitingly signposted with only the words: "Entrance Here". He could not see any exit, perhaps there was none at all. But without alcohol, without the same or even greater (but never lower) intake every day, his soul began to quiver, like a half-torn piece of tin on an old abandoned roof. It frantically shakes, screeches, flutters, preparing to break off and fly away, then with its sharp, rusty edge cuts through anything that is inappropriately situated along the path of its swift flight. Only alcohol, poured in time from a cold, indifferent glass onto this surface that is roaring from pain, can magically pacify it. So, until next time, until the next day. It was frightening, but at the same time it was clear that things could not be otherwise. The pain roaring inside him could be burned away only with a flame of the same degree, the same mercilessness and ardor: in alcohol.

But in this he still had to know his limits, to control himself, for in spite of the pain, he still wanted to live. These limits were so unsteady, barely graspable, a slippery ooze that trickled through his fingers.

Once he and Nikolai Eliseyev decided to get drunk together. There was no special reason for it, but they ran into each other and thought it would be fun. Grisha was driving, but that did not stop them. Granted, with age he had established a good habit: it is okay to drink behind the wheel, but without driving. Therefore, a place was always found in the neighborhood where they could park the car, without being too far from his house and from the shop. A point of intersection between three forces: being homey, riotous indulgence and a tiny bit of adult sobriety left in his head. Usually this plan worked, they could drink, sit in a warm place, listen to music, talk and then go their separate ways home. There was some well-established comfort in this.

But life is complicated by the fact that even the best-laid plans are laid to waste. Plus, it is not complicated by the situation but by one's own self-awareness, a surge of a different mood that was not needed on a given day, a wringing of the soul, such that it cracks, the poor thing, is twisted. The soul is an unfathomable phenomenon. You cannot compress it, just like water, like anything that is even slightly liquid. That is why it stretches out with effort from an uncomfortable, unnatural position. It is such a strong force that you had better stay back: it will tear you apart if you have not learned how to slow down. That is what happened back then, too, word for word, somehow the conversation turned to some uncomfortable topic, some sore part was touched and you could not hide from the pain. That means you need to heal. Well, they went to it. The first bottle went by in a flash, they did not even taste it. They had food and some good conversation, not in the sense that it was a calm, orderly conversation, but one that involved empathy, the sort of thing a person lives for sometimes. Grisha quickly ran to get a second bottle – thank goodness the shop was nearby and money was not an issue for a person of a certain age. An age when you know how little money is really worth. It is not worth the paper it is printed on, or the metal used to make the coins.

The second bottle went more slowly, with reflections, debates, conclusions and suggestions. Complex ones. Then things sped up again. After a person has half a liter in them, things are already good, that suffices, then he starts to burst into tears or laughter, or partial or total blackouts. Grisha was well aware of this. But on that day, he did not have the strength to stop. For example, if a heavy blue wave grabs you and carries you along and you do not try to resist, because you see it taking you the right way. He had earned this. After all his stupid life to date, he had earned this. He felt an excitement at having earned it. A cheerful desperation and recklessness together with his friend. Shall we have another one? Sure, why not!

They went together to get the third bottle, holding each other up by the armpit and laughing. Suddenly a sense of being such big heroes awoke within them, such a desire for justice, that if they were to meet someone along the way who was unrighteous, they would thrash him.

But this desire was emanating around them with such a bright light that justice was established miraculously by itself. Praise be to God!

When they bought the fourth bottle, Grisha noted through his narrowed but still focused field of vision, that the cashier was looking at them strangely. Grisha himself had sold alcohol in the past, so he noticed this. But he could not manage to pick himself up; the wave was already crashing and frothing on the sand. Shining friendship was revealed to the world out of the foam. The pain subsided. It was a holiday all around them, people were dancing, firecrackers were going off, the night was flowing past, daybreak was on its way, but their happiness would never end. Happiness was possible. Life was possible. With these feelings they went to get a fifth bottle. They bought it without any hassle. Then they got back into the car and opened the bottle. They popped the cap off, but under it there was no safety closure in the neck of the bottle. Yet the bottle was the same as before, as was the cap and the label. Everything looked like it normally did, just without a safety closure. If Grisha had been sober, he would have been on guard. He actually was on guard if he had noticed it, registered it, but now there was no longer any reason to end the drinking, no stop sign. There was a sign, but maybe he just did not understand it. Maybe it was the opposite: everything was perfectly fine. So, they drank this fifth bottle. But in their stomachs they felt that something was off. That cheating fucker had tricked them into buying counterfeit vodka. He had found a good moment and plied them with fake stuff. This became clear the next morning.

Before that, Grisha had had to die several times: from horror, from love, from a terrible illness that simply went away on its own. But never had it been something so real, so definite. The next morning he did not wake up, he came to, at home on his couch. How he got home, he did not remember and it did not matter. Because in his head a gigantic bell was ringing. He would shatter it to pieces, but it would slowly come together again, so that it could be shattered again with the next blow. His heart was beating hard and wearily. Everywhere – in his arms, in his legs and in his chest, Grisha could feel his pulse, fast and full, so hard that it was like a steel rope that tightened under his skin with every beating of his heart, then slackened without disappearing entirely. Grisha tried to stand up but was unable to. His body would not obey him. It seemed to have grown faint, to be half dead and it only had life in it in his clenching, groaning muscle pains. Yet these pains were not especially strong, for the heavy ringing in his head drowned out everything.

A stench hung over the room, so strong that it constantly gave Grisha an urge to vomit, although ordinarily he never noticed the smell of his own breath after drinking. Now it was as if he had burned his entire being in a stinking, greedy flame and this chemical burning was so terrible that it smothered his willpower and any thought that he might even try to save himself. Grisha felt completely immobilized by the pain and the horror of what was happening. Through incredible effort, which sprang from some supernatural striving to live, he managed to reach for the telephone and dial the number of his doctor girlfriend.

"Marinka, I'm dying," he spoke hoarsely into the phone.

Resuscitation is a complicated word, but it can still save your life. Marinka rushed over, thank goodness she lived nearby. She had with her everything she needed: a drip, saline, syringes. She grabbed his wrist right away and felt his pulse, then said "Uh-huh" in a doctorly way. She measured his blood pressure and turned serious.

"Two-hundred and sixty, dear. What did you drink?"

"Vodka. The bottle must have been refilled with fake stuff." In spite of the deathly pain he felt, Grisha was ashamed at how he looked, at the things being done around him. He tried to stand up.

"Lie down, I'll organize things here. Did you go to the bathroom, urinate?"

"No, I didn't feel the need to for some reason."

"I see." While Marinka had asked him, she was setting up the drip. She put the needle in a vein. Saline started to murmur down from the drip. "Hello, emergency room? Get the dialysis ready, you might have a patient in about an hour."

"What's that for?" It might have seemed that Grisha no longer had the strength to get scared, but indeed he could. Now he felt not a hot fear, but one that was somehow cold, piercing. He understood how it was.

"We'll see. If you don't urinate within an hour, we'll drive you to help." Marinka had always been a firm woman. That is why she had succeeded in many things, saving people's lives when others were just standing there at a loss. "Let's deal with the blood pressure. What have you got here?"

"Berlipril."

"Fine, take a double dose. One more under your tongue. That's it. I'll make some magnesium solution, roll over on your side. Don't groan, we'll get you through this."

After ten minutes had passed, they had done everything possible. Marinka spent another ten minutes putting the place in order:

she opened the windows, wiped the floor and threw his vomit-soiled blanket in the bathroom. She then covered him with another one and brought him a washbowl. Grisha periodically threw up into this too, then she took it away, washed it and brought it back. She changed the IV bag. She kept an eye on him.

Grisha, for his part, lived his life, or rather his death. He really did not want to die, but death was close, he would feel it. He knew that in this moment, without pain or fanfare, his kidneys were dying. That's it, the end. Nothing could be done. There are no limits to perfection and death is the greatest of all perfection. Without it, he would be a swollen, yellow cripple going in for dialysis once a week. He would not go on like that for long, only long enough to realize that death is better than a life like that. Everything was being decided now, in these very minutes.

"Marinka, am I dying?" he asked in a stupid, pitiful tone.

"You don't want to go to the bathroom? Listen to your body." She answered his question with another question, but she was already looking at her watch.

Then suddenly things began working down below. Something barely graspable, like in a dream in childhood, when it seems like you are doing everything right, but then you wake up in a wet bed.

"Marinka, its working! Disconnect the drip, I'll run to the bathroom."

"Lay back down, you runner." In a womanly, shameless way she unzipped his trousers, and set the washbowl in front of him. "Try now."

It flowed freely, ringing on the enamel surface. He closed his eyes from shame. He only opened them again when she returned with the bowl, now clean. She measured his blood pressure, it had fallen little by little. She called the emergency room again and called the dialysis off. Grisha began to fall asleep. The pain in his head had become huge, soft and constant. The last thing he remembered was her pulling the blanket up over him and tucking it under his chin.

He lay in bed for several days. He could not believe he had been so lucky again. That he had come to the brink, teetered there, but did not fall. That there must be a God.

But he was still being suffocated by hatred. While he was weak, it had barely moved inside him. It now came back along with his own strength. It grew stronger and vaster.

"What did you do that for, you fucker?" Grisha would ask that bastard, that weasel standing behind the counter, whose shifty eyes would never let Grisha sleep at night.

"What for?" Everything would flash before his eyes, beginning with his happy and then unhappy childhood, his whole swaggering, lascivious youth where his main goal was to hide from himself all the dark things that had happened in the past, all his adult years, experience, fighting, victories and pain. At the end came the black eyes of the weasel that lacked any hesitation, any sense, waiting to kill a man just like that. To take advantage of you when your guard was down. To make another fifty rubles, a hundred, or even a hundred thousand. The fucker!

"But I'll show you, you bastard! You don't know who you're dealing with, fucker. You must have gotten away with it until now, that's why you're unafraid. But you'll be afraid of me, you creep!"

Grisha recognized this violence inside him. Several times in his life, when he was not able to control it, it had betrayed him and left him feeling ashamed. But there were also many times when it came to his rescue, saved him, simply enabled him to do what was right. At those moments, it seemed to him like he knew what was right. Something was leading him. Or someone. Now with all his pain from the past, all his hurt at the present, he realized what he needed to do.

He no longer wanted to drink. He wanted to kill. To bring justice to the world. To spill blood, so that amid the horror of the past he would also see his own abomination and he would rise up again, cleansed. He wanted light.

He had a good knife. It was homemade from a truck's leaf spring, with a handle carved from Karelian birch. With a guard, with a fuller on the blade, everything that it should have – perhaps Russian craftsmen aren't the world's best, but they know weapons. The blade was good steel – he could swing it at any piece of iron and a deep nick would be left on the iron while the blade remained flawless. Many times he had lovingly sharpened it and polished the tight, heavy, shiny surface with a fine-grained whetstone. Then he would test it out on a nail: the nail would be cut through like butter.

Grisha rarely used the knife. He was wary – this knife was, by all standards, a weapon. Therefore, he would only take it along to the forests, to the White Sea, where there was freedom, there were no limitations, where the sea is the law and the only prosecutor the bear. For gutting fish, for cutting light undergrowth and rope for nets, there was no better tool. Now, too, he needed nothing else. The knife should solve everything.

It was very simple: he would punish evil. Otherwise the evil would happen again. The state, for various reasons, sometimes does not do anything. Then you have to calmly and carefully take matters into your own hands.

Grisha planned everything. For several days he would walk by the shop and learn its shifts, its closing times. He watched the weasel activate the alarm on the door. The weasel did not recognize Grisha. Why should he? Grisha was only one customer among many. That is where the man made his mistake. Weasels should be very careful.

During winter it gets dark very early in the North. At eight o'clock everything is already cast deeply into night and only the streetlights on the snow fend off the darkness. The rare passersby are wrapped up in furs and their only hope and yearning is for their warm homes. The only thing they care about is getting there as fast as possible. This was true of this time. Right at eight o'clock the shop closed. Five minutes later, two shop girls happily popped out from its service entrance and scurried off in different directions. Another ten minutes later, the weasel was held up by something in front of the door. He opened the door and started fussing around with the key still in it. Just then Grisha walked up to him from behind. He bluntly shoved the man back into the shop. Grisha himself then leaped in, pushed the weasel against the wall and pressed the ice-cold blade against the man's trembling cheeks. "Easy now, easy," Grisha said, while he felt behind him for the latch and closed the door.

"Now we're going to have a little chat." He saw at once a puddle form under the weasel and flow along the floor.

"What are you scared of, buddy?" Grisha said, already relieved. It had been hard to decide whether to do it, but if you decide and then you see that you planned everything correctly, then things are easier. If you seriously frighten a person, then you can do whatever you want – he falls into a strange stupor, is reduced to a rag doll. Especially if the person is an easily scared one. The weasel had turned out to be such a person, Grisha had seen it earlier in his eyes and he saw it now in the man's frozen pose, from the puddle that was starting to steam in the cold entryway.

He gave the shop owner a shove. "Where's your stockroom?"

"The money, I'll give you the money, whatever else you want…" the man prattled without taking his eyes off the burning blade. In the half-darkness the blade really was magnificent – narrow, stinging, evil-looking.

"I don't need your money, buddy." Grisha was pleased to see the man's fear. Having a power over another that is direct, right there, is a source of great satisfaction. It is flattering. Enthralling. When a creature is trembling right next to you, you feel that you are its master. It will do anything you tell it to. Its life, its death is in your hands. Grisha shrugged off these thoughts, these feelings that had leaped up suddenly from some dark depth within man. It wasn't this that he had come for. Nor the man's money; after all, money is always divided into your own and someone else's. "Take me to where you keep your stock. Where is it?"

The weasel began to fuss and fidget. He had only now noticed his wet trousers and was trying to cover himself with his hands.

"Take me to your stockroom, I said!" The man could not be allowed to snap out of it. Grisha needed him to constantly be doing something and quickly. Otherwise, he would start thinking and not feeling. That wouldn't do any good at all.

The owner of the wet groin hurried forward with a hobbling motion. Grisha followed him. He kept the knife always visible and the weasel's pathetic glance fell on it now and again. A weapon is a powerful thing.

Finally, down a long dark hallway they came to a large stockroom in the cellar. The weasel turned the light on.

"What's your name, buddy?" Grisha allowed himself to relax a little, as everything was going as planned.

"Vasily." The weasel suddenly understood for the first time that no one was going to kill him.

"Here's the thing, Vasily: you're trading in fake vodka. Where is it?"

The man did not even try to deny it. He quickly nodded towards the room. There, in the musty, still not fully lit space were several rows of boxes. About five hundred units altogether.

"That's not mine, they made me do it," the weasel prattled on, already aware of what Grisha was getting at.

"I didn't ask you. I don't care. Go on, start."

"Start what?" The man still did not understand.

"Start pouring it all out. Where's the toilet, nearby? Great. Get going!"

"But I… How? I'll owe them for it."

"You owed people as soon as you agreed to do it: you owe everyone that got poisoned. You owe me. Come on, get going, or I'll stab you!" He needed to spur the weasel on, otherwise there would be unnecessary talking and crying.

The crying started all the same, once the first bottle of fake stuff had gone down the toilet. A smell rose up – the place stank to high heaven. In general the entire atmosphere of the cellar became something unreal, otherworldly. The dim lamp illuminated the walls of a green, hopeless color. Shadows swept along it, like on a battlefield. The smell rose in eddies and smoky bursts. It stung his eyes and nose and made it hard to breathe.

Vasily now and then began to whine at the sight of his ruin. "But it's not my fault! It's not my goods! I'm only a salesperson!" Having tried whining, he moved on to threats: "You don't know who you're dealing with! These are serious people. They'll avenge their own."

"It's only their own when it doesn't harm other people. Otherwise it's nobody's. Come on, keep working."

Grisha had initially sat down and drove the man on whenever the latter seemed to slacken, but then he started to help himself. Things went much faster once the two of them were doing it. But although they were working together, Grisha did not forget to keep the weasel afraid. Once you relax, it is hard to get you back in working condition.

"Why don't you call home and tell your wife that you're doing inventory tonight. You have a wife?"

"I have a wife and kids. And you're pouring our livelihood down the drain."

"Come on, call her, you poor starving man. You should have thought about what you've been doing."

This business occupied them until morning. They put the empty bottles back in the boxes and piled them up along the free wall. During breaks, when they no longer had the energy to labor at this, Grisha made the shopkeeper sign two papers. "So, you'll sign this statement to the police that you've been trading in fake vodka. You signed it? Great. Give it to me, I'll hold on to it, so that you don't try anything funny. Now, sign this receipt that you got money from me in exchange for the goods. That's for your bosses, in case you try any tricks. Now write a paying-in form for the money. That will do it. Did you understand everything?"

"What about me? How am I going to deal with everything?"

"You'll find a way, buddy. If you managed to rise to the owner of a shop, that means you know how to think. Just keep thinking. Solve your own problem. I've already solved mine. You just remember that if you don't show some concern for other people, it'll all come back to you."

The remainder of the night flew by. The amount of counterfeit swill boggled the mind. Grisha's head bubbled like a cauldron from the smell. Finally, they were finished. Grisha got ready to go. Vasily looked tired, but some thoughts were roaming in his mind. Grisha took the papers and neatly hid the knife away.

"You'd better watch out," Grisha said. "I'll be around and I'll be checking to see that you've understood." Then he stepped from the musty space into the open air.

It was dark. A handful of people were rushing about on their own business. The morning rush hour had not yet come. How wonderful it was to breathe fresh air! How invigorating the light frost was after the oppressive heat! How sweet it was to look up at the starry sky! Even with an unusual, winged delight. It must have been the alcohol fumes that still lingered in his head.

1935, VOLOGDA DISTRICT

I walked through my own country and I couldn't recognize it. Everywhere it was Russian people, but the further away I went from the North, the more incomprehensible they became. "The sea makes the man," the old men used to say and I was truly made by it. The beauty and severity of the sea left no room for strife among people, there was none. We spent our days laboring freely and our nights in love; we would ride out storms with a desire to live and spend our holidays in celebration. There was no more room in a person's heart for evil. In the entire history of the Pomor lands, the elders could remember only a few criminal, evil deeds. Once some workers had stranded the owner of their *karbas*, their Pomor boat, on Grumant and then took possession of his boat. They were caught and condemned for it. Killing another human being, that was something that never crossed our minds. Priest Varlaam had given everyone a firm lesson. Stealing is something I had never heard of. All the evil forces within a Russian – and there are quite a few in each person – vanish in the course of living at sea. After all, when you spend days, weeks heaving on the seas, you come back and the only thing you have strength left for is giving thanks to God. Then you rest a bit, the sea calms down and becomes so beautiful that it involuntarily brings tears to your eyes. You just want to ask, "Why were you spinning me around and spraying me yesterday, you gorgeous thing? Why did drain us of everything, crush our hearts with fear?" Then you realize it yourself, you see that two sides of things have been revealed to you: a mortal terror sent by the enemy, a divine beauty that celebrates life. You rise and your heart is warmed by the simplicity with which the truth is revealed to you. The world becomes clear to you, everyone who lives here understands it too, so there will be no strife between brothers, because it wouldn't do any good, it would be senseless, wrong.

The further I went from the North, the more I could see that people didn't know this, didn't understand it. Brother growls at brother like a wolf, ready to tear the other apart. No one lives in harmony with anyone else. The simple folk are kinder, but the officials are evil like devils. But where do the officials come from? From among the simple folk, from their own. How many times did I see it: the most humble person, the most gentle, would turn into a beast after only catching a whiff of power and authority. As if he is getting revenge on everyone for his former humbleness. He doesn't have a wise thought in his mind, that tomorrow everything might be turned around. If not him, then his children would suffer. I just couldn't understand my nation. Life was hard and evil for those who didn't know the sea. Everything revolved in a senseless vortex, revealing time after time a new circle of evil ignorance. Many people didn't have the strength to stop, reflect on things, remember the old ways and come to the light.

I saw much of human ways. I realized many things and learned a great deal. I became wicked myself – a solitary sheep won't survive long among a pack of wolves. But always, when I reached the edge, I was able to stop. I remembered the White Sea and the black barge. I stood there on the edge, rooted to the spot. I looked down, I had the strength to take a step back, then another one. This is important, to have such strength. It is important to know where to draw that strength from. After the Great War I went back, to Keret.

Many years later, Grisha learned that his grandfather had died. He was alone at home then, then the phone rang. He picked it up. "Grandpa Fyodor is dead," came the voice of one of his uncles' wives down the line. The news stunned Grisha and he froze. After he hung up, he did not know what he should do. A strange feeling came upon him, one of emptiness and sadness; that probably he had something to do with it. For the first time the abstract word had become a poignant reality. For the first time, something cold flew right by him, he felt the biting wind from the beating of its heavy, silent wings. He sat there for half an hour, then managed to call his parents. They quickly got busy. Adults always know what to do in the event of a death. "Are you going?" his father asked him and Grisha shook his head sadly. He was very afraid. Afraid of seeing a man whom he remembered differently now lying in such an ugly state. During that half an hour over which he ruminated on the news, he remembered clearly and in vivid detail the last time he had gone fishing with Grandpa. They had taken an overnight trip to a distant lake. Grandpa was already slow on his feet and it took them a long time to get there. True, when they did get there it was still light out; during summers in the North it does not get dark. They set up their camp. It was simple: a campfire and a few spruce branches on the ground. Plus, a pole to hang the kettle over the fire. Along with some thick smoke to keep the mosquitoes away. That was their whole setup.

Grisha quickly caught some perch for bait, while Grandpa set out traps. A lot of them, about twenty. They were the simplest traps possible: a forked branch with a cord wound around it. The end of the cord went into the split end of one of the fork prongs, not tightly but so that it could be easily pulled out by a man's hand, which was equal to a pike's strength. The bottom of the forked stick was tied to a long pole stuck in the ground. At the end of the cord was a big, rusty hook, sometimes a triple hook but most often a single one. The hook would be stuck through the dorsal fin of a perch. The important thing was to avoid the spine, then the fish would go on living for a long time. Perch are a better fish for bait than roach, the latter quickly fade away. The pole would be set into the ground at an angle, so that the fork attached to it reached the water with the far end of the cord with the bait and the hook. The far end of the cord was slightly submerged in the water, so that the bait fish stayed at the surface and only it's back stuck out above the water. The bait perch would live for a long time there, swim around in circles, flop around all night and attract the attention of pike, who were greedy for any helpless fish. The big fish would grab the bait, swallow it and pull on the cord. The end of the cord would slip out of the gap in which it was lodged and then the cord would unravel. The pike, dismayed at the pain and the sudden captivity, would tug strongly on the cord several times and splash mightily all around. Then it would retreat to the depths and wait there in the hope that everything would somehow be resolved. Morning would come and the cord unwound from the forked branch would be visible from afar.

They did everything quickly then. Twenty traps on the shore is no small feat for an old man and a small boy. Grisha was tired. They drank tea that was thick and dark, like swamp water and smelled of smoke and wild rosemary. A few mosquitoes had been careless and now swam in the brew. "With meat in it," his grandfather joked.

Then Grisha fell asleep. It was hard to get to sleep, he felt anxious. To one side the campfire was flickering with a hot flame, to the other side was the cold, nighttime silence. Sometimes that silence was broken by indistinct sounds, splashes, a whisper, talking and in his sleep Grisha saw terrible things – a boat had come to shore there with strange men and they said some loud, angry words, a fight broke out and they tried to take Grandpa off somewhere. Grisha would awake with a start and always glimpse above their campfire the laughing eyes of his unsleeping grandfather. The old man knew everything and about forest dreams, too. Then Grisha would fall asleep again, at first everything was fine in his dream, even happy, but again anxiety overtook him, black inconsolable birds were crying loudly and he heard the heavy footsteps and whispering of strange, threatening men walking boldly over the earth. They came treading towards them, these dark, honest, deceitful men. Closer and closer, the heavy footsteps were now inside him, deep in his chest and Grisha again woke with a start and once more saw the smiling eyes of his grandfather.

Then he fell into a deep sleep. He was disturbed no longer by the heat, nor the cold; his body had accepted nature and become one with it. He plunged into an oblivion that happens when you know for certain that there are no other people around, which means there are no enemies either. Even the gaze of a big or small animal peering at you through the bushes does not bother you, for the animal is itself afraid of you. It really wants to eat something of what smells good from the pot. But the smell of smoke is unpleasant to it. The body lying by the fire might suddenly jump up and attack, with a flash of fire and a defending boom, inflicting an unexpected and mortal pain. The animal knows this and so it quietly, enviously roams at a distance. Only sometimes, after pondering and rolling its hungry saliva around its mouth, will it step on a dry branch with a crunching sound, scare itself and try to silently sink into the night so as never to return.

Grisha slept soundly as the morning came and he woke up only when the fresh, pure sun began to shine bright on his face, but through his back, which had slid from the spruce branches, he felt the cold morning ground. He opened his eyes. The sun was still quite low in the sky. Over the lake hung a light, low mist. It covered the entire surface of the water with a fluffy, thin layer, like cotton wool. There in the mist, knee-deep in it, his grandfather was walking in the shallows. He seemed to be walk-ing on water, slightly sinking into it but effortlessly gliding right along, without stumbling. In each hand he held three pikes by their jaws. They were already dead, he had killed them, but they had managed to bite his fingers and blood dripped from his hands. It mixed with the blood of the fish and fell in drops into the water. There it slowly dissolved in ghastly red circles as if they were the gleams of a flame on the water. Only the light splashing of his steps reached Grisha, only the brightly lit figure of his grandfather could be seen against the background of the distant dark coast and the bright blue sky. It even seemed to Grisha that he could hear the subtle round sounds of the red drops falling into the water. But it only seemed like that. Grandpa was coming ever closer. Grisha lay there watching motionlessly. It all took his breath away: the sun, the sky, this dear and strong relative – a man with his prey that he had won in battle and the vague mist. Closer to the shore the mist had dissipated and with a suddenly expanded view Grisha saw how the red drops of blood, falling into transparent water that was penetrated by the sun's rays, would – for a moment before they died – be diluted to form a small, round rainbow of red hues in the water that parted in front of them. "Get up, little fish, let's have breakfast," his grandfather shouted loudly, with a youthfulness in his voice and the faint echo answered from the far shore.

His parents left for two days for the funeral. During this time Grisha stayed at home with his little brother Konstantin. The latter still did not understand anything. They played, ate, fought – as an elder brother often does with a younger one, until some adult age when suddenly affection arises out of somewhere. During this time, Grisha tried not to think about his grandfather. He locked up all his thoughts about Grandpa in some distant, secret place of his soul, along with all his fears about what had happened to Grandpa and what would happen to him someday. It was easier to not think. In general, to not think is always easier. It is just that without that, somehow one cannot live one's life.

His parents came home with photos of the funeral. They let the children look at them. Even after he grew up, Grisha could not understand what they had taken them for. Why photograph dead, departed people. It is clear that people had an external justification for this – they wanted to preserve to the end the image of a relative, a progenitor, someone who had raised them and preceded them with his own departure. But this justification was awkward, absurd even – love is stronger than optical illusions and there is no beauty in death. In the photos the coffin was placed on chairs, some people stood around it with predictable faces, mournful, but for that reason not particularly expressive – at funerals one has to mourn. Grandpa was lying in the coffin. Rather, it wasn't Grandpa, it was just his body lying there. It did not look like him, just like an abandoned chrysalis does not look like a fluttering butterfly. There was one good thing about these photos, perhaps: nowhere else could one see what that container had consisted of. However, Grisha only understood this later, after he had grown old, but back then he had pushed the absurd, unwanted photos away in horror. The impression on his soul was more important, more correct and the photos sought to destroy it. He did not let them. So, he did not begin to examine them, only quickly looked over them and saw Grandpa's high forehead and lips pressed together sternly. He also knew about the three holes in Grandpa's back.

"Can you imagine, the nurse said that towards the end, he kept asking to go out to sea. Take me out, he said, to get a glimpse of it for the last time. Ha, he suddenly wants a vacation," Grisha's father laughed in a spasmodic and mysterious manner. He had said this to Grisha's mother, but Grisha heard it and for some reason remembered the words. Only after several years had passed did he learn from his father that Grandpa, before he died, had fought with all his relatives, with his sons. He kept demanding to be heard, he shouted that they didn't understand anything that he needed to explain something. That the sea doesn't accept murderers. That God and death aren't the same things. As well as other ravings.

His sons, after having suffered from his strict authority and his temper in bygone years, now felt that they were the stronger, so they simply smiled and nodded. "We understand, old man! You don't need to explain." So often, people feel no need for truth. None at all. They do not even require knowledge – things are easier without it.

Grandfather would get angry and fall into his usual rage, albeit one that was now feeble and powerless. Then everyone would leave him with a feeling of resentment. When they put him in the hospital, no one wanted to visit him. Let him lie there alone and suffer. He'll get softer, he'll learn to speak more gently in his old age.

When they came for the body, the nurse who had tended to him looked at them with amazement. "I thought he was all alone," she said. "No one came to visit him."

Grisha's father recounted all this calmly, but he hid his reddened eyes.

Grisha did not like to visit the cemetery. It took him a long time to get ready. There was some adult, grown-man duty in this, to gird one's loins and go down to the place where they have buried something that lives in you, in your heart, from childhood; it lives on brightly, angrily, unpredictably, happily, merrily. It lives desperately and hurriedly, greedily, in spite of its own death. He took a long time to get ready, then he got in the car.

Everything around was like it was usually. His eyes were used to seeing it and it bored him. He drove down a road lined with bleak marshes that occasionally gave way to stunted, mossy spruce groves, their twisted, tortured nature mirroring the life here. Among the swamps there were sad dead trees that seemed to have chosen the freedom of this open space, but then they were withered at the roots by the unpropitious, rust-colored soil. Often this sickly forest was cut open by brutal clearings, where merciless iron had destroyed, had mixed with the soil an order of things that had formed over centuries. In these clearings everything was brown: the crooked branches, the stumps of trees, the huge, age-old trunks thrown into a wild disorder. Mankind did nothing about this, the forest stood silent and nature, with a shameless tenderness, had exposed its lacerations and tried to lick its wounds with some young, timid undergrowth. Grisha drove by and looked at all of this and felt a chill in his heart. "Is it really always like that, is there really no end to it, no way out? Is there no way for the soul to burst forth? Is it really that way, why? Why do we live such resigned, evil, reckless and absurd lives? We live lives where we blame others and find excuses for ourselves in everything. We live without fearing anything and yet being afraid of everything. Without trusting in the horizon and noticing the earth under our feet. Grandpa's life was like that too…"

Here he told himself, "Stop!" It was not even he who said it; rather something powerful spoke up inside him. As if it came of its own accord and not voluntarily on his part. Because the first part was true, but from that moment it had ceased to be truth. From the moment when he had started to talk about Grandpa. It was wrong to muse on humility or faithlessness. It was not appropriate for him. It did not fit in his train of thought or the surrounding nature. The nature too had suddenly changed. Grisha parked the car at the path leading to the cemetery. Driving further was not allowed, he had to go on foot.

A sandy hill and below it, at a small distance, a lake. High, red pine trees that shot into the blue sky.   The sky had cleared just like that. Water, the same blue color, was melting below. The black rectangles of headstones. Occasionally, pillars with red stars on them. Crosses, most of them new. Grisha remembered that until quite recently, there were no crosses at all, only on the oldest graves of all. Now there were more of them, they had appeared and were now mixed with the stars and the black rectangles. All of this was correct. Wrought-iron fences surrounded the tombs of loved ones. The solitary, abandoned mounds that interested no one quickly fell level with the earth and were overgrown with grass. Featureless graves of a red color with names and dates deteriorated, rotted, fell apart. There was a certain truth in this, too. It was quiet. Even the mosquitoes buzzed in a timid way. Only the birds were unafraid of death. They fluttered around, chirped and pecked at the humble foods left on graves.

Grisha spent a long time looking for his grandfather's grave. Finally, he found it. It was the same as many others, a black stone at Grisha's feet. A local worker had hastily carved a portrait of Grandpa. In his army tunic, with medals on his chest. A stern gaze that suggested a knowledge of many things. Thin, pursed lips. A mocking, slightly snide expression in his laugh lines. A firm, stubborn chin.

Grisha suddenly thought that this uniform did not suit his grandfather. People inadvertently find themselves wearing it and few of them enjoy it. Much more appropriate for Grisha's grandfather would have been hunting or seagoing clothes – an old, reliable waterproof cloak, a sailor's striped shirt and long boots. Freedom and necessity.

He stood there looking at the grave. He said nothing. It was always strange when someone came to the graves and greeted the dead, talked with them. He just could not understand this. To this day. Therefore, he stood there without speaking, only looking at the grave and trying to observe the finer details, the insects and the pine needles on the cold, smooth stone. Otherwise it would have been very painful. Many questions would have arisen, ones without answers to them. Therefore, he only looked on wordlessly. He stood like that for a long time. He had not taken anything to eat or drink – that had also seemed a strange thing to do. But now, all of a sudden it became something natural. But there was no one with him. Therefore, he simply stood there. Then he turned around and walked away. Only at the end, he ran his hand along the gravestone. He touched something cold, within which there was something warm. His hand shook at the unexpectedness of it. But no, a ray of sun had only warmed a small part of the stone, its right corner, so it became oddly warm. For some reason Grisha regretted that no cross stood on his grandfather's grave. He really liked the Pomor crosses that he had seen in his trips to the North. Eight-pointed Orthodox crosses, generally ordinary ones, but on top there would be a little house that was clapped together from two boards and protected the cross from the brutal sea weather. Something necessary. The cross itself had words carved all over it. Sometimes words impossible to understand, sometimes he could decipher old, long-forgotten ones. Grisha somehow regretted that his grandfather's grave had no such cross. It needed one somehow and no one had known, had guessed. It needed one.

With effort, Grisha turned his back to the grave and walked off. He left without looking around and tried to slow his involuntarily quickening step. He had been moving quickly because the path went down from the hill, so steep that it was almost straight down. Towards the lake and along it, with bushes around him. Only suddenly, as he quickly moved along into the small meadow reaching to the lake shore, he stopped in his tracks: a white swan was launching itself from the shore and then it swam on, the water swirling behind it from its motor-like feet. With a good splashing, one as vigorous as a large boat's. It made a lot of noise as it went. The water behind it was split into two waves by an arrow at whose tip was the swan. Grisha had seen swans along the White Sea, but never here. He stood frozen and could not take his eyes off it. It was as if the swan had been waiting for it, but now its work was done and it hastened towards the North. It swam on faster and faster, then it started to beat with its wings to help. It now put its full strength into it, though it was still in the water. Then it strained and ran over the surface. It ran flapping its wings. But what splashing and spray of watery joy came from it! Suddenly Grisha saw in this cloud of spray what the swan itself had made: a rainbow shimmered. It was small, like a solemn arch. Now the bird flew into it. Through it, higher and higher, towards the North.

"Fly, little fish, fly!" shot up from his heart just like that.

                                * * *

The bear has many names. The Russians know it as the stomping one, Mikhail, the flatfooted one, the master of the forest, the brown one. The Karelians call it *karhu* and *konti*. Among the Finns it is *tapio*, the spirit of the forest. All these names are used in order to avoid accidentally calling it by its real name. And that name is Beast.

Its claws are as long as a man's hand. Its teeth are blades. Its legs so thick that you can wrap your hands around them. It runs through the forest faster than a horse. With one blow it can shatter a moose's spine. To it a human being is just a thin reed. Only once it is skinned, does its body greatly resemble a person's, to a degree that is scary. The arms, the legs, the belly. A dead man, whether one who has hung himself there or who has died for some other reason, is generally a treat. Free, legal loot.

The bear walks without making a sound, without the crack of a twig. It can climb a tree in a flash. It can spot a hunter and come so close that no weapon will help.

Old people say that when St. Varlaam of Keret lived in his forest cell, the Beast came to him in a bear's guise. It roared, dug at the ground and swung its head in fury. But Varlaam made the sign of the cross over it and then placed his hand on its head. The Beast fell quiet then, calmed down. It went off without making a sound.

The North is the end of the world. An end where the dreams of freedom can come true, the only place where a man is not subject to the whims of another. Whether this is on the sea, in the forests, in the tundra or among the wild rocks – his life, his death depend only on God and the man himself, nothing stands between the two. The man needs to only heed God within him, nothing will hinder him from walking his own free and right road. The North is a border between light and darkness, any words, any crafty designs are vain – people can see right through you and you can see right through others. It feels easy, because what is it, if not happiness, to not live among lies but among brightness, among the cold, hard truth. What is it then, if not happiness, to know that you are free, that you are the master of your own self and your destiny, you are your own steersman and tailwind. The sea is your father and the earth your mother, there are no limits to your freedom and curiosity.

So, a thought came into my head, dear friends, of a difficult business but one so pleasant among my inquisitive dreams. I was restless all the long winter and mild summer and I kept thinking that thought. I have been to many lands: down the Norwegian way and in the city of Arkhangelsk. I have spent the winter in Novaya Zemlya and I have gone many times to Grumant to hunt for sea creatures. Here is what came into my head. Beyond Norway are the Danish and Hanseatic lands, as everyone knows. Our men have traveled there too and told us about life in the West. People there live well, but it is a life too boring for us, one without bravado. Things in the North are also clear: there is perpetual ice there, the kingdom of the walrus and the white bear. Men cannot reach farther than Grumant, regardless of what mariner you are, for you will reach the icy limits and then involuntarily turn back. In the South matters are also straightforward: there is the Russian land, Novgorod and the tsardom of Muscovy. They are our own people, Russians, though not the same as us. They live without the sea and they do not know freedom, for they are all under some master, the tsar there and his servants. That is also clear. Towards the East, however, is an obscure direction, one unknown and alluring. When you pass Novaya Zemlya and the Matochkin Strait you head out into the sea – there the Kara Sea begins and the land of the Samoyeds. Our men have traveled there too and then recounted fantastical tales of the numberless herds of sea animals, about incredible schools of fish. There are so many fur animals that one can catch them by hand. You can knock birds down with a stick as they fly by in thick flocks. Reindeer numbering into the many thousand wander across the tundra. Black oil, the blood of the earth, rises on its own from under the marshes. Gold nuggets lie on the banks of the great rivers. But what is found even further beyond that, no one knows – no one has ever gone there. They feared to go. It frightens me too. But I am sorely fascinated by what there might be in the distant East, what outlandish beasts and lands lie there. What do I have to lose? We only live once. One must think, prepare well and make a ship ready. Go with God, to His glory. I resolved, my dears, to head east out of my interest in many things, to the lands where the sun rises, whence the cold wind comes, sometimes bringing what sounds like a fearsome, drawn-out call.

The preparations were long but we were glad to undertake them. There is nothing better in this world than when you make a decision, get to it, prepare, trust in God and make no mistakes yourself. The first task was to assemble such a crew that was young at heart and experienced in these affairs. There are plenty such men among our own. After all, you are not a Pomor if distant lands do not call to you and you will not become experienced unless you study the things of the North in all their finer details – you would not even survive to maturity of body and soul. But if a fine reward is promised, then it is a rare man among us who will hold back. That is the way we live: our freedom, our business and feeding our wives and children.

I remember like it was yesterday the moment when I definitively resolved on my course. It was a bright day, mid-March. Where we live, winter always still reigns fiercely in March, it is a month more vicious than February. But on rare occasions, the sun looks out from behind the dark clouds and sometimes the sky clears entirely and it is celebration then in heaven and on earth. It is white everywhere around you, peaceful. Only the snow shines so violently and silently, like the eternal flame of desire that burns silently and constantly within a man. A desire for a new, interesting life, for strength and freedom. You are blinded, you lose your wits from the unbearable yearning for it. You cringe from this pain which is called happiness, then open your eyes and a wind – ever so light – blows by and a light, hardly noticeable drizzle falls from unseen mountain clouds. As if God is shaking the dust from His weary feet, the mud on the merciless roads turns incredible, bright silver, which shines to praise the rightness of divine providence. I stood thus, frozen to the spot and struck by the vast distances suddenly revealed to me, by the noble and gladsome yearning I felt, a bright splendor came into my head. I considered this instant to be a blessing, wiped the grateful tears from my eyes, put my hat on and began to think seriously about the journey. It is no wonder that our family's name is Shaloumov, for there is indeed a *shalost'*, a mischievousness among us, but we have our wits about us too, for you cannot get anywhere without that. You cannot throw yourself blindly into the ocean and without a jaunty courage you will be sitting on the shore, scratching yourself and letting your soul rot away slowly.

Indeed, the men were resolved to go with me on this long journey! There was Senka Oshkuy, who with his brother had hunted the bear without a gun many a time – his brother would goad the bear, cause it to rise up on its hind legs, then he would get the creature on the bear spear. Senka would then beat the bear over the head with the butt of his axe; with the first blow he did the bear in, for there could be no second – the beast is so fierce and fast. Vanya the Rower, the most boisterous man on the Murman Coast, who could travel the sea for days on end without sail and row the fishing boat that we call a *shneka* thirty miles. Petka Shueretsky, the most eager hunter of sea creatures – I used to go with him to hunt and I admired how he could take out a seal from far away with just one shot, then he would ski towards it through freezing, icy water, stepping on the sea like on dry land. He would direct the ends of his skis by pulling on strings attached to them, all the while whistling gaily, as if he was not facing deadly danger on the sea but was merely on a light stroll, waving a stick and warding off flies. Seventeen more men contracted to go with me, each one stronger than the last and capable in affairs. We were a band of renown, and with such men my confidence grew by one hundred times and our journey began to seem not so terrible. With those lads, even hell would not be so bad and heaven was not too far. They believed in me and chose me to be their helmsman, so they began to prepare for the journey. We dubbed our ship the *Varlaam Keretsky*.

TROPARION IN THE FIRST TONE

Enlightened by God's grace from above, O venerable father, thou left the earthly sorrow of all the tumult of the world. Out of love of Christ thou didst reject it all defiantly. Thou followed Christ according to the Gospel and didst obey His will in all things, and relied upon him with all thy mind and heart unequivocally, and thou renounced the flesh with fasting and vigil, and in prayer unceasing thou begged for God's mercy and the intercession of the Most Holy Theotokos. In return God granted thee strength against the fierce enemy. Without fear of the cold, heavy wind and the harsh sea, thou humbled thyself still more, and thou didst make a journey in a small boat over the depths, through the turbulent sea, inspired by divine providence, and thou made the impassable sea way at Svyatoy Nos safe from the sea worm and safely passable by men without any harm. Leading an angelic life, also after your death thou dost distribute the blessing of miracles, and thus we come in faith to the reliquary with thy venerable relics, most blessed Varlaam, our father, and we cry out to thee: pray to Christ the Lord that He may save our souls.

* * *

Travel is exciting. Whether you are driving or going on foot or in a boat, the landscape changes but nature remains eternally the same. What makes it so great is that, along with your awoken interest in things, there is something unshakable, something that you can rely on. One wants to rely on something, for life is constantly changing and unpredictable, death is always near and unexpected, only faith in something will help you avoid panicking before the fast and successive change of generations and fates. Travel is exciting: you meet new people, discover new cities and countries and, after you have heard a countless number of life stories, you come to one conclusion: we all have something in common. After you have suffered various things from other people and from yourself, you suddenly grasp the simple things, they prove to be so deep that divine providence can be seen in them, even by simple mortals. Any sort of journey is good in that you begin it at one time and always finish it at another, you can look back and appreciate the path you have traveled. Then you can look ahead without fear. You are attentive and you notice how you yourself have changed, what barely perceptible joys and sorrows the people you meet have experienced. Like in your wildest dreams, you are carried across time and you travel only a small part of the way. The most important thing is that you realize that your soul ripens from experience. Whether you have traveled a simple road or a complicated one, just look, a simple, eternal unity will appear before you, inseparably linked: space, time, human beings. You are amazed that you never realized this before. You feel happiness, but then you are saddened. But it will be a good sadness; the experience of your journeys will give you the strength to rejoice at the living and not fear the dead so much. As an observant person, you will become stronger and brighter. Complicated things will not become simple, but you have the strength and mind to get to grips with them. Travel is exciting.

2005, GREMUCHA

They say that love for one's country is ultimately based on chemistry. Just like all other human sensations. Let it be so, let it always be down to hormones at work, but the instant that Grisha first saw the Keret, his eyes immediately filled with unbidden tears and his chest breathed in the fresh sea air deeply, so deeply that his ribs ached. Perhaps this was just a sudden emotional outburst – they say that happens too. But now every time, every year it seemed to him, to someone coming out of forested and marshy places, that his life was in vain, if he did not make it to the Keret. How this happened, where it came from, he did not know. The memory of his forebears told him nothing about any preserved images and legends. His previous life had drawn him towards completely different places: deserts, mountains and other exotic locales. Big cities and faraway countries were a spicy attraction, representing uncharted possibilities and delectable promises. A sensual, heavy desire to embrace the entire world, to taste it in full and, in its individual parts, long took hold of him, until suddenly in one of those moments of his varied life he caught a whiff of the light smell of the northern sea. Unexpectedly, inconceivably, but like a salmon that could still seek out its native river from hundreds of miles away, he was drawn northwards. If earlier, his body had led him headlong and gloomily, now his soul was tense, it froze in anticipation and suddenly began to sing, he had no strength to resist this bright, joyfully ringing song. He went off, swam towards it and into it, against his will, in spite of his persistent need for comfort and warmth, he ended up in a strange, wild place where the turbulent Keret River falls into the sea; in the midst of the ruins overgrown with various kinds of grass, in the wasteland, a bright chapel stands. Here the torment and the fear have ended and grace filled his soul like the sea breeze. He suddenly felt at home here.

The Keret always accepted him. Or rather, it seemed to study him. In the North it is always like that: no man rushes towards you with arms wide open. But he will not reject you, either. At first he will examine you and direct a couple of words your way. He is wise – there is no use hiding – and he will know what kind of person you are. This is where the secret of their piercing blue eyes lies: Pomors can look straight into your soul. They have a subtle feel for people. If something is not right, they will not yell at you or try to set you straight. They will simply turn away. They are finished dealing with you.

That is how the Keret examined Grisha, scrutinized him. With a smile hidden deep in its gray breakers, it watched him learn to build his first boat. It watched as Grisha's fishing skills came back to him, as if from scratch, after so many years of living in civilization, he prepared his fishing rod. With a stern, disapproving glance it watched him try fishing with a net, wondering if this man would know his limits. But once, when Grisha and his brother Konstantin had left their net in the water, just carelessly departing without raising it, the Keret frowned. For an entire year after that he dreamed that the Keret was looking at him, without speaking, from under the gray moss of the overgrown rocks. The next year, Grisha spent a long time looking for that net so that his soul would be released from the guilt. When he found the net and raised it, he caught a glimpse of a half-rotten salmon in it. That is how the Keret had punished him, he always remembered this lesson. His hands, which were slipping on the slimy loops of the fishing net, all covered with a morbid sludge, remembered too, as did his nostrils breathing in the hellish smell. Grisha and his brother struggled with the net and finally hauled it up, then they sunk it by rolling it into a ball and attaching a weight to it. The next morning, the Keret sent a huge black snake to his campsite, so that it could once more make clear the rules of life in the North.

Only in the fifth year did the river give Grisha his first wonderful fish and it came as an enormous pleasure. He rejoiced, feeling like he was the first man ever in the northern lands, until he read the old Pomor tale: "Only in the fifth year does the White Sea give a fisherman salmon…"

Slowly, carefully, they studied one another. The sea and the river showed forth all kinds of wonders, yet there were also trials. But everything went peacefully for the time being. So smoothly in fact that Grisha was convinced that the river had accepted him, had murmured about this to the sea and that he now belonged here.

The weather this time spoiled them. It was a quiet, sunny evening. There was a thick smell of vegetation, sweet, almost to the point of revulsion. The Keret babbled its eternal song as it flowed over the rocks and entrusted its happiness and its sorrow to the sea. The incredible sky hung light blue over all of this and the setting sun shone softly. Grisha, feeling in his usual good spirits, made a campfire. His brother was busy nearby with their canoe and Nikolai Eliseyev was sitting in a folding chair. Nikolai was sitting on the bank of the river where it rushed into the sea. He was looking around him with eyes wide and then said aloud, "Pity I didn't bring a *kohta* with me. My wife told me to bring a *kohta* along, but I guess I forgot it. It'll be tough without a *kohta*."

Finally, Grisha turned away from the fire and towards Nikolai. He was already used to his friend's constant joking and talk of how everything should be done in life, but now he was happy to hear a new word. "Nikolai, what's a *kohta*?" he asked. "Is that something Karelian? I've never heard that word before."

"You don't know?!" Nikolai burst out. "It's made from wool, thick to keep the rain off. And warm!" He seemed to be lost in old memories.

Now Grisha got it. "You mean what Russians call a *kofta*?"

"Some people might say *kofta*, but for me it's *kohta*, a Karelian word, not a Russian one." Nikolai's mood had changed quickly and sharply, but he never got truly angry. His heart ached for all things Karelian.

Grisha tried to hide his smile and asked, "Do you remember when you taught me and my Dad how to eat salted pork fat the Karelian way?"

Nikolai frowned. "I don't recall anything like that."

"We were eating lunch in the village and you had come. You saw how we were cutting it and you said, 'You aren't eating it right. I'll show you how you ought to do it.'"

"And?" Nikolai was now curious himself.

"We were cutting off thick pieces and putting it on bread, but you said we had to cut it thin, so that it would melt in our mouths. 'So you don't have to chew it. Don't chew it,' you said."

"Yes, that's right. It tastes better that way."

"My dad is also Karelian. He watched your little lesson with a frown, then he said, 'Nikolai, you chewed it. You said not to chew it, but you chewed it.'"

"That's not right! It's not right!" Nikolai cried.

Grisha and his brother could not hold back. "You taught us not to chew it, but you chewed it!"

After they had eaten dinner, Grisha could not resist stripping naked and going into the water. The water in the river proved to be cool, but not the painful, stinging cold that makes bathing in the North a matter of true courage. It was impossible to swim anywhere – the rapids were roaring all around –so he stayed in the water at the bank, grabbed onto the branch of a bush growing alongside and lay still. His body was washed by lively, tickling streams and it immediately tensed somehow after its relaxation on the ground above. The sun warmed the top of his back. An incredible and delectable smell of freshness came from the water. A light fog rising from the surface of the water wafted in his nostrils with a sensation of calm and happiness. The eternal roar of the foam separated his hearing and his consciousness from vain things. Grisha froze in the water. Then he felt happiness. Never before had it been such a complete happiness. There had always been something slightly in the way. Now, as he merged with the river, he seemed to absorb its impetuous bliss. As if he had come back to something forgotten. The sun's rays shone softly through the little pool where he swayed in the water. A short distance away, the rushing stream turned white, opaque, savage. From the corner of his eye he suddenly saw a small fish jump out and pass right by his face. The silver fish froze and barely moved its fins. Grisha froze too. For a long minute he stared at it, then he turned silly: he let go of the branch, kicked at the water and tried to catch the fish with his mouth. The fish easily slipped away, back into the depths, but Grisha was already caught in the current and had to get back to shore with two hectic strokes. Out of the terror and excitement he ingested some water that went right to his lungs. Coughing and laughing at his own self, he again, with some difficulty, grabbed hold of the bush.

"Hey, Aquaman, come on out of there!" His brother had remembered him. Meanwhile, Nikolai had lost his wariness at new places and shouted enthusiastically, "Come forth, my son!" A happiness had overtaken them, too.

Grisha got out of the water reluctantly, feeling the drops of water roll down his rejuvenated body. He looked at the shouting men with a hostile stare. "How noisy they are. People!"

Then there was some talking, liberal drinking and lying in the grass. Some light walks in the surrounding area.

"It's like a resort. A real resort," Nikolai could not get enough of these new places.

However, as soon as Nikolai had said this in a relaxed tone, Grisha suddenly tensed. Even he did not initially understand what it was that had frightened him. The sun seemed to be shining just the same as before. Maybe the wind had slightly changed direction and a slight chill had come. He looked around, baffled. Then he saw it. On the other bank of the wide river, a big, triangular rock rose. Whether the sun was now shining at a different angle, or whether they simply had not noticed it before, a demon sat on the smooth surface of the rock, facing them. It was small, hunched and black, it propped its horned head up with its hand and stared at them. Grisha shuddered.

"Look, guys!"

"What? Where?" They remained as carefree as before.

"Over there. You see? To the left of the big fir."

"Oh my!"

They fell silent. The demon did not move either.

"It's just a shadow, a black one," his brother said with a lowered voice. "I'll get a photo of it now." He crept over to grab his camera and began to fidget with it. The sun disappeared behind a small cloud. The demon disappeared. For all three of the men, their spirits had fallen.

"Alright, resort guests, let's hit the hay. We've got a long day ahead of us tomorrow." Grisha suppressed the unease he felt and crawled into the tent. "It was just a shadow," he told himself before he fell asleep.

The next morning, they awoke in a fantastic mood. Though they had difficult work ahead of them, everything seemed great. Can it really be called work when you are on the road! A journey on the sea is the greatest joy a man can experience. Towards uncharted worlds.

They set up their canoe quickly and energetically. They threw their things inside as if it was the easiest thing in the world, then they just as easily took their own places there. Their shotgun, fishing rods, tent, various food – it had seemed to be a lot and the whole car had been packed, but everything fit in their little canoe and there remained room for themselves too. They carried it into the water carefully, so that they would not scratch it on the stones, they managed to establish a rhythm right away. They were doing very well now that there were three of them. "And one, and two, and three." The sea foamed at the canoe's nose. The ancient shores dwindled behind them. A wake trailed at their stern. "And one, and two, and three."

They were now out at sea and gently moving along the rocks. One has to be very courageous to take a canoe far from the seashore. A whole host of such courageous men now lie at the ocean bottom. It is better to proceed slowly, with awareness and caution. Grisha was their steersman, he sat at the stern and controlled the rudder. He sought constantly not to lose his sense of responsibility and to think carefully despite the emotions he felt at being at sea. The other two in front laughed, chatted, rowed vigorously. It was good that they had a lot of youthful energy in their arms and adventures were awaiting them. Grisha himself was still troubled constantly by the sea demon's appearance the day before. It did not augur well. They should expect tricks in store.

They quickly slipped through the Uzkaya Salma strait and came out into the open sea. It was lovely all around them. Red rocks, dark-green forests, the open blue of the boundless surface. But Grisha knew already that things here were not so simple. From some barely noticeable clues he could guess that once, a sawmill had stood here. There had been a fisherman's wharf, where they hauled fish in and gutted it. In another place a salt works had been located before and Pomor salt had fed the entire nation. Soon the first fishermen's shack should appear, where in times past men had caught fish like vegetables in the garden – they came, took it out of the ocean and then went off with their catch. Where did everything disappear to? Where did all the life go from these places? The silent rocks said nothing in answer and the age-old fir trees only swung their branches sadly.

The sea began to rock them ever more strongly. A bad wind had come, from the north east, the *polunoshnik* as it was called in olden times. The waves danced. Grayish clouds flew in the sky above. All this had happened quickly, in not even half an hour. They looked down and spray was already flying into their boat. Their trousers were drenched and it was uncomfortable to sit there all wet. Grisha suffered it for a long time. It was thirty kilometers altogether to the mouth of the Letnyaya River. There they would quickly reach the protection of its high banks and calmly reach some lovely places. Already, they were halfway there if they just thought about it. Gremucha now appeared. Some called it Gremucha, others called it Kapucha. It was a high mountain right on the shore, with high, precipitous cliffs plunging right into the sea. The sea was deep here, it was scary even to think about it. It was called Gremucha for the way it thundered during storms. The name Kapucha came from the sea kale that the waves cast up onto the rocks in bunches, with the sea kale lying in wild curls after the strong winds. Now too, Grisha looked and saw how the cliffs were beginning to rumble. Foam swirled around the foot of the mountain. Water was already fiercely lashing over the sides of their canoe. Regardless of their desire to immediately reach their goal, they would have to wait this one out. It was not for nothing that Grisha had felt a heaviness in his soul since that morning. It was not for nothing that the little demon had teased them the day before.

"Guys, that's it, we're turning to shore," he said in a tough, commanding voice.

The others tried to argue. "Why? We're moving quickly. It's summer, not autumn. We'll make it there in a flash."

"You want to try landing on those cliff faces if something goes wrong? Are you going to cling to them with your fingernails?" Grisha had already made his decision and turned the rudder sharply towards shore without listening to their objections.

They reached the shore quickly and managed to find a flat spot at the foot of Gremucha. While they were getting out, the waves lashed the canoe hard several times and filled it halfway full with water in a mere second. Thank God they had made it out first.

"The storms don't last long in the summer, so it'll calm down, maybe by this evening," Grisha tried to console them, though he kept looking towards the east. Heavy gray clouds were coming across the sky from that direction.

The weather was as if it was unleashed and the bright sun suddenly gave way to darkness. The wind howled shrilly through the pine trees and along with the rain, which now came parallel with the ground, it brought spray from the ocean waves and with a roar they crashed on the rumbling cliff. The large sea pebbles, in these parts are called *areshnik*, the size of babies' heads, rustled as they rolled back and forth on the gently sloping shores of the small coves wedged between the cliffs of Gremucha. Their rustling was dangerous somehow, like the rustling of the scales of a big snake. Gray foam extended in strips across the entire sea and beyond the horizon. The sky seemed to be lying on the earth and crushing her with its gray belly. There was not a single patch of light on its dark-gray skin.

The danger of despair spoke all around them in different voices.

Good thing they had a canister of pure alcohol with them. It was small, about ten liters and it was now the only white spot against the background of the surrounding twilight. They quickly diluted the alcohol with water in the proportion "for facing adversity" and got down to setting up camp for the storm. They pitched their tent on a slope which was slippery with wet moss. They then made a fire from the bleached driftwood that had accumulated everywhere, dry branches that had been brought here from some unknown country. From the thicker pieces of the driftwood they cut some sticks, Nikolai used his Karelian cleverness and stuck them vertically into the gaps between the stones. With grunts and sometimes slipping on the rocks, they then hauled over some logs that were just as bleached and washed clean by the sea and created a wall from them, affixing them to the driftwood pieces with rope at some points and nails at others. Though the sound of their hatchets could not block out the howling of the elements, it still instilled their low spirits with a certain confidence and a feeling that all would be well. In less than an hour, a log wall stood on the rocks and shielded the fire and the backs of the men sitting at it from the wind and the low-flying rain. The fire flickered in circles from the gusts of wind, but it burned hot and bright, holding firm behind the age-old, dry branches which shined white everywhere, like dug-up bones. Their sleeping bags were already snug in the tent, which was now fluttering like a sail under the nearby pines. Water was boiling in a kettle over the fire and their pot exuded the familiar smells of an expedition: tinned meat and pasta.

"Look, what's this?" Grisha's brother turned over in his hands a piece of wood with remnants of old writing on it.

"I don't know," Grisha said. "It looks like part of a ship, like a bowsprit. What's written on it?"

"Well, I don't know, it's hard to make anything out. I can see something like 'arlaa'. Oh, here's clearer: 'keretsk'."

"Alright, let's not worry about it. Better we down some booze." Grisha was itching for a drink.

"If you say so," said Konstantin, who was not opposed either. He threw the chunk of wood into the fire, which immediately flared brightly.

"Shame I didn't bring a *kohta* along," said Nikolai dreamily, as he wrapped his canvas raincoat tightly around him.

"Again you and your *kofta*," Konstantin said laughing and warmed his frozen hands at the fire.

"Being without a *kohta* means death for a Karelian," Konstantin said as if giving them a lesson, then they all allowed themselves a second big draft of liquor before dinner.

That night the sound persisted. The very low howl that the rocks gave off seemed unbearable. But they had nowhere to go, they just had to be patient and get through this.

"Just like the old Pomors," Grisha tried to cheer everyone up the next morning as the dark, leaden grayness of the night gave way to the light-gray dawn. "They would spend months living on Grumant during the winter, or on the Murmansk coast, or Chukotka. Without the sun rising at all. What saved them from losing their minds in that darkness were the tales that they would tell each other. As well as the work they had to do."

"Where do you know that from?" Konstantin mumbled discontentedly. For all three of them, their mood resembled the weather.

"I read it," Grisha answered, slightly proud at this knowledge. "I've read a lot of stuff… How they would take cottage cheese and lettuce with them to protect themselves against scurvy. How they drifted on ice floes while pursuing animals, how they made hearths from clay that they had brought with them, they burned wood that they had brought and made their fires under their boat which was turned over. How they would wait out snowstorms in the Kola Peninsula under their *keryozhka*, which was a kind of sleigh that was shaped like a narrow boat…"

"Alright, then," Nikolai shivered. "Enough talking. Let's go try and catch some fish."

No fish were caught. The rough waves threw their lure back onto the shore before it even got a chance to sink. The animals and birds had also all gone away to hide from the bad weather. Around them was only the wind and the raging waters, plus, the endless downpour reigned.

"Ugh, the *polunoshnik* is blaring in the middle of the summer," Grisha again showed off his knowledge. "The Pomors had a name for every wind. The *polunoshnik* was the northeast wind, the fiercest one of all. The *gorny* came from the shore, the south. The *shelonnik* blew from the southwest, it was a good wind. It got its name from the Shelon River that's near Novgorod. There was a battle there once with the Muscovites, when they massacred their own people, fellow Christians."

"That is how it has always been for us Russians, brother fighting against brother," Konstantin said gloomily. Things between him and Grisha had also not been easy.

"Oh, come on! Who cares? Nikolai, come on, I want to show you how *rhodiola rosea* grows. It's also called northern ginseng."

"Does it have healthy properties?" Nikolai asked.

"Does it! If you boil it and then drink it, then you won't get any hangover the next morning, even from the strongest liquor. It's also good for your stomach and your immune system. For just about everything."

On the morning of the third day Grisha again headed over the rocks for *rhodiola rosea*. They had drank such good tea from it the evening before. But on the small meadow there was nothing at all. Not even the slightest bush. He returned to their camp astounded. "Can you believe it, it has disappeared somewhere!"

"Yeah, somewhere," Nikolai flashed a Karelian grin. "We've got to have something to bring home from here. Since we don't have any fish, or meat…" With satisfaction he patted his backpack, which was near to bursting. His face radiated such a joy at his collection that it was impossible to be angry at him. The three of them had a good laugh for the first time in several days.

"Maybe we should walk back along the shore and haul the boat and our stuff?" Nikolai was tired of sitting still.

"That would be unrealistic," Grisha burst his bubble. "The stones, pebbles, the driftwood and the wet rocks. We'd break our legs."

Moving on was truly impossible. Nowhere to go.

On the sixth day Grisha's tooth started to hurt from the constant damp, from the wet tent and sleeping bag, from the piercing summer wind. The only thing that helped was a drink mixed to the proportion "for surviving a long spell of bad weather". Even that would only help for a while.

He could not sleep. At night he would constantly roll around in the tent. The roar along the rocks became completely unbearable, it weighed on his soul as if he had been pulled somewhere under the earth. In the middle of the night his brother suddenly mumbled something.

"What's wrong, Konstantin?" he asked as he shook him by the shoulder.

"Don't go there, black water. Black water…" his brother moaned in a heavy voice without opening his eyes.

A sense of horror ran down Grisha's spine. He felt a chill on his skin. For the rest of the night he did not close his eyes at all.

"What happened, last night I mean?" he asked Konstantin as soon as he got up.

"That constant roar. The rocks are shaking. The vibrations…" His brother's face was haggard now, with sunken, unhealthy-looking eyes. "I started to have bad dreams. As if we got to the mouth of the Letnyaya. We get there and there's someone in white lying on the shore, face down. I go up to him, turn him over and it's me." Konstantin's voice was shaking.

"Oh, come on! Seems like the wind has started to drop. Please God, let it calm down by tomorrow."

On the morning of day seven it really did calm down. The waves were still big, but already easier to tackle. The savage white crests had disappeared. The wind had practically stopped. In the gray sky a slight, dark-blue dawn came.

"Well then, we've got to pack up. Maybe we can get out of here." Grisha remembered again that he had been their steersman. "We might not get another chance for a long time."

"Ha, then our bones will bleach here just like the driftwood." His brother was in a dreary mood after the difficult night.

"Let's just have some tea, for the road." Even bad weather could not dampen Nikolai's Karelian habit.

They quickly lit a fire. It took them less than half an hour to pack up, throw their things into the canoe and head out to sea.

At first the waves seemed fine, not too high. They did not lash their canoe, only moderately knocked against the sides and the boat moved quickly, with an unpleasant rocking from side to side. But as soon as they were about five hundred meters from the shore, instead of the slackening *polunoshnik*, suddenly a westerly began to whistle past them. It rose up quickly, in just five minutes or so, it whipped up waves from the west. It was a headwind, coming right along their bearing, it immediately made the canoe jump up over the crests. Their boat would then be thrown back down and their stomachs dropped. This shaking was no fun at all and Grisha was scared again. He could see that the wind was rising. The cold water began to lash their boat again. The most terrible thing of all was that it was too late to turn back, they could not return to shore, because the waves had become so strong that their canoe would be overturned in an instant if they tried to change direction. "These are called short waves," he quickly recalled something he had read. "This is why they are considered the most dangerous!"

They rowed madly, but no longer aware of where they should be rowing to. The wind again rose to hurricane force. Their fishing rods flew from the boat into the sea, along with some clothing, there was no time to catch them.

"Turn to shore, damn it, we're going to drown out here!" Konstantin screamed.

Grisha, however, understood that in no circumstances should he turn the rudder. That if he did so, the next moment their boat would be upended like a mere splinter. That they would not be able to swim to shore; their muscles would immediately cramp up at the cold water.

"Come on, keep rowing, no talking!" He shouted, then directed a string of profanity at them to convince them. Meanwhile, he was feverishly, desperately thinking about what he should do.

"What should I do? Lord, what should I do? Help me, our Father who art in heaven. Have mercy on us sinners…" Where did he find the words with which to pray, words that he had never learned, or had forgotten, or came to him just like that? "St. Varlaam, protect us! St. Nicholas, rescuer of seamen, save us!"

He could see that his friends still did not realize the full danger, the entire horror of what was going to happen to them in several minutes. They were still rowing, albeit spasmodically and swinging their oars past the water. They were still fighting.

"That's it, don't be afraid! No need to panic! Don't give up! Just hold on!" He whispered, if his hands had been free, he would have slapped himself in the face. "Just hold on!"

He looked around in search of some salvation, some way out that might suddenly appear. Then he suddenly saw that the forest-covered island at the entrance to the Uzkaya Salma strait shielded a small portion of sea from the westerly wind. "It's a *zaveter'*," he thought, remembering the old word. They could try to head for it.

Little by little, literally in one-degree increments so that the side of their canoe would not face the waves, he began to turn their bearing.

"Row harder, damn it!" He shouted to his men. "We'll get out of it now!"

Indeed, as soon as their canoe came into the shielded stretch of water, the rocking stopped. The surface of the sea grew calm, as if by magic. He even dared to turn the canoe's side to the open sea and head for the entrance to Uzkaya Salma. Birds flew over the calm water. It was as if they were carrying the boat over the water with their six hands. Quickly, in just a few minutes, they approached the sandy shore. Only at the last minute did Grisha glimpse on the island's cape an old Pomor cross. It wasn't a votive cross but an indicator.

In a couple of hours they flew all the way to the mouth of the Keret. They rowed laughing and bantering. Life again became something joyful and fun. The past now seemed like an easy adventure.

On the shore they were met by old Savvin. He looked at these wet, filthy men with a smile. "Well, did you get a taste of our little sea here?"

"Did we!" Nikolai Eliseyev was beaming with happiness at again being on solid ground. Grisha, however, turned back towards the way they came. Fog crept along there like a thick wall, as if pushing down on the water that was growing calmer.

Old Savvin caught his glance.

"The priest brought his wife…"

"What does that mean?" Grisha asked, astonished.

"Well, have you ever heard of St. Varlaam of Keret?"

"Oh, I asked him for help when things were a real mess!"

"A man hasn't really prayed unless he has been at sea," the old man smiled. "You folks head into the house, I'll get the stove lit."

Grisha's toothache had arisen anew, but now it quickly abated when he pressed his swollen cheek to the warm side of the stove. The old man made them beds in an old home he owned, not the one he lived in now. At night Nikolai grounded his teeth in his sleep, while Grisha dreamed of black cats. There were a lot of them in the room, but they did not dare approach him.

ANOTHER MIRACLE WORKED
BY THE VENERABLE VARLAAM

The same man told us this story. A certain man from the river Dvina, whose name was Nikifor, was coming back with his companions from fishing in Murmansk. And when he approached Svyaty Nos, a windstorm came their way, and it broke their mast, and the sail was taken away by the sea, and waves were pouring into their boat. And the waves took everything away from their boat, and they were borne in their boat into the depths of the sea, and they were all afraid for their lives, and they were carried into the depths of the sea.

And after many days passed, the venerable father Varlaam revealed himself to Nikifor in a dream and he spake to him thus: "Why do you despair and you think not about saving yourselves? Your sail is near the boat, and the mast is also near the boat, and you are not putting the mast in place. Labor, do not be idle, and God will rescue you!"

Nikifor was bewildered by the vision, and he began to tell his companions of it. "Where is the sail, brother? We cannot see it." And they began to look for it in various places, and then they found the sail near the boat and barely managed to drag it back onto the boat, and there were their oars and the rudder too. After they thus labored, they were tired and fell asleep. And then the same man revealed himself to them, and he spake, "Labor, ask God for help, and God will rescue you." And Nikifor asked him, "Who art thou, master, thou who comest in our dreams and carest for us?" And he answered, "I am Varlaam of Keret." Nikifor did not know of him, and so he began to ask his companions, but none of them had heard of Varlaam. They began their usual preparations on the boat and thought about their journey further. And they saw the ice parting before them, and making way for them. And a tailwind began to blow, and on the third day they reached the mouth of the Dvina. In the second year after this revelation, Nikifor came to Keret and asked, "Who is the man called Varlaam, and where is he?", thinking that he was still alive.

One whose abode was there said to him, "That holy man came to thee in thy sleep, and God rescued thee from drowning thanks to his intercession." And the man showed him the tomb of the saint. Nikifor brought many candles and placed them on the grave and he prayed to the venerable Varlaam for his salvation.

*   *   *

All people today who consider themselves educated know well what adrenaline is. "That's easy," they exclaim. "Adrenaline is the hormone that causes excitation. That's important. It's emotions!" Some who are especially informed will even recall endorphins. "The pleasure hormone," they will say, as their eyes lightly glaze over as they look back on sweet memories. It will all be true. It will be knowledge of life. Indeed, all human sensations, sad as it might sound, have a basis in biochemistry. Love, hate, excitement, a drive for new sensations. A good life, a craving for which is inherent in all human beings. A good, rich, primitive life.

But there is one substance that one prefers not to think about. It is so much easier to know of alcohol dehydrogenase, a means of breaking down alcohol. They say, incidentally, that for Russians it is produced not only by the liver but also by subcutaneous fatty tissue. There is quite a bit of evidence for this. Or perfume dehydrogenase, peculiar to the French. Or binge-eating-dehydrogenase, the joy of Americans.

It bears a romantic name, the slow-reacting substance P. Why P, I have no idea. It could hardly stand for "Poets". I suggest that you, my honorable reader, think up your own version and use that. It is easier for me. I do not know what it means. Substance P is the pain threshold hormone. The one that lets a person survive critical situations. The one that lets you withstand enormous physical trials, deprivations and cataclysms. The one that saves you from death until the last moment. It is this that is peculiar to northerners. Russians, Karelians and others. Its spiritual analogue is faith.

It happened thus. Or it did not. There was a rumbling and a roar. The water of the sea in January is black. Kola Bay is usually calm, but this time it was raging like a madman. The waves beat on the rocks as if they sought to shatter them. There was no sky at all. Snow flew along the ground. The wind tore at my cassock, trying to tear it away and leave me naked, shivering and fallen. I cannot remember how I ended up here, at the very cape. Salt spray flew at my face. Tears welled up in my eyes. I could hardly see anything, whether near or far.

Suddenly the dark clouds parted and everything was bathed in a bright light. It was cold, green and blue. Flashes passed over the sky. They danced a hellish dance, shimmered and changed color. This demonic and overwhelming phenomenon wearied me.

The wind grew ever stronger and drained my spirit. I heard a voice in this deathly light, under this threatening sky. A voice that was sibilant and whispering. It pierced me to the bone, worse than any wind could. "Who are you, Russian men? Why have you come here, to the edge of my land? What are you seeking, what do you want? Why are you destroying my fortress and disturbing my peace?"

I had nothing to answer it, I lacked the strength in my throat to form sounds and in my heart to live. Horror had wrapped around my entire body like a harsh icy robe, pierced through with sharp needles.

"You remain silent? In that case, I shall not let you pass further. You will not make your way out to sea by my paths!"

A crash resounded everywhere around me. I saw the rocky islands at the entrance to the bay suddenly shift from their places. They were driven like light boats by the howling wind. I knew that across the entire North, at every one of its rivers, the islands had moved to the river mouths in order to block them. The wind, the waves, and the hellish cold I saw too.

But with frozen lips I managed to mouth a prayer. Then another. And again. My frozen hands took strength from somewhere. I grabbed my axe and began to fashion a wooden cross.

Around me everything had lost its mind and was howling, rolling, hissing. The sky raged with a cold flame. My eyes were stuck with snow.

The wind tore the axe from my hands. But I continued to pray and to chop and chop. I was sore at heart.

Although, as soon as the timber cross stood firmly among the rocks, the wind suddenly calmed. As if they shuddered with their rocky bulk, the islands stopped. The hissing voice along with the dreaded white light crept away towards the horizon. The voice whistled its last words, "Do not rejoice so soon. I will stay with you and your people forever. You will forget your forebears just like your children will forget you. Brother will hate brother always, holding grudges and doing harm. Your women will forget about your kindness and they shall do greater harm to you than your enemies. Your houses shall disappear under weeds. It shall be so forever. For ever…"

An eerie calm reigned around me. I staggered off to my home, where my wife was waiting for me rolled up in a bundle. Such a warm bundle.

2005, KERET

Grisha sat on a hillock in the shadow of the chapel built to St. Varlaam. It was a recent construction, its wooden boards had not yet had a chance to age and in spots resin oozed from the fresh cracks. "It's strange," he thought. "There was once a huge stone church here. It burnt down, lightning struck it. Then there were a few chapels, smaller ones. They say that people burned those down, but someone would remember and again erect a new chapel. I ought to ask Savvin who did that."

A few Pomor crosses stood firmly there. They were of the old style, with a little roof made from boards at the top. Other crosses had already tired of standing vigil and now lay on the ground. Lingonberries and crowberries sprouted through their decrepit bodies. A large stone, bearing names that had long since been effaced and could hardly be made out, was overgrown with gray moss. Captains, navigators, merchants, steersmen… It had not interested anyone for a long time now. A warped iron cross, which had fallen once upon a time from a high bell tower, looked like an outsider among its wooden brothers planted on the ground.

The weather became heavenly. An awesome blue sky with cirrus clouds, in a pearly color tinted by the high setting sun that was ready to become, right away, the dawning sun, as if it were merely going for a dip in the calm sea. Nearby the Keret, whose name had come from the Saami for 'high river', roared in its last rapids before it poured into the White Sea. The light and warm wind called the *shellonik* blew the mosquitoes towards the water, here and there little salmon splashed. The tall, succulent grass and thick juniper nearly hid the light-gray, silvery remnants of the houses that had once stood here and only a distant black boat on the smooth sea served as a sign of human life.

Grisha made his farewell. His things were already packed and loaded into the car. In his hands he held an old map, worn at its folds. He took one last look at it. The map was beautiful but changeable like a woman, it showed roads that were already overgrown, rivers that had dwindled and turned into mere streams, lakes that had become marshes. But the names of villages were continually tagged with the same word: "unin-habited… uninhabited… uninhabited…" Only the hard, rocky shore stood steadfast against the onslaught of the sea and time.

Old Savvin was standing silently nearby, looking out at the waves. Then he said to no one in particular, "We have come to a time when even fire is cold."

Grisha gave a start. "I wanted to give you a book. *Dictionary of the Spoken Pomor Dialect*, it's called. Have you heard the story about it?"

Savvin gently accepted the dark-blue volume. He stroked the cover with his well-worn hands and peered at the letters. "I've heard of Ivan Durov. He achieved what he worked for. Good job!" Then he nodded and walked with bent back towards his little home, one of the last left in Keret.

Grisha, without even understanding why and unprepared for it, sud-denly cried after him, "Forgive us!"

Savvin merely waved a hand without turning around. "God forgives!"

Grisha said his goodbye. Many things were clear to him, he had tramped over them on foot, raked through them with oars. Still, a few questions spun in his head. "Where are you all?" He asked the White Sea. "Where are you, captains of the polar seas, steersmen, merchants, builders of boats and houses? Where are you, fishermen and keepers of saltworks, white-headed brotherhood, warriors, widows, brave lads? Where are you, cream of Russia? Who did you confide in, you unyielding men? Where did you all go? What demons did you admit into your bright hearts?"

With his wet, clouded eyes he suddenly seemed to see them in the patches of sunlight, in the shadows of grass, they were walking from the ruins of the houses to the sea, these hardened men with ample beards, young ladies in pearl-embroidered sarafans and headdresses, old wom-en in black dresses and dancing adolescents. They slipped down to the shore and went out into the sea. Children played like merry salmon fry. The adolescents dove in like fast grilse. Like silvery ice-followers and *zakroyka* salmon, the young Pomor ladies wriggled. Like *listopadki* the old women walked away gravely into the depths. The northern men split the waves like royal herring.

A fast golden cloud came. A light, bright drizzle passed by. A bright rainbow lay over the water of the White Sea. "A flame out at sea," Grisha remembered.

The Flying Dutchman

by Anatoly Kudryavitsky

Some time in the 1970s, Konstantin Alpheyev, a well-known Russian musicologist, finds himself in trouble with the KGB, the Russian secret police, after the death of his girlfriend, for which one of their officers may have been responsible. He has to flee from the city and to go into hiding. He rents an old house located on the bank of a big Russian river, and lives there like a recluse observing nature and working on his new book about Wagner. The house, a part of an old barge, undergoes strange metamorphoses rebuilding itself as a medieval schooner, and Alpheyev begins to identify himself with the Flying Dutchman. Meanwhile, the police locate his new whereabouts and put him under surveillance. A chain of strange events in the nearby village makes the police officer contact the KGB, and the latter figure out who the new tenant of the old house actually is.

Buy it > www.glagoslav.com

Nikolai Gumilev's Africa

Gumilev holds a unique position in the history of Russian poetry as a result of his profound involvement with Africa. He extensively wrote both poetry and prose on the culture of the continent in general and on Ethiopia (Abyssinia, as it was called in Gumilev's time) in particular. During his abbreviated lifetime Gumilev made four trips to Northern and Eastern Africa, the most extensive of which was a 1913 expedition to Abyssinia undertaken on assignment from the St. Petersburg Imperial Museum of Anthropology and Ethnography. During that trip Gumilev collected Ethiopian folklore and ethnographic objects, which, upon his return to St. Petersburg, he deposited at the Museum. He and his assistant Nikolai Sverchkov also made more than 200 photographs that offer a unique picture of the African country in the early part of the century.

This volume collects all of Gumilev's poetry and prose written about Africa for the first time as well as a number of the photographs that he and Nikolai Sverchkov took during their trip that give a fascinating view of that part of the world in the early twentieth century.

Buy it > www.glagoslav.com

A Brown Man in Russia
Lessons Learned on the Trans-Siberian
by Vijay Menon

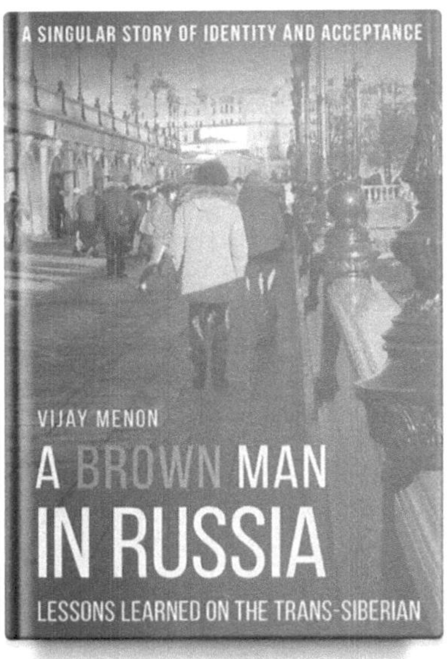

A Brown Man in Russia describes the fantastical travels of a young, colored American traveler as he backpacks across Russia in the middle of winter via the Trans-Siberian. The book is a hybrid between the curmudgeonly travelogues of Paul Theroux and the philosophical works of Robert Pirsig. Styled in the vein of Hofstadter, the author lays out a series of absurd, but true stories followed by a deeper rumination on what they mean and why they matter. Each chapter presents a vivid anecdote from the perspective of the fumbling traveler and concludes with a deeper lesson to be gleaned. For those who recognize the discordant nature of our world in a time ripe for demagoguery and for those who want to make it better, the book is an all too welcome antidote. It explores the current global climate of despair over differences and outputs a very different message – one of hope and shared understanding. At times surreal, at times inappropriate, at times hilarious, and at times deeply human, A Brown Man in Russia is a reminder to those who feel marginalized, hopeless, or endlessly divided that harmony is achievable even in the most unlikely of places.

Buy it > www.glagoslav.com

Glagoslav Publications Catalogue

- *The Time of Women* by Elena Chizhova
- *Andrei Tarkovsky: The Collector of Dreams* by Layla Alexander-Garrett
- *Andrei Tarkovsky - A Life on the Cross* by Lyudmila Boyadzhieva
- *Sin* by Zakhar Prilepin
- *Hardly Ever Otherwise* by Maria Matios
- *Khatyn* by Ales Adamovich
- *The Lost Button* by Irene Rozdobudko
- *Christened with Crosses* by Eduard Kochergin
- *The Vital Needs of the Dead* by Igor Sakhnovsky
- *The Sarabande of Sara's Band* by Larysa Denysenko
- *A Poet and Bin Laden* by Hamid Ismailov
- *Watching The Russians (Dutch Edition)* by Maria Konyukova
- *Kobzar* by Taras Shevchenko
- *The Stone Bridge* by Alexander Terekhov
- *Moryak* by Lee Mandel
- *King Stakh's Wild Hunt* by Uladzimir Karatkevich
- *The Hawks of Peace* by Dmitry Rogozin
- *Harlequin's Costume* by Leonid Yuzefovich
- *Depeche Mode* by Serhii Zhadan
- *The Grand Slam and other stories (Dutch Edition)* by Leonid Andreev
- *METRO 2033 (Dutch Edition)* by Dmitry Glukhovsky
- *METRO 2034 (Dutch Edition)* by Dmitry Glukhovsky
- *A Russian Story* by Eugenia Kononenko
- *Herstories, An Anthology of New Ukrainian Women Prose Writers*
- *The Battle of the Sexes Russian Style* by Nadezhda Ptushkina
- *A Book Without Photographs* by Sergey Shargunov
- *Down Among The Fishes* by Natalka Babina
- *disUNITY* by Anatoly Kudryavitsky
- *Sankya* by Zakhar Prilepin
- *Wolf Messing* by Tatiana Lungin
- *Good Stalin* by Victor Erofeyev
- *Solar Plexus* by Rustam Ibragimbekov

- *Don't Call me a Victim!* by Dina Yafasova
- *Poetin (Dutch Edition)* by Chris Hutchins and Alexander Korobko
- *A History of Belarus* by Lubov Bazan
- *Children's Fashion of the Russian Empire* by Alexander Vasiliev
- *Empire of Corruption - The Russian National Pastime* by Vladimir Soloviev
- *Heroes of the 90s: People and Money. The Modern History of Russian Capitalism*
- *Fifty Highlights from the Russian Literature (Dutch Edition)* by Maarten Tengbergen
- *Bajesvolk (Dutch Edition)* by Mikhail Khodorkovsky
- *Tsarina Alexandra's Diary (Dutch Edition)*
- *Myths about Russia* by Vladimir Medinskiy
- *Boris Yeltsin: The Decade that Shook the World* by Boris Minaev
- *A Man Of Change: A study of the political life of Boris Yeltsin*
- *Sberbank: The Rebirth of Russia's Financial Giant* by Evgeny Karasyuk
- *To Get Ukraine* by Oleksandr Shyshko
- *Asystole* by Oleg Pavlov
- *Gnedich* by Maria Rybakova
- *Marina Tsvetaeva: The Essential Poetry*
- *Multiple Personalities* by Tatyana Shcherbina
- *The Investigator* by Margarita Khemlin
- *The Exile* by Zinaida Tulub
- *Leo Tolstoy: Flight from paradise* by Pavel Basinsky
- *Moscow in the 1930* by Natalia Gromova
- *Laurus (Dutch edition)* by Evgenij Vodolazkin
- *Prisoner* by Anna Nemzer
- *The Crime of Chernobyl: The Nuclear Goulag* by Wladimir Tchertkoff
- *Alpine Ballad* by Vasil Bykau
- *The Complete Correspondence of Hryhory Skovoroda*
- *The Tale of Aypi* by Ak Welsapar
- *Selected Poems* by Lydia Grigorieva
- *The Fantastic Worlds of Yuri Vynnychuk*

- *The Garden of Divine Songs and Collected Poetry of Hryhory Skovoroda*
- *Adventures in the Slavic Kitchen: A Book of Essays with Recipes*
- *Seven Signs of the Lion* by Michael M. Naydan
- *Forefathers' Eve* by Adam Mickiewicz
- *One-Two* by Igor Eliseev
- *Girls, be Good* by Bojan Babić
- *Time of the Octopus* by Anatoly Kucherena
- *The Grand Harmony* by Bohdan Ihor Antonych
- *The Selected Lyric Poetry Of Maksym Rylsky*
- *The Shining Light* by Galymkair Mutanov
- *The Frontier: 28 Contemporary Ukrainian Poets - An Anthology*
- *Acropolis: The Wawel Plays* by Stanisław Wyspiański
- *Contours of the City* by Attyla Mohylny
- *Conversations Before Silence: The Selected Poetry of Oles Ilchenko*
- *The Secret History of my Sojourn in Russia* by Jaroslav Hašek
- *Mirror Sand: An Anthology of Russian Short Poems in English Translation* (A Bilingual Edition)
- *Maybe We're Leaving* by Jan Balaban
- *Death of the Snake Catcher* by Ak Welsapar
- *A Brown Man in Russia: Perambulations Through A Siberian Winter* by Vijay Menon
- *Hard Times* by Ostap Vyshnia
- *The Flying Dutchman* by Anatoly Kudryavitsky
- *Nikolai Gumilev's Africa* by Nikolai Gumilev
- *Combustions* by Srđan Srdić
- *The Sonnets* by Adam Mickiewicz
- *Dramatic Works* by Zygmunt Krasiński
- *Four Plays* by Juliusz Słowacki
- *Little Zinnobers* by Elena Chizhova
- *We Are Building Capitalism! Moscow in Transition 1992-1997*
- *The Nuremberg Trials* by Alexander Zvyagintsev
- *Duel* by Borys Antonenko-Davydovych
- *The Hemingway Game* by Evgeni Grishkovets
- *Mikhail Bulgakov: The Life and Times* by Marietta Chudakova

More coming soon...